THE GREAT SMOKY MOUNTAIN BANK JOB

AND OTHER SAM JENKINS MYSTERIES

WAYNE ZURL

First Printing: 2017

ISBN: 978-1-68046-529-7

Melange Books, LLC
White Bear Lake, MN 55110
www.melange-books.com

Published in the United States of America.

Cover Design by Lynsee Lauritsen

CONTENTS

To Stephen King for suggesting a few twists to incorporate into *Murder in a Wish-Book House.*

To my Uncle Al, for providing me with a basis for Det. Albert Mueller.

To the real Chip Gunther, for what reason, I don't know.

To my old classmate who joined the Weather Underground. You should have gone to jail.

To my friend, Rich Greco who, if asked, would have given Bettye Lambert advice on what fishing tackle to buy her son.

To my wife, Barbara, for suggesting we take a ride into the southeastern Kentucky coal country one November day.

And to all the members of SCPD who looked long and hard under their unmarked police cars during those tense days in 1990.

MURDER IN A WISH-BOOK HOUSE

The farmhouse on Doc Beasley Road didn't look like the ramshackle, gothic home Norman Bates inhabited in the movie. But I wouldn't have been there at eleven on a November Sunday morning had the resident not been victim of a slash-and-stab, *Psycho*-like killing.

I turned left into the driveway and parked my unmarked Ford near the morgue wagon, crime scene van and a Prospect PD cruiser.

"Hey, boss," PO Bobby Crockett said. "Sorry ta bother you, but you'll wanna see this. Or maybe you won't."

"That why you're out here?"

He nodded.

"What happened?"

"The vic's name's Richard McBath, a teacher at Heritage High. His daughter did a sleepover at a friend's house. This mornin' 'bout ten, the girl-friend's mother brings the kid home and finds Richard stabbed to death."

"Where's that woman now?"

"Junior escorted her home. The McBath girl's with her."

"Hear anything about Richard having a wife?"

"Not a word."

"The ME and crime scene guys been here long?"

"Half an hour."

"A bad one, huh?"

"Ain't never seen nothin' like it. Lord have mercy. The blood. The smell. It's a mess."

"I'll hold my nose and take a look."

I'd seen houses like that before, not only in Tennessee, but back on Long Island where I'd worked as a cop for twenty years. One of the kit-homes people picked from a Sears Roebuck catalog since the 1920s.

Entering the side door, I found myself in a large eat-in kitchen. In the living room, I found crime scene investigator Jackie Shuman and his partner, David Sparks, dusting for latents and taking blood samples.

"Jesus H. Christ," I said. "How many people got killed here?"

Jackie was kneeling near me, dusting a lamp table.

"All this blood—looks like a bunch o' people, but it's jest one. You doin' aw rot today?"

"I was before I got here. Who's the ME?"

"Doc Rappaport's upstairs. Earl's with him."

I pulled on a pair of latex gloves and started up the stairs. On the third step, I stopped. "Jackie, you photograph the staircase yet? I don't want to tromp on this blood before you do your thing."

"Did it first off. Y'all think yer dealin' with an amateur?"

"Perish the thought."

I continued up the stairs and found lots of blood splattered on the runner. Red smears and hand prints showed on the wall along the staircase.

The previous day had been cool, but not cold. Luckily, the heat hadn't been turned up. But the unmistakable smell of a violent crime hung in the air. A warmer house would have created a nasty-smelling environment.

Strictly from the look of the old blood, I guessed our victim had been butchered sometime during the previous afternoon or evening.

The further up I went, the more blood I saw. More intense splattering augmented the smeared handprints on the walls. On the upstairs landing, it looked like the victim slammed into the wall, leaving a red smear where his shoulder hit the sheetrock.

To my left was a bathroom. To the right, the largest of three bedrooms. The medical examiner, his helper and our victim were all in that big room.

"Hey, Morris, what's a nice Jewish boy like you doing in a place like this?"

The doctor said, "This is a bad one, Sam. Such a mess. I haven't seen many like this."

I looked around the room. The victim, a medium-sized man, lay on the floor next to a queen-sized bed. From the bloodstains on the coverlet, I knew he started off on the bed, got stabbed and then slid off onto the floor. A night table stood next to the bed, its top drawer still open.

"I'm not pushing you, Mo, but can you give me something?"

"Sure, he's dead."

"And you know this after how many years of experience?"

He ignored me.

"I haven't counted yet, but I'm guessing thirty to forty stab wounds and who knows how many cuts."

"Find the weapon?" I asked.

"Yeah, in the shower...a butcher knife. Jackie says it fits the wooden block in the kitchen."

I pointed at the night table. "Why's the drawer open?"

"Who knows?"

"If you want help getting him downstairs, give a shout. I'll muster the troops."

"Thanks. And my lower back thanks you, too."

I began my search with the bureau. In the top drawer, among T-shirts and boxer shorts, I found a box of Remington .38 Special cartridges. Twelve of the original fifty rounds were missing.

"You guys come across a handgun?" I asked.

Neither Morris nor Earl had seen one. I checked the night table with the open drawer and found only the personal trinkets that end up in everyone's night table. No gun.

I tossed the closet. Looked under the mattress and under the rug. Examined the bottoms, backs and sides of all the drawers. Searched everywhere else in the bedroom someone could look for clues—nothing.

I tried the second bedroom and found the closet full of women's clothing, neatly arranged. Four empty hangers hung on the pole. When I opened the bi-fold doors, the heady smell of lavender attacked my senses. All the drawers in that room contained more women's clothes. I thought it strange, a young couple with separate bedrooms, and so far, no mention of a wife.

I looked at a nine-inch chef's knife that lay on the shower floor. A shower still wet from use. I opened the glass door and smelled lavender—not as strong as the sachet in the closet, but unmistakably the same, perhaps from a soap or shampoo.

I made my way into the third bedroom—the little girl's. I found nothing related to the crime.

Downstairs, in a storage room adjacent to the kitchen, I found lots of cardboard boxes with items unnecessary to everyday life in the McBath household. But I noticed an interesting thing: two suitcases—one large, one medium—and a void. A space that made me think a third suitcase had been removed. A smaller one.

I went through the kitchen door and out to the side yard.

"Bobby," I said, "did you run the plate on that truck in the driveway?"

"Yessir. Comes back to the victim."

"You check the garage?"

"Yeah. Nothin' 'cept all the garagey stuff you'd expect."

"You get any more info on our guy or his family?"

"Not yet."

"I'm going to call Bettye and get her to fire up the computer. How do I find the woman who called this in?"

———

I called Sergeant Bettye Lambert, my desk officer and occasional partner when I need help on an investigation. Her husband answered.

"Hey, Donnie, Sam Jenkins. Sorry to bother you, but may I speak with Bettye?"

"Sure thing. You got somethin' big goin' on?"

"Yeah, one of our local residents got himself murdered."

"And you want Bettye ta he'p ya do some detectin'?"

"No, I was going to invite her to one of those Gatlinburg motels with the heart-shaped hot tubs. If she says okay, remind her to bring her swimsuit."

"Shoot, I know that's a lie. If y'all were takin' her to a mo-tel with a hot tub, you wouldn't want her ta have no swimsuit."

"Oh, Donald, you can see right through me, can't you?"

He laughed. "Y'all hang on. I'll git her."

In a minute, Bettye answered the phone.

"Hey, Betts. Sorry to interrupt your Sunday."

"That's okay, darlin'. What have you got?"

"Bobby caught a homicide. If I were Sherlock Holmes, I'd think Jack the Ripper was back in business. Wanna go to the office, and run a complete background on the victim, and look for a wife? There's a daughter, but I haven't heard anything about a wife."

"Soon as we hang up, I'll be on my way."

"When you get in, call Bobby, and he'll give the details. When you finish the computer work, you and I have to go see the woman who reported this. She's got the daughter with her. I'd like a little help speaking with the girl."

"If you were going to take me to a motel with a hot tub, I'm surprised you need help talking to a girl."

"Donnie told you that?"

"Uh-huh."

"Remind me never to tell your husband a secret."

She laughed. "Sammy, darlin', I'll see you at the office."

"Give me another hour. I'll pick up lunch."

I went back into the house and asked Mo and Jackie for their take on the murder. Piecing their stories together, along with what Bobby knew, I inferred that the murder happened between eight and eleven the night before.

We had no idea what McBath did between 1 p.m. and when he ate dinner. We assumed he settled down to read a book. That book lay on the floor with several pages roughly folded over.

Richard had defensive wounds on his forearms and hands. He started defending himself where Jackie found blood splatter and moved up the stairs—bleeding like a stuck pig.

He made it to the second floor, ricocheted off the wall and stumbled to his bedroom. There he went to the night table, perhaps trying to reach his gun as a last defense. Stabbed again numerous times, he slid off his bed and died on the floor.

Some conjecture: The killer, covered with blood, showered, changed into clothes found in the house, washed out the shower, cleaned up the murder weapon and took a suitcase to carry away the bloody duds he or she wore when they killed Richard.

In my opinion, it would take a cold customer to hack someone to death and then blithely spend time spiffing themselves up before leaving the scene.

I got the keys David Sparks recovered and opened Richard's Dodge Dakota. Aside from the normal items found in almost everyone's vehicle, I found nothing in the cab or the truck bed.

I lifted both garage doors to get as much light as possible. From the wear on the floor and the two sets of dirty tire tracks, I assumed the Dakota and another vehicle were parked in the garage regularly.

What happened to that second vehicle? Where was the wife? Was there a missing gun? Why a separate bedroom for a couple in their thirties?

A breeze blew into the empty garage. Golden leaves fell from the trees, and I smelled a faint odor of lavender. I closed the doors. Jackie and David still had to process the extended crime scene.

Halfway down the driveway, I stopped and called my wife. With work ahead of me, I suggested not planning an elaborate evening meal. If she'd be content with a TV dinner, an appropriate bottle of wine would make me happy.

A second call went to my friend in the news business. Rachel Williamson was the senior news anchor at WNXX TV in Knoxville. I've known her since my first week at Prospect PD and always give her a call about anything exciting in Prospect. Rachel never fails to reciprocate with a favor. Being a beautiful forty-year-old woman who's fond of me had nothing to do with it.

Her voicemail came on. I waited for the beep.

"Hey, woman, if you're there, answer the phone. This is your informant in Prospect. My apologies for interrupting your Sunday, but you'll want to be the first one on the air with this story." I heard a connection click in.

"Hi, Sammy. Do they have my poor boy working on his day off?"

"Yes, ma'am. And a grisly job it is. Got your shorthand pad ready?"

"What's shorthand? Hang on. I'll hook up my iPod."

"What's an iPod?"

"Don't be silly. Even you know what an iPod is."

I gave her the details exactly as I'd put them into a press release in an hour or two.

"If you want footage of the house, get a cameraman rolling. I'm guessing the other networks will have this story by two o'clock at the latest. Someone at the sheriff's office will leak the news."

"I'll call John. And, Sam, you're so sweet. Thanks for calling. You're my favorite police chief."

"I'd better be your only police chief, momma."

"You know you are. Come into Knoxville, and I'll let you take me to lunch."

"Isn't that supposed to work the other way around?"

"Of course it is, Sammy, but you're too old-fashioned to let me pay."

"Okay, kiddo, I'll let you take me for granted. Now get on the air, and scoop the competition."

"Scoop the competition? You sound like Walter Winchell."

"Gotta go. Bye."

I hung up, called Mayor Ronnie Shields and told him one of his constituents had been murdered.

———

After lunch, Bettye tapped away on her computer keys. From Motor Vehicle records, she learned Richard Lee McBath was thirty-two years old, had a clean driving record, and in addition to the Dodge Dakota, he owned a Chrysler minivan—the missing vehicle.

By running a group search on McBath, Bettye found Jane Dulcie McBath, the other licensed driver at 462 Doc Beasley Road—the missing wife.

The Tennessee Bureau of Investigation told her Richard's name came through their system for a background check when he purchased a .38 caliber Smith & Wesson—the missing pistol.

From Robert Dillard, principal of Heritage High School, she learned that Dick McBath (*Dick and Jane? Where's Spot?* I wondered) was an English teacher, well liked by his peers and popular with the students. McBath volunteered to conduct English workshops for those needing or wanting them. Dillard offered only sketchy information, but he knew Jane had been hospitalized nine months earlier for stress and other emotional problems.

An important bit of information came from running both names through NCIC, looking for a criminal history and any wants or warrants. Dick's name came back clean.

Jane presented another story. She'd recently been convicted of driving under the influence of alcohol and prescription drugs. And stemming from another incident at a restaurant where she assaulted Dick, an order of protection had been lodged against her in county court.

More interesting was her voluntary committal to the Peninsula Psychiatric Hospital in close-by Louisville, Tennessee. And even more exciting: News of her escape on Saturday night.

The reports said Jane and two other women fled the facility long before their scheduled release dates. In effecting their getaway, the ladies ran into an unforeseen problem. Confronted by an elderly security guard, one of the absconding girls smacked the poor guy on the head with a metal bar she broke off a towel rack. The guard suffered a massive coronary and died before a supervisor found him. Jane was still at large.

———

"I thought the tourist booklets call us the peaceful side of the Smokies," I said.

Bettye said, "Every once in a while we get a doozie, don't we?"

I sent out our alarm for Jane McBath, augmenting the earlier bulletin wanting her for escape and the death of the guard. I added the possibility she may have taken the family minivan and be in possession of a handgun. Then, after putting out the obligatory press release, Bettye and I left the office.

———

We drove north on Prospect Road, turned onto Humphrey's Lane and found the Tillis residence.

Vibrant maple and sweet gum trees lined the quiet residential street. Yellow, orange and red leaves broke from the branches and floated, swirling in the light breeze. The Tillis' two-story brick home sat on a well-groomed lot. A man answered the door.

"Hello, I'm Chief Jenkins. This is Sergeant Lambert from Prospect PD. We'd like to see Mrs. Tillis and speak with the McBath girl. I don't know the girl's first name.

"Sure, come in," he said. "The girl's name is Nell. I'm Woodrow Tillis. Good ta meet y'all."

Dick and Jane and now their daughter, little Nell? Where the hell is Spot? I wondered yet again.

"Thanks, Mr. Tillis."

"This is jest terrible," he said. "Dick was a nice guy. Let me get Vanetta for ya."

Bettye and I stepped into the living room and sat on an Early-American sofa. Woodrow disappeared for a few moments.

Vanetta Tillis came in. She was a good-looking brunette in her late-thirties and nicely dressed in a print blouse and black slacks.

I made the introductions.

She forced a smile and sat across from us in an upholstered chair.

"We know you've already told Officer Crockett what happened," I said, "but would you start again and tell us what you saw?"

Vanetta went over the whole story. After driving young Nellie back home, she got no response knocking on the unlocked back door and entered the kitchen. Once inside, she received no answer to her calls and upon entering the living room, saw the blood. She began to panic and screamed for McBath. Hearing no answer, she dragged Nell and her daughter, Tammy, outside and called 911. In a few minutes, Officers Bobby Crockett and Junior Huskey arrived. The rest we knew.

"We've learned that for several months Jane had been hospitalized," I said. "Do you know anything about that?"

"You mean hospitalized until the other night."

"Exactly. Know anything about the order of protection and the fight at Aubrey's restaurant?"

"That fight wasn't the start of their problems, it was just the peak. Jane was on anti-depressants. And she wouldn't stop drinking. The two didn't mix. You must know about her DUI arrest."

Bettye and I nodded.

"I think the combination of pills and wine made her paranoid. Or maybe she was paranoid, and the pills and wine made it worse."

"Tell us about this paranoia," Bettye said.

"Jane always thought people were talking about her behind her back. Worse than that, she thought Dick was interested in other women. Any women and one in particular."

"Who was that?" Bettye asked.

"Myra Witford. She's a guidance counselor where Dick worked. Myra and a friend of hers were in Aubrey's the night Jane created the scene and hit Dick with a plate of food. Dick said hello to Myra, and Jane went out of control. The restaurant manager called the Maryville Police."

"What happened then?" I said.

"Since it was a domestic violence thing, they had to appear in court. The judge issued an order of protection to keep Jane from abusing Dick. Lot o' good that did."

"Will you explain that?" Bettye asked.

"Well, not too long after being in court, she showed up at school, found Dick and began screaming at him, accusing him of spending his time after classes with Myra instead of at the extra activities he volunteered for. The principal called the county police. Jane was so violent they put her in a strait jacket and took her to a psychiatrist. Dick and the doctor convinced her to go to Peninsula without a fight."

"It seems," I said, "because the committal was voluntary, she didn't have to escape from the hospital. She could have gotten out with a doctor's permission, even on a temporary basis. The other two women who left with her were there by court order."

"Yes, I guess so. Jane didn't like being in the hospital, but she went to her sessions and didn't fight the medications."

"Do you think Jane's paranoia made her escape for some reason other than just wanting to get home?" I asked.

"I do. She wanted to get back to Nellie. I also think she went there to kill Dick."

"How is it you know so much about Dick and Jane? I assume you're very close?"

"Chief, Jane is my sister."

I shot a quick glance at Bettye who raised her eyebrows.

We talked more, but the only revelation came when Vanetta said Jane might seek assistance from their brother, Yancey Sumner, one of the more infamous characters of Blount County.

When Vanetta looked tired of our questions, I asked to speak with Nell. Woodrow brought her in and stayed with us, while his wife took a break.

Nell was a cute little girl of five. She held her head down and looked at Bettye and me with her eyes staring upward, her face framed by long brown hair.

"Nellie," Woodrow said, "these people are from the po-leece. They'd like to talk with you. Okay?"

Nellie nodded, but she didn't smile or answer.

Bettye knelt down two feet from the girl's chair. I knelt also, but gave her more space.

"Hi, Nellie. I'm Miss Bettye, and this is Mr. Sam. We're sorry about what happened to your daddy. Can we talk about a few things?"

The girl nodded.

"When you left home to visit your Aunt Vanetta, did you know what Daddy was going to do?"

Nellie nodded again and continued to pout.

"What was that, darlin'?" Bettye asked.

"He wanted to read his new book."

"That's all? Just read?"

Nellie nodded.

"He didn't say he needed to go out somewhere?"

She shook her head.

"Did he say a friend was going to stop by and see him?"

She shook her head again.

"Nellie, when was the last time you saw your mom?" I asked.

Tears began to well up in the kid's eyes. She looked down and wrinkled her lips. Then she looked up at Bettye who smiled at her and then at me.

"Today," she said.

I don't think I've ever seen more sadness in a child's eyes.

"Where was that, Nellie?" Bettye asked.

"I didn't really see her. But she was in our house."

"How do you know that?" I asked.

"I smelled her," she said.

Lavender.

We thanked Nell and Woodrow. He took her back to play with Cousin Tammy, and Mrs. Tillis rejoined us.

"I have just a few more questions," I said.

Vanetta nodded and took a sip from the glass of sweet tea.

"When you last visited Jane, how did she seem?"

"The more we talked, the angrier she got. Not angry at me. Just angry at the world. At Dick. At people in general."

"Did she mention Myra Witford?"

"She did. She thought Dick was seeing Myra while she was in the hospital."

"Do you think Jane wants to harm Myra?"

"That wouldn't surprise me."

"Do you know where we can find your brother?"

"Not exactly. We haven't spoken in almost two years."

"You said Jane and Yancey were close. Would he help her even if he knew all the circumstances?"

"You don't know Yancey very well, do you?"

I shook my head. I looked at Bettye; she nodded. She knew better.

"Our little brother couldn't care less what's legal or right. If something seems like a good idea to him, Yancey will do it. And Jane can twist that fool around her little finger."

"Thanks, Mrs. Tillis." I said. "We appreciate your help. Will you be taking care of Nellie, or should we arrange for the county to get her a place to stay?"

"No. Nellie is our responsibility. We love her, and we'll give her a home as long as she needs one."

"Thanks again. We'll be in touch."

———

We had a dead English teacher and a sad little girl who might have thought Mommy offed Daddy with the family butcher knife. And we had a troubled woman, a former part-time real estate agent, now a full-time head case, possibly joining forces with her asshole brother to evade capture. And maybe Jane wanted to add another notch to the handle of her knife by cutting up a guidance counselor.

Back at the municipal building, I called in PO Joey Gillespie to work overtime sitting in his personal car, watching the Tillis home. I'd provide security as long as Jane roamed freely.

I called the sheriff's duty officer, a Lieutenant Garner, and told him about the possibility of an attack on Myra Witford who lived in a section of Maryville patrolled by county deputies. When I suggested he assign someone to keep an eye on Myra, he complained about being short of personnel. I impressed upon him how embarrassing it would be if Myra got carved up on his watch, especially after I told him Jane might be thinking vendetta. It became unnecessary to explain vicarious liability.

After that, Bettye sent out an alarm for Yancey Sumner as 'wanted for questioning' about his sister, my murder suspect.

I wanted to speak with Myra Witford, so Bettye and I drove to the Fort Gamble area of Maryville.

Her modest brick house sat in a subdivision which only a few years earlier had been a corn field. When Myra answered the door, it seemed like she'd been crying. She was in her mid-thirties and, at first impression, didn't look like a home wrecker.

She heard about Dick's murder on the news bulletin broadcasted during the afternoon NFL game. She then got scared when Lieutenant Garner told her Jane McBath might want to punch her ticket, and he'd only send a deputy to watch her house when he could spare a man.

"Ms. Witford, we're sorry you lost a colleague," I said.

"Thank you. It's a terrible shock. How could they let Jane escape like that?"

"I'm sure the hospital has someone looking into that. Just a few questions if you don't mind."

She shook her head.

"We know about the trouble in Aubrey's restaurant. Did Richard ever mention Jane accusing other women of having affairs with him?"

"I think she often accused him of being unfaithful, but I'm the only one she named."

"Forgive me for asking, but were her accusations unfounded?"

Myra hesitated.

"Dick and I were having an affair. But we were very discreet. No one suspected. I'm sure of that. I don't know why she accused us. She couldn't have known. I chalked it up to her paranoia."

"How long were you two together?" Bettye asked.

"A little more than a year. Dick was a wonderful man. The students loved him. I loved him. I'm sure he loved me."

"What did you know about his home life?" I asked.

"That's how we became close. One afternoon, after classes were over, I passed his room and found him at his desk. He was sitting there bent over, as if he was sleeping. I went in to see if he was all right. When he picked up his head, I saw tears in his eyes. I felt so sorry for him. We sat there, and he told me everything.

"After Nellie was born," she continued, "Jane suffered from post-partum depression. She never shook it off, even with medication. The pills didn't do much good, so Jane started drinking. You can guess the two didn't mix. As time went by, she became more paranoid. I believe she never saw the right doctor and never got the right medicine. Now this."

Myra's tears began again. She wiped her eyes with a wrinkled tissue that looked as if it needed replacing.

"Ms. Witford," I said, "Richard was killed in our jurisdiction. We wanted to speak to you, but you live in the area patrolled by Blount County. I can't send a Prospect officer here to watch over you. I also can't determine what the sheriff's manpower situation is like. So, I would suggest if you have a relative or a friend to stay with, you do so. And if anything scares you, call 911 immediately.

"I have no one close by, but if I see any trouble, I'll call."

Before we left, Bettye and I handed her business cards with the office and our personal numbers on them.

On the way back to the barn, Bettye said, "I've never thought catchin' your husband with another woman was a killin' offense, but this sure casts a new light on our case. I wonder how Jane found out."

"Probably a hundred ways. Or it was just conjecture, magnified by paranoia. Who knows?"

We got back to the Municipal Building just before five-thirty. I watched Bettye drive off, and then I drove back to the Sears Roebuck wish-book house.

Dick McBath had been tagged, bagged and transported up to the University of Tennessee Forensics Lab for his postmortem exam. Bobby Crockett still stood guard.

"We almost done here?" I asked.

"Uh-huh. Jack and Sparky'll be finished soon."

"Did Mo tell you when they'd get to the autopsy?"

"Said tomorrow afternoon earliest. He'll call you."

"Okay, I'll give you a holler when he's ready."

"Aw, Sam! You ain't gonna make me go to an autopsy, are ya?"

"Not me, kid. The Tennessee court system. You were first officer."

"Aw, man, them things are disgustin'. I hate lookin' at a cut-up body. And it stinks."

"I know. Stick some Vicks up your nose, and close your eyes. I'll look for both of us."

Bobby accepted that idea.

By six-thirty, the crime scene investigators had finished and cleared out. Bobby and I wrapped the farmhouse with yellow tape. He got two and a half hours of overtime, and I got bupkis for working on my day off.

———

I parked in our driveway and headed toward the front door. The air smelled like autumn. Far off, someone was burning leaves.

When I opened the door, Bitsey, our old Scottish terrier, attacked me. As soon as she recognized me as her father, she flipped onto her back and encouraged me to scratch her belly. While I crouched down close to the dog, my wife walked into the living room.

"Hello, Sambo. How's my hotshot detective?"

"Wow, you look good," I said.

Kate wore tight navy slacks and a light blue knitted blouse.

"Aren't you nice?"

I stood up. She kissed me and touched my cheek.

"Of course, I'm every girl's sweetheart. You're the lucky one who gets to live with me."

"You're not just good-lookin', big feller, you're modest, too."

"Thanks. How about a drink?"

"Follow me. I'll show you what I've got."

A bottle of Laphroaig single-malt whisky stood on the kitchen counter next to a crystal glass. Just beyond, a dish filled with mixed nuts waited for me. The table setting included a tall candle. All the accouterments to make a meal sat on the range or the counter.

"This is more than a TV dinner. You've been busy," I said.

"Not really. It's Veteran's Day. This is for my ex-soldier boy. How about linguini and clam sauce? That's easy."

"How about white clam sauce? I've seen enough red today to last me a while."

"White it is. I've got a bottle of Pinot Grigio icy cold for us. This won't take long. A salad is made, and the bread is ready to be warmed up."

"You're not only beautiful, you're useful, too."

"Such a smoothie." She kissed me again.

I grabbed her around the waist. "If I'm your soldier boy, you wanna be my doughnut dolly?"

"I'm already sleeping with a handsome officer, I guess I qualify."

"Caustic, aren't you?"

"Have your drink, sweetie. I'm getting hungry."

During dinner, I told Kate what happened, sparing the gory details. "The skell brother is MIA," I said. "Who knows where Jane the head case is lurking?"

"How do you plan to find her?"

"Beats the hell outta me. How do you find a homicidal lunatic in the mountains?"

"Do you remember when we first got Bitsey?" she asked, sipping her wine.

The 60s station played Johnny Rivers singing *Mountain of Love.*

"She was horrible. If we left her home alone, she'd wreck the house."

"And when we hired that man to train Bitsey, what was the first thing he said?"

"I don't know. Walk softly, and carry a big stick?"

"Don't be stupid. He said get a training cage."

"Yes, he did."

"And how did we get Bitsey to go into the cage voluntarily?"

"Tossed in a chunk of hot dog."

"Right, Sammy. Now you have to find a hot dog Jane McBath responds to."

"And what makes you so wise in the ways of catching killers?"

"I've been married to a big-time cop for forty years."

———

At nine o'clock, we settled down to watch TV. At quarter to ten, I received a phone call. Myra Witford sounded hysterical.

"Mr. Jenkins, someone broke into my home! I heard glass break, ran to the front window to call for the policeman, but he was gone. I called 911 like you told me, and I ran to my neighbor's house. Why did that policeman leave?"

"Where are you now, Myra?"

"Next door at Mrs. Plemmons' house."

"Is a police officer there?"

"Yes, two of them."

"Did you see the person who broke in?"

"I didn't see anyone. I just know it was Jane McBath."

"Let me speak to a cop."

"They're in my house."

"I'll be there in ten minutes."

I hit the main road and flipped a switch to activate the flashing lights behind the grill of my Crown Victoria. In nine minutes, I pulled up behind a county sheriff's patrol car. An unmarked Ford, like mine, sat at the curb behind it.

A uniformed deputy met me at the front door of Myra's house. I showed him my ID and continued into the living room.

A detective named Bo Stallins walked from the kitchen. He was around forty and about six-two. He pulled off a pair of latex gloves that made a snapping sound and stuck them in the pocket of his leather jacket.

"Hey," he said, "You out for a ride and decided to stop?"

"The woman who owns this house is sort of a material witness of mine."

"Sort of?"

I explained.

"Y'all like the McBath woman for this?" he asked.

"Either Jane or her brother, Yancey Sumner—or both."

"Whoa. Now there's a real good ol' boy for ya."

"So I hear. The break look like much?"

"Look fer yerse'f. Broken glass, a flipped lock bolt and in they walked."

It was neat and simple. Shards of a broken door pane lay on the tile floor. The open door swayed slightly. Nothing more.

"I'd appreciate it if you have a crime scene guy check this over," I said.

"He ain't got much else doin' t'night."

"The complainant called me, said a patrolman had been here and left. You know what that's about?"

"Not yet, but he'll be back, an' you kin ask him."

In the living room, we found a second cop standing there—young, with a shaved head and the bulk of a weightlifter.

"Hey, Dwight," Stallins said, "this here's Chief Jenkins from Prospect. He needs to talk with ya."

Dwight walked over.

"I'm Sam Jenkins. Good to meet you."

"Dwight Cluny. You doin' aw rot today?" He spoke without friendliness.

"I'd like to know what happened. I think that elopee from Peninsula Hospital came here after Ms. Witford. You know we like her for killing her husband last night?"

He nodded, showing a little attitude, but said nothing.

"I'm not trying to second guess you, but where'd you go tonight?"

"We's shorthanded," he said. "I had ta take me a leak. So, I went down ta the Walland fire station."

"You could have used the bathroom here."

He made a face.

"Did you notice anyone drive by or slow down? Someone who looked interested in the Witford place?"

He shook his head.

"Jane McBath probably took her green minivan after she killed her husband. See anything like that drive by?"

He shook his head again. Dwight was a man of few words.

"How about a car that passed by more than once?" I wanted him to at least grunt.

"Nope, no ve-hickles."

I was getting nowhere. I envisioned a stunning career in law enforcement for Dwight Cluny.

"Okay, thanks for your time," I said. "Bo, would you send me a copy of the crime scene report?"

"Sure thing."

"Ask them to tape a piece of cardboard over the open pane. Save her having a cold house in the morning. I'll take her to a motel in Prospect and have a guy watch the room."

"I'll git'er done."

Cluny smirked. I ignored him but said, "Thanks, Bo," as I left.

───────

At Mrs. Plemmons' house, I spoke to Myra. "Okay, let's go to your place and grab whatever you need for a night. I'll find you a motel in Prospect and have a cop watch your room. Detective Stallins will make a temporary repair and lock up your house the best he can."

On our way to the Foothills View Motel, I asked, "Did you see any vehicles pass your house? I'm particularly interested in a green minivan."

"I was pretty nervous, so I looked out the windows off and on all night. A couple of times I thought the cop looked like he was sleeping. I saw a Camaro twice. Once parked up the street, maybe visiting someone. Then I saw it again, driving by."

"How do you know it was the same car?"

"It was an older car, like one my brother had years ago. This one was red with a gray front fender."

"You notice a plate number?"

"Sorry."

I told the motel clerk what I needed. He gave me a voucher to sign, gave Myra a downstairs room, and assured me he'd be awake and on duty until 8 a.m. when the manager came in.

I called in PO Harlan Flatt who was scheduled to work a midnight shift and told him to park his cruiser in front of room 104 and not to leave unless Al Qaeda attacked the Municipal Building.

Sergeant Stan Rose met me after Myra was tucked in for the night.

"Will you keep an eye on her until Harley gets here?" I asked.

"Sure. My motto: protect and serve—and save gas. I'll park right here. I'm tired of driving."

"Oh great, an ambitious supervisor."

Stanley grinned. "Make up your mind, fearless leader. You want me burning up the roads or protecting our endangered species?"

"Watch her. And, hey, didn't we agree you'd call me bwana?"

"What else y'all need, massah?"

"Search the computer for vehicles owned by Yancey Sumner. See if there's an older red Camaro in the woodpile somewhere. A current address for him would be nice, too."

"As you wish, sahib."

———

The next morning, I escorted Myra to school where Principal Dillard assigned a security officer to watch over her.

Then I drove to Peninsula Hospital. A talk with the administrator and his security chief confirmed that Jane McBath had a volatile personality and often became uncooperative.

Staff members noted that unlike many patients, she was careful of her grooming and appearance, and had an obsession with lavender perfume, shampoo, and soap. When Jane escaped, she took a pillowcase with a few articles of underclothing and all her cosmetics and toiletries.

According to her attending psychiatrist, she harbored enough anger and instability to attack another person, especially her husband, who she spoke of often in therapy. They were convinced that Jane posed a potential threat to anyone she disliked. Doctor-patient confidentiality was set aside because of that probability.

———

B ack at the PD, Bettye handed me a note from Stan Rose.
Yancey Joe Sumner had a record that included numerous arrests by Blount County and the surrounding PDs for the typical package often attached to your average Appalachian moron.

From burglary, larceny of a vehicle, criminal trespass and misdemeanor assault to possession of drugs and DUI, Yancey amassed a fine collection of charges. Several times, he'd been a guest of the county jail. I assumed the judges were sick of seeing Yancey's face in front of their benches.

Besides the Tennessee arrests, there were others in Harlan County, Kentucky. The co-defendants there were locals from that jurisdiction. I wondered if Yancey would take his sister up north to hide her.

Also of interest was his 1984, red Z-28 Camaro registered to an address in Prospect. I sent PO Vernon Hobbs to check. Vern learned we were eight months too late looking for Yancey at 1824 Boling Road.

We made progress, but none of it got us any closer to finding Jane McBath.

Myra Witford remained in jeopardy. Little Nell McBath might be abducted by her mother or her shithead uncle, and Mayor Ronnie Shields would get upset if he had to spring for too many motel bills to house my material witness.

I amended my alarm for Yancey Sumner, added his '84 Camaro and his possible complicity in the burglary of Myra Witford's home.

Then I called Ralph Oliveri at the FBI office in Knoxville.

"Sure, we'll consider this a possible interstate flight, but you know what, goombah?" he said. "You oughta start paying for all the favors you get from me and the Bureau."

"Ralphie, how can you say that? I thought FBI assistance to local agencies was standard procedure. Besides, I'd never ask this favor if I thought cops would pay attention to a small department like us. When something comes from a Fed, it gets results. If we catch this bad girl, you'll get an honorable mention."

"Easy, Kemosabe. More bullshit like that and I'll need hip boots."

"Ralph, you misjudge me."

"Nuts. This makes three big favors for you in the last couple of months. How about that lunch you promised?"

"Jesus, Ralph. I'd need an expense account to handle all the lunches you want. I work for Tennessee wages. I'm no GS-13, you know."

"My heart bleeds for you. Your big New York pension plus the contract you negotiated with Prospect. You're in some tax bracket. I'm a school-trained accountant, remember?"

"Okay, quit crying. I'll take you to the Villa Napoli. Will that soothe your black, Sicilian heart?"

"That's a nice place...like being home in Queens."

"Okay, we'll go, right after I find my mental patient and her jerk-off brother."

"Deal. You get all the cooperation the government can offer."

"You're a prince, Ralphie."

———

It was time to discuss the *hot dog* for which Jane McBath might jump into a cage. I left my office and stood in front of Bettye Lambert's desk.

"You know, Betts," I said, "you look really nice today. You do something different with your hair?"

"Sam Jenkins, you know damn well my hair is the same as it is every other day. It might have been a little different on Sunday—when you didn't say a word—but not today. And don't you make eyes at me, mister. You want something. What is it?"

"Bettye, if I had feelings, they'd be hurt."

She squinted at me.

"Okay, I have an idea, but I'll need your approval."

"You're the boss. Why do you need my approval?"

"Because I need you...and your husband...to volunteer for something that will help us capture Jane McBath."

"Sit down, Sammy, and tell me about it."

I explained. It didn't take much convincing and a quick call got Donnie Lambert on board. I only needed a little more assistance to orchestrate my cunning plan.

I called Rachel Williamson at home.

"Wow, calls two days in a row," she said. "I'm excited. You have more news?"

"I need a favor. And you can help me apprehend Jane McBath."

"What favor?"

"Televise a story, saying Donald Lambert from Prospect and his wife are going to provide foster care for little Nell McBath. Give their address and hope Jane tries to break in and abduct her kid. Then, voilá, we collar her in the act."

"Isn't Donald Lambert Bettye's husband?"

"Uh-huh."

"Is this a true story? Will they really have the girl?"

"Of course it's true. Would I lie to you? Well, they'll have her for a while. Then she'll go back to her aunt and uncle."

I waited for a reply.

"You have to think about this? Rachel, this is another chance to get a great story. You and me, kid...we'll make history."

"Yeah, right." She paused. "Okay, I think I can sell this one. This is how we do it." She explained.

———

Bettye e-mailed a photo of Donnie for Rachel to use on TV. Starting at noon, every newscast gave the story I explained. Donnie's smiling face appeared, as did their address. After the second spot aired, all the other networks picked up the story, and every broadcast in the Knoxville area relayed the same message. I hoped Jane was watching.

At 3 p.m., the alarms Ralph and I sent out paid off. A Fayette County cop in Lexington, Kentucky spotted Yancey Sumner's Camaro just outside the city. He caught Yancey with switched plates and a bag full of marijuana. They held Yancey for our questioning and their arraignment.

At 3:45, Stan Rose reported for his evening shift. I told him about the plan.

"Sounds cool. I'll bring a shotgun," he said.

"Yeah, a shotgun's always a good idea. But how'd you like to take a ride up to Lexington and see what you can squeeze out of Yancey?"

"Oh, man, how come I gotta miss all the fun?"

"Because you're the best man to interrogate a hardened criminal."

"Hardened criminal? Man's only a pimple on a good crook's ass."

"Be that as it may."

"Lexington's three hours away."

"Might be a good idea to get started, then. Go home, and change into your detective clothes. Take my car. You'll look cool in a big gray Ford."

"Your new car?"

"Sure."

"Okay, sounds good."

Before dark, Woodrow and Vanetta Tillis delivered Nell to the Lambert home. If Jane was watching, we wanted to make sure she had a clear view of her daughter. After dark, Bettye and another officer hid Nell in Bettye's minivan in the attached garage and secretly took the kid back to the Tillis home. I didn't want her to witness her mom getting arrested. The switch of our young decoy went off without a hitch.

I wanted to speed up Jane's attempt to kidnap her daughter, so at 10 p.m., we turned off all the lights on the first floor. Bettye and Donnie went upstairs and turned off those lights fifteen minutes later. PO Harlan Flatt and I watched the two doors, waiting for some action.

I sat in the kitchen, in the doorway next to the laundry room. I had a good view of the back door, but I wasn't visible to the outside. Harley and his shotgun waited in the living room, watching the front door. Officer Len Alcock hid outside with a pair of night vision glasses.

We all carried closed-circuit radios. The plan called for the first person who saw Jane to signal the others, not by speaking into the radio—that might be heard—but by simply 'breaking squelch'. That meant just a signal of static created by clicking the transmit button. Lenny's signal was one. I was two, and Harley was three clicks. If Jane got past all of us and showed up on the second floor, Bettye would key the mike and scream her head off.

Just before midnight, I saw a silhouette at the back door. I drew my pistol and knew where to find the closest light switch so I could surprise our intruder. I waited. The seconds seemed interminable.

Then I heard a muffled thud and broken glass hitting the floor. The figure I saw looked female-sized. I turned my radio volume down and depressed the key twice, alerting the others that someone was in the kitchen.

A small arm reached in and flipped the lock bolt. The hand withdrew, and the knob turned. The spring-loaded bolt clicked. The hinges creaked. I turned the radio volume back up. The door opened slowly. The figure took a step into the kitchen, stopped, listened and waited. She took another step. Glass crunched beneath her foot. She stopped. I heard her push the broken glass aside with her foot. Carefully, she took a step then another.

The intruder stood ten feet from the door, far into the room. The smell of lavender traveled to where I crouched. I pointed my flashlight at her head and pressed the switch. A beam of light hit her in the face. She used a hand to shade her eyes.

"Police, don't move!" I shouted. "Put both hands on your head!"

She didn't move. I saw a gun in her right hand.

Before the woman could react, Harley Flatt threw open the door from the dining room. The frightening sound of a pump action shotgun racking a round into the chamber echoed in the room. I flipped on the lights, set aside my flashlight and keyed my radio.

"Okay, everyone into the kitchen. Lenny, check the outside for another subject."

I spoke to the intruder, "Officer Flatt is not a compassionate man. I believe he's looking for an excuse to blow you up with that shotgun. Put your gun on the counter... slowly...and put your hands on your head."

Myra Witford placed a small semiautomatic on the countertop and both hands on her head. Len Alcock stepped through the kitchen door. Bettye and Donnie stood just behind Harley.

"Lenny, cuffs!" I said. He holstered his Glock and handcuffed Myra.

She and I looked at each other. "Surprise, surprise," I said, "You come here often, miss?"

Harley put his Remington 870 at port arms and clicked the safety. Alcock led Myra into the living room. Bettye stood there with her Glock at one side, Donnie at the other. Everyone looked at Myra in surprise. I slipped an old Browning .32 into my jacket pocket.

I spoke to Myra. "You mind telling me what's going on?"

Arrogantly, she said, "I believe you're supposed to say I have the right to remain silent. I'd like a lawyer."

We all left Donnie at home and adjourned to the PD.

———

While we waited for the attorney Myra called, Stanley came in fresh from Kentucky.

Besides telling me the traffic on I-75 was reminiscent of the Santa Monica Freeway, he said the Fayette County cops confirmed Yancey Sumner had been staying with friends in one of the lower-class neighborhoods of Lexington. He arrived in town early Sunday evening and couldn't have been near Myra's home when the burglary occurred.

Yancey told Stan he harbored his sister after her escape and provided an address in Prospect. With luck, we'd find Jane there.

Since Myra exercised her constitutional rights and her mouthpiece hadn't arrived, I mustered my troops, called in the county crime scene investigators and headed for Yancey's place.

———

A bright blue mailbox stood at the driveway of 5440 Chilhowee Road. Sixty feet off the blacktop, a single-wide mobile home waited for us.

No light showed inside the trailer. A wooden stairway led to the front door. Alcock and Flatt jogged around back to cover the rear. Stan and I went up the steps. I hit the door with the side of my closed fist several times. Nothing. I tried again.

"Open up, Jane, this is the po-leece!"

Stanley snickered. "Po-leece?"

"Use your bulk for some good, Stanley." I gestured toward the locked door.

I moved out of the way. Stan reared back and snap-kicked the door. The frame cracked. The door swung inward. I stepped into the doorway. A blast of heat hit me. The smell overcame us.

"Whoa, shit!" Stanley said.

"Son-of-a-bitch!" I added.

I fought back the impulse to become violently ill. We pulled out handkerchiefs, covered our noses and entered the trailer with guns drawn. Harley and Len heard us and came trotting around front. They started up the stairs.

"Boss, they's a minivan around the back...Yow!" I heard.

The smell of death and the beginning of putrefaction was overwhelming.

"Stay outta here," Stan told the others.

I flipped a light switch. A female body lay on the floor of the living room. I found the thermostat and turned it off. It had been set at ninety.

I knelt next to the body, turned the head and recognized Jane McBath from her pictures. There was a single bullet hole in her temple.

Stan helped turn her over. A second shot went through the center of her breast. Blood had flowed everywhere on the dirty, shag carpet. I stood up and pointed to the opposite end of the trailer. Stan followed.

We checked the two bedrooms, the bathroom and closets, but found no one else. Dick's Smith and Wesson revolver lay on the dresser in a bedroom. A faint smell of lavender and a few of Jane's cosmetics were in the bathroom.

"Screw this," I said. "Let's go."

At the entrance, two Prospect cops and two crime scene investigators waited for instructions.

"Lenny, call for the ME." Turning to the evidence technicians, I said, "Gents, I apologize, but this one's yours. Hold your noses. Harley, you two stick around here, and make yourselves useful, but don't go inside."

"10-4, boss. Gotcha covered."

———

Back at the PD, we found Myra in the squad room and Bettye standing guard. A meek-looking guy sat next to Myra. I recognized him as an attorney more suited to writing wills than defending murderers. Albert Beckwith was high alphabetically in the Yellow Pages and possibly the first guy Myra called.

"You're her lawyer?"

He nodded.

"I'm Sam Jenkins, the chief here."

Albert nodded again.

"How much you wanna bet the two bullets in Jane McBath came from the little Browning I took from your client?

His mouth opened.

I was mad, at Myra and at myself. I fell for her snow job. "Don't say anything—either of you."

He frowned.

"In case your client hasn't told you, we found the body of Jane McBath in a trailer. I have no doubt Ms. Witford killed her."

"How do you—"

I interrupted. "You get one offer, so listen carefully." I looked at Myra. "You tell me exactly what happened, and I'll let the DA offer you a deal you don't deserve. If either of you think I can't put her away for life, do a little research. I don't lose in court. It's your choice, Counselor. Talk to your client while I'm in the men's room, washing the stink of death out of my nose."

I left the squad room, and Stanley stayed. When I came out of the washroom, Bettye waited for me in the hall. I knew my blood pressure had risen.

"Sammy, you okay?" she asked.

"Yeah, Betts, I'm fine."

"This really bothered you, didn't it?"

She touched my cheek.

"Yeah, kiddo. This bothered me. Give me a minute to get it together."

"What can I do for you, darlin'?"

"Nothing. I'm okay. Go inside with Stan. I'll be with you in a minute."

Bettye walked back to the squad room. I went to my office, took a bottle of Glenfiddich from my drawer and poured an inch of scotch into a coffee cup. To say I was mad at Myra and myself wouldn't do justice to the feelings built up within me. Anyone can be fooled, and I'm certainly no exception. Twenty years ago, I would have shrugged off Myra's duplicity, said, "Screw you, lady," and gone for her throat. But at my age, things like that tend to create a greater bother—something Bettye obviously noticed. Unfortunately, Ms. Witford's attorney would feel the verbal brunt of my anger. I sent the whisky down the hatch, took a deep breath and joined the others.

"Okay, Counselor," I said, "what's the story? Do I give her a break or go for the max?"

He looked at me for a long moment.

"What are you offering?" he asked.

I snickered. "You think this is an episode of Law & Order? What am I offering? You gotta be kidding! Last time I looked, Tennessee still had the death penalty. What do you think I'm offering? I'll give you her life—if she confesses. One offer. Ten seconds. Take it, or leave it." I realized I'd been shouting.

Beckwith put his head next to Myra's. They took nine seconds.

"Okay," he said. "Can you get an ADA down here at this hour?"

"You bet."

He nodded. I walked out. Bettye followed.

In my office, I picked up the phone to call the Justice Center. Bettye came around behind my desk.

"Sam, I'm worried about you. You sure you're okay?"

"Yes, I'm fine. I was just posturing for the lawyer."

"I've never seen you this angry before."

"Sorry. I didn't mean to act volatile. I'll calm down."

She touched my cheek again.

"You helped her out, and she lied to you. No one broke into her home. And I feel bad for you. But it's okay. No matter what, I'm your friend. I'm here with you." She hesitated and added, "So's Stanley."

"I know. Thanks."

She smiled.

"Ask the duty officer to get the on-call ADA to come down." I handed her the phone. "I'll start her on a statement."

Bettye nodded. I walked back to the squad room.

"You two have an opportunity to converse?" I asked.

Myra nodded.

Beckwith asked, "Is the ADA coming?"

"Being called now. She ready to start her statement?"

He nodded.

I pushed a lined pad and pen toward her. Myra began to write. Beckwith stood looking over her shoulder.

At 3:45 a.m., Beckwith slid a finished statement across the desk at me. I took a few minutes to read it.

"I have a few questions," I said, beginning a question and answer page attached to the handwritten statement. "Did anyone try to break into your home last night?"

"No," Myra said.

I made the appropriate notation.

"Did you break the glass in your door and falsely report the incident?"

"Don't answer that, Myra," Beckwith said.

"Albert, we're talking about a lousy misdemeanor. My concern is the underlying Class A felony. Gimme a break."

Beckwith nodded at Myra.

She said, "Yes."

"When you confronted Jane McBath in the trailer on Chilhowee Road, did you ever intend to call the police to have her arrested?"

"No."

"You went there for one purpose—to kill her?"

"Myra." Beckwith cautioned.

"Goddamnit!" I said.

"Yes," she said.

"How did you know where to find her?"

"I thought she'd be with her brother. Richard told me where he lived. He wanted me to know where Jane might go if she took Nell from him. I saw Yancey's red car then."

"When did you go to the trailer to kill Jane?"

"Early last night before you came to my home."

"You had already killed Jane when you staged the break-in at your house?"

"Yes. I'm sorry."

"Why did you turn the heat so high in the trailer?"

"I'd seen on TV if you did that it'd be hard to determine the time of death."

Beckwith said, "Myra, you don't have to elaborate."

I ignored him.

"Why did you break into the Lambert's home tonight?"

"I wanted Nell with me. I wanted her...for always."

"She's not your child. Why did you want her?"

"Richard is gone now. She's a part of Richard. She should be mine. Richard and I loved each other."

"Did you think you could hide her from everyone?"

"I would have found somewhere to live. I would have brought her up and loved her. And she would have loved me."

I tried not to react to her insane ideas.

"Is there anything else you want to say before you sign this statement?"

She thought for a moment. "No."

I drew a line under her last 'No' and wrote 'end of statement'.

I passed the pad to her attorney. He read over the questions and responses. He pushed the pad to Myra. She signed it and pushed it back to me. I finished my work by writing 'Witnessed by legal counsel for the accused', turned the pad around and motioned for Beckwith to sign.

Bettye came in and said the ADA had arrived.

A moment later, Shelby Johnson, a young black man dressed in sports clothes and a tan windbreaker, walked into the squad room. I introduced him to the defendant. He already knew Beckwith.

I took Myra's statement and made copies for the prosecutor and the defense. I gave the original to Bettye.

I sat at my desk, yawned and roughed out a list of crimes I would charge Myra with and my sentence recommendation. I'd see if Shelby Johnson would accept it and sell it to his boss.

I started with murder 2nd degree, my gift rather than murder one. I added aggravated burglary for breaking into the Lambert home with the intent to kidnap Nell. Then I threw in attempted kidnapping 1st degree, possession of a deadly weapon during the commission of a felony and falsely reporting an incident.

Under that list, I scribbled: Plead guilty to all the above and allocute—twenty-five to life, in satisfaction of all—sentences to run concurrently. I photocopied the page. On the original, I wrote in red pen, "He hasn't mentioned an insanity plea *yet*."

I walked back to the squad room and handed both pages to the ADA.

He looked at me.

"This is a gift," he said.

"The holidays are coming. I'm in a festive mood. Will it fly?"

"It'll save time and money. I think I can sell it if you're satisfied."

"I am. Give him his copy." I pointed at Beckwith.

"Twenty-five years is a gift?" Beckwith said.

Shelby was about to speak. I didn't let him.

"Albert, I've been up for twenty-two hours. I'm tired and irritable. You fuck around with me once more, and I'll throw away my offer, and we will prosecute Ms. Witford for murder one, with all the trimmings—and I'll ask the DA and the judge to consider the death penalty or consecutive sentences."

He tried to look annoyed.

"Perhaps you see I'm getting a little emotional here," I said. "You do anything other than roll over and say yes, and I'll do everything possible to see your client gets the big sleep. Do we understand each other?"

"I'm acting professional here. There's no reason to speak to me like that."

I glared at him, unimpressed by his rhetoric.

He lowered his eyes and nodded. "We agree to twenty-five to life in satisfaction of all charges. Will you oppose parole when she's eligible?"

"I'll be too old to care. Don't sweat it."

"All right then. Can we wrap this up shortly?"

"Sergeant Rose and I will complete the paperwork. I'll have Ms. Witford transported to the sheriff's facility, the documents taken to Mr. Johnson's office and the arraignment will take place in the morning. You may stay with your client while the sergeant completes the arrest report or leave—your choice. I'll be writing the prosecution worksheet and composing the court information. Mr. Johnson, you stayin' or goin'?"

"I'll be in my office until arraignments. You seem to have everything under control." He extended his hand for me to shake.

"Thanks for coming out."

"Good job. See y'all later."

Stanley took a spot at the computer terminal next to Myra. I walked out with Shelby. Beckwith stayed, perhaps wanting to run up the billing.

When the ADA left, I sat down in a chair next to Bettye who sat reading *Northern Lights* by Nora Roberts.

"Hey," I said.

"Hey, yourself."

"That any good?"

"Uh-huh."

"What's it about?"

"A big city detective who takes a chief's job in a little town and finds himself a girlfriend. I don't think you'd like it."

"Maybe I would. By the way, you did one hell of a job tonight."

"Thanks."

"You bet. And now it's about wrapped up."

Bettye marked her place in the book and stood up to put on her jacket. We walked to the back door together.

"Good night, Sam."

"See you tomorrow."

"I'll be here."

I waited there until she drove out of the lot, locked our door, the public back doors and finally settled in to do my paperwork.

At six-thirty, two cops escorted Myra to the Justice Center. Albert Beckwith left, and Stanley mumbled something about seeing me at 4 p.m.

My last business was to leave a note for the day shift to have one man stay in the office until either Bettye or I got back. I turned out the lights and went home.

———

At seven o'clock, I parked my car and looked toward the sunrise. Chickadees and cardinals and a few cedar waxwings flew around the yard. A hint of sunlight showed above the trees. It was cool and damp, and the sun gave the autumn leaves a golden glow.

I needed breakfast and a shave. I looked like a derelict. I wanted to brush my teeth and see my wife.

Up in the bedroom, I put my hand on Kate's cheek and waited for her to wake up. Bitsey, the savage guard dog, snored peacefully on her bed ten feet away.

"Hey, where have you been?" Kate asked, still half asleep.

"You don't want to know."

I sat on the edge of the mattress, bent over and kissed her forehead.

"What time is it?"

"Seven. You gonna sleep all day?"

"I guess not. You've had a long night. Are you ready to sleep?"

"Too hungry. Maybe later."

"When later?"

"This afternoon or tonight. I couldn't sleep now."

"What were you doing?" She rubbed my chin. "You look like a hobo."

"Tossing out hot dogs—figuratively."

"Did they work?"

"Like a charm."

"My hero."

"You had the good idea. I'm just the guy with technical ability."

"Like a surgeon."

"You betcha."

"You want breakfast?"

"Sure."

———

At arraignment, Myra Witford pled guilty to murder, accepted her deal and was initiated into the criminal justice system.

Little Nell McBath stayed with her aunt and uncle.

I bought lunch for my team—and my favorite FBI agent—at the Villa Napoli. Life in beautiful downtown Prospect went back to normal.

THE END

V IS FOR... VITAMIN?

Bettye Lambert and I walked arm in arm along the Prospect Greenway at 6:15 on a moonless Thursday night. Leaves from poplar, maple and elm trees floated down, littering the isolated blacktop path, illuminated only by the occasional overhead mercury vapor lamp.

Further up the trail, we stepped over golden-brown sycamore leaves, some the size of dinner plates and all garnished with julienned slivers of willow.

"You walk too fast," she said. "It's more romantic to walk slowly."

"Yeah, I guess you're right."

"Then let's slow down."

"You want to *look* romantic? Let's sit on the next bench and neck."

"Sammy, darlin', it's not even forty degrees out here."

"I know. I'm from New York. I walk fast and the cold doesn't bother me."

We walked for another hundred yards. Bettye told me how her son signed up for freshman wrestling at Heritage High School and I told her I just bought a new set of Pirelli radials for my '67 Austin-Healey.

"Not many people are out on a Thursday night," she observed.

"Yeah, people are funny. If they walk or run or bicycle three times a week, they do it on Monday, Wednesday and Friday. The other days don't get much action."

The Smith & Wesson Chief's Special in my jacket pocket felt cool from the brisk evening temperature. Acorns crunched under our feet as we walked on and passed a narrow path leading to McTeer's Station Pike.

Sixty seconds later I said, "I think we've got company." Footsteps slapped the pavement behind us. I whispered, "I'm turning around. Take a quick step forward and to the right."

"Okey dokey."

I spun around abruptly and looked at a stocky man not more than ten feet behind us.

"Excuse me," I said. "What time is it?"

He stopped in his tracks, his unshaven face partially hidden by a hooded sweatshirt worn under a brown Carhartt jacket.

The man looked shaken, but recovered quickly and stared into my eyes. He stepped closer and whipped a hand out of his jacket pocket. I heard the sharp click first and then saw the brushed silver blade of a push-button knife shine in the lamplight.

"It's time to gimme your wallet." His voice sounded low and menacing.

"Hey, take it easy," I said. "What do you want?"

"I want ya money, stupid. Gimme yer wallet and yer watch, or I'll cut yew and yer perty woman here."

He was now no more than four feet from me with the blade pointed roughly six inches above my stomach.

"Oh, I'm so glad you cleared that up, asshole." With a quick move, I leveled my stainless steel .38 at his chest. "You're under arrest."

"Oh, shit!" he said and tossed the switchblade at me, the point making a short slice in the cloth of my new ninety-dollar Storm Chaser jacket.

Looking down at my ruined windbreaker, I said, "Son of a bitch!" As the man took off, I shouted, "Don't you run on me." I fumbled momentarily getting the revolver back into its holster as I began running. Bettye followed close by with a small blue steel .38 in her hand.

"Are you hurt?" she asked.

"No, but I'll kill this bastard for cutting my jacket."

I sprinted off after our would-be robber.

"Police. Stop!" I yelled as the chunky felon ran awkwardly along the path.

He had nowhere to go but straight ahead. To our left, Crystal Creek gurgled along over rocks and tree roots. To our right, beyond thirty feet of woodlands, a six-foot chain link fence blocked access to the road.

As we approached a dog-leg to the left and a wooden footbridge over the creek, the tarmac walkway puckered in all directions from the overgrown roots of a giant tulip poplar. The cracked pavement offered an obstacle to the fleeing subject. I was only twenty feet behind him when the toe of his sneaker caught the elevated blacktop and sent him sailing.

He landed on his stomach, letting out a loud "Oof," as he hit the ground, but immediately he began low-crawling toward the grass verge and the woods beyond.

I caught up to him before he wiggled ten feet.

"Stay where you are, damn it." I said, puffing from the run.

As he continued his comical escape, I lunged forward and caught a handful of his hoodie. He struggled and grunted, and I slammed my fist into his kidney.

"Goddamnit, you prick, hold still," I said.

But he still tried to crawl further, arms and legs flailing in four directions, no doubt hoping to escape the inevitable. I heard Bettye's footsteps behind me, and I hit him twice more, same spot.

"Oof! Oh! Je-sus have mercy!" he cried. "Okay, okay. No more. I give up. You got me."

From behind me I heard, "For God's sake, Sam. Don't beat him to death."

"Bastard ruined my new jacket, and he thinks I'll let him get away!" I slapped him on the head and yanked his left arm behind him to hook up a handcuff.

Less than five minutes later, Officer Will Sparks met us in a marked Prospect PD cruiser idling at the main intersection of the four trails that made up the city's greenway.

I led our defendant toward the open back door of the police car, his hood now hanging behind his head.

"Hey, boss. Hey, Miss Bettye. Y'all got yerse'fs a perpetrator." Young Sparks sounded cheerful. He looked like a thirty-year-old version of Opie Taylor.

When we reached the cruiser, Will said, "Hey, I know this ol' boy."

The man in cuffs hung his head. Will took off his PPD ball cap and ran a hand through his red hair.

"Uh-huh, name's Virgil Terp. I locked him up once fer... Cain't remember. Stolen property or some such."

"Virgil Terp?" I recalled a historical character with a similar name.

"Yep, that's him," Sparks said.

"He matches the description of the subject in one of the robberies on the greenway," Bettye said. Her blonde hair looked shiny in the bright parking lot lights.

"We've got three more stick-ups done by someone three inches taller and forty pounds lighter," I said. "Will, you know if he hangs out with someone about that size?"

Virgil stood about five-nine and weighed at least 200 pounds. We needed someone closer to my height, six-foot or taller and thin, no more than a 160.

"Got him a brother named Morgan," Will said. "He's taller and perty thin."

"Morgan and Virgil Terp?" I said. "You gotta be kiddin'."

"Nosir. The Terp family's been around Prospect fer years."

"Is there a third brother named Wyatt?" I asked.

"Not that I know of," he said, missing my implication.

Bettye smiled, and her hazel eyes showed a spark of recognition to my reference to the old western hero.

I pushed Virgil into the backseat of Will's car and slammed the door.

"Take him in, and start the paperwork," I said. "We'll be back at the barn shortly. I'll write the prosecution worksheet. On your way in, call Stanley, and ask him to meet us at the PD. And call in the next cell guard on the list. This guy's not going anywhere tonight."

As Will drove away, Bettye and I took the short walk to my unmarked Ford.

"You may want to spend some time on the treadmill, darlin'. You were puffin' by the time you caught ol' Virgil," she said, sounding all bubbly.

"I don't like treadmills," I growled. "I get up early three days a week and walk."

"Then maybe you ought to run."

"Gimme a break."

"Bein' tall, dark and handsome's not enough, Sammy. You need to be healthy."

"Are you my sergeant or my mother?"

I don't know why she laughed at that.

"Have you gained weight recently?" she asked.

"I have not, and you know it. I'm the same hundred and eighty pounds I've been since I was a kid."

"Just askin'." She chuckled.

"You were just harassing me."

"Sammy, would I do that?"

"Yes."

"I said tall, *dark* and handsome, sugar. But there's a lot more gray up there since you started workin' here."

"That's because of you. Now leave me alone."

She laughed again. I wished I had Virgil handy. I would have smacked him.

———

When Bettye and I walked into the squad room, we found Virgil Terp shackled to a steel ring on the sidewall of a desk. Will Sparks typed away at the computer, and Sergeant Stan Rose, all six-foot-four inches of him, stood looking down at Virgil.

As Bettye and I shook off our coats, Stanley broke out in a wide grin.

"You do good work for two old white people."

"Hey," Bettye said. "I'm only forty-five. That's not old."

"Thanks for sticking up for me, Mrs. Lambert."

"Sorry, boss."

I whispered in her ear. "You may look a lot younger, but check the calendar, love, you're forty-six."

"Oh, shut up, Sammy." She didn't whisper.

I pulled up a chair facing Terp.

"How old are you, Virgil?"

"Twenny-two."

"What a shame. A young life cut short by the criminal justice system."

He wrinkled his brow and squinted at me.

"You're being charged with armed robbery, possession of a deadly weapon and attempted murder of a police officer. How's that sound?"

"Murder? I didn't try ta murder no-body."

"Not the way I see it, nitwit. And I'm the cop. You threw a knife at me. Knives kill people. And you ruined my new jacket. I want to see you do life in jail."

"Life," he croaked. "I don't think ya kin do that."

"Who cares what you think, stupid? Can you afford a good lawyer?" I didn't give him time to answer. "No, of course not. You'll get a public defender. And everyone knows they're so inexperienced they have trouble finding the courtroom."

Virgil seemed to lose some of his attitude and hunched forward hanging his head.

"The only way I'd cut you any slack, Virgil, old buddy, is if you name your partner. Who did the other three robberies on the greenbelt?"

He lifted his head to answer. "I don't know what yer talkin' about."

"Yes, you do. Make a statement, and I might do something about that attempted murder charge."

"I ain't writin' no statement." His attitude came back.

"You're protecting your brother, aren't you?"

"I want a lawyer."

"You need at least one. Last chance, moron. Talk now or no deals."

"Lawyer."

He actually smiled. I actually didn't smack him.

I wanted to strangle the smug bastard, but settled for retreating to the front of the squad room.

"Attempted murder?" Bettye said. "Really? Maybe attempted assault?"

"Yeah, well. He's an imbecile. He didn't know. It was worth a try."

I looked at Stanley standing there grinning. "I may be white," I said, "but I am not up tight. So, my brother, how'd you like to do some detective work tonight?"

"My great white leader speaks like a poet. Whatcha need?" Stanley, who usually speaks with no accent at all, lapsed into his Uncle Remus act for our entertainment.

"Pull a motor vehicle photo of Morgan Terp off the computer, and make a six-pack of pictures to show the victims of the other three robberies. Maybe we'll get lucky."

"Will told me this desperado here didn't even wear a mask," Stan said.

"Yeah, he should have read a Jesse James comic book before embarking on his life of crime. No other vic mentioned a mask either. Obviously, intelligence wasn't issued to the Terp boys. Let's hope someone recognizes brother Morgan.

Later that evening, Stanley hit the jackpot. All three victims positively identified Morgan Terp as the person who robbed them at knifepoint along the Prospect Greenway.

After picking up an arrest warrant at the Blount County Justice Center the next morning, I met Officers Junior Huskey and Billy Puckett at Prospect Pines Nursing Home and Assisted Living Facility where Morgan Terp worked as a maintenance man.

I sent Puckett to guard the rear entrance with PO Johnny Rutledge who had watched Terp's home overnight and followed him to work earlier that morning. Rutledge was tired, but eager to work. Junior and I checked in with the administrator.

After a quick chat with the man who governed the home of more than two-hundred senior citizens, Junior and I followed the facility's security chief, looking for Morgan Terp.

In the second-floor library, a room no more than eight by twelve, we found Morgan on a six-foot step ladder changing a fluorescent bulb in a ceiling fixture.

I nodded to Junior who stepped off to the right and drew his .40 caliber Glock. I took the left, while the security man blocked the doorway.

"Morgan Terp," I said. "Prospect Police. Down off the ladder. You're under arrest."

He thought quickly—or perhaps not at all. Morgan jumped from the ladder and turned in one motion. He stood less than six feet from us holding a three-foot fluorescent tube at port arms like a riot baton. His face was contorted into a virtual snarl.

I drew my pistol and brought it up to a perfect point-shoulder position. If Morgan were a silhouette target, it would have been pointed directly at his X-ring.

"We've got guns, you fool. You've got a light bulb. Are you nuts?"

The tall, skinny Terp looked at me and then Junior, who resembled a big high school linebacker and could have broken him and his light bulb in half even if he didn't carry a gun.

Terp's shoulders relaxed and dropped a few inches. He lowered the light tube and shook his head. "Okay. I ain't gonna fight."

"Hand me the bulb slowly," I said. "Then turn around for him to cuff you."

Morgan offered no resistance. Junior cuffed and frisked him. I handed the security chief the light bulb.

Fifteen minutes later, Junior led Morgan Terp out the front door, and my cell phone rang. Two people in the lobby frowned as an instrumental version of *Paint it Black* played inside my jacket pocket.

"Hi, sweetie," Kate said. "I think there's a problem at the assisted living facility. Can you meet me there?"

My wife and a few other local women did volunteer work entertaining the residents at several senior citizen facilities in and around Prospect.

"You're at Prospect Pines today, right?"

"I am," she said.

"Then, I think your problem is me. Junior and I arrested one of the staff for robbery. We may have gotten a little noisy. Trouble's over."

"Different trouble, Sammy. We've got a dead body over here, and a man in a wheelchair says it's murder."

———

It only took five minutes to walk from the administrator's office to the lobby of the assisted living wing. Kate and the activities director, a young woman named Allison Gamble, stood there waiting.

"Hi, Allison," I said and then looked at Kate. "What's up, kiddo?"

"They found Mr. Cumberbatch dead in his room," Kate said. "He always comes to our programs so Allison sent someone to get him."

"Mister who?" I asked.

"Wallace Cumberbatch," Allison said.

"And how old was Wallace Cumberbatch?" I asked.

"Seventy-eight," Allison answered.

"Kate, sweetie, I know these old gents love looking at you and wouldn't miss one of your dog and pony shows for all the money in the state, but this is a nursing home. People die here all the time."

Kate put her hands on her shapely hips, and her dark eyes showed annoyance. I know it's cliché, but she is beautiful when she's angry. Other times, too. The old men at Prospect Pines probably liked her snug turtleneck and designer jeans. I certainly did.

"The doctor says he had a heart attack," Allison said.

"That's bullshit." The voice came from behind me.

I turned around.

"Wally was no ath-a-lete, but his heart wasn't that bad," said a man sitting in a motorized wheelchair.

"Really? And you are?"

"Al Mueller, Detective Sergeant, Michigan State Police, retired."

Mueller looked big even hunched into the wheelchair. His hair was all white, and he had the mottled nose of a heavy drinker.

"Sergeant Mueller, I'm Sam Jenkins, chief at Prospect PD."

He stuck out an oversized hand for me to shake. Mueller wore a red plaid shirt and khaki pants.

"You ever do any detective work?" he asked.

"Yeah. Just a little."

"Whereabouts? You don't sound like a local."

"New York. Twenty years worth."

"Pick up any rank?"

Maybe he was writing a book.

"Yeah, I was a lieutenant. A section commander."

"Good. We can talk about it. But now we gotta secure the crime scene. Come on. Follow me."

Mueller used a two-inch joystick to spin his wheelchair on its axis and blast off down the corridor like someone leading a column of mechanized infantry. I looked at Kate and Allison, shrugged and followed the old man.

Two orderlies had pushed a rolling gurney into Wallace Cumberbatch's room sometime before I arrived.

"I told them to wait for the cops," Al said. "Don't let'em touch the body."

I looked at the two men dressed in sage green hospital scrubs. "Hang on a minute, guys." I flashed my badge. "Let's see if we can resolve this situation before you do anything."

Obviously not piece-workers, the orderlies seemed happy to wait. They backed up and leaned against the wall.

"Okay, Al, why do you think he was murdered?"

"He was in good shape for his age. Uh... What did you say your name was?"

"Sam."

"I'm tellin' you, Sam. He walked a couple miles every day, went to their goddamn exercise classes, ate a fistful of vitamins each morning and danced with the old broads in this place every time they held a get-together."

"He was seventy-eight. These things happen," I said.

"Yeah? And I'm eighty-four. You see me croakin' in my room?"

"The doctor seems to think he died of natural causes."

"That asshole didn't spend two minutes with the body. Look at the eyes, Sam. Tell me what you see."

Wallace Cumberbatch lay across his bed in a fairly natural position.

Unless someone moved the body, he just collapsed on the mattress and died.

I pried up Wally's eyelids. "You're right. He's dilated to about the size of a .38 wadcutter. He take any medication?"

"There are some bottles over there." Mueller pointed to several amber-colored plastic vials sitting on a maple dresser. "I don't know what he takes, but I never seen his eyes look like that. He's gooned up on something."

I looked at the orderlies. "Sorry, guys. I've got reason to look closer at this one. Tell whoever you work for I'm making this room a crime scene. No one but police personnel comes in."

Mueller looked at the two workers. "See. I told you so."

One of them said offhandedly to the other, "Shit. Ol' man be pissin' in the wind."

Al just couldn't let that one go. "Shut up, you black bastard."

The orderly turned and locked eyes with Mueller, but Al was no slouch in a staring contest.

I held up a hand before the confrontation could escalate. "I'll take care of this, gentlemen. Thanks."

The two men left, taking the gurney with them.

"You know, Al," I said, "I won't mention anything about what the new generation calls political correctness, but it's never a good idea to piss off a guy who can spit in your soup."

"Ah, fuck him, that cock-a-roach. Let's get the coroner down here."

I laughed. "We've got medical examiners in Blount County, not a coroner. Like I told the orderlies, I'll take care of it."

Al looked mad. His face had turned a little red, and he sat there, shaking his head. "You believe that bastard? When I was on the job, somebody talked to me like that, I'd put him through a wall."

I nodded, knowing how he felt. "Yeah, but times change. And maybe he meant me. I'm an old man, too."

Mueller laughed. "Yeah, right. You look young enough to be my son. When you're ready for my statement, I'll be in my room—number 124. See ya later, kid."

———

The county sheriff sent me two crime scene investigators to handle my forensic work and Doctor Morris Rappaport showed up representing the medical examiner.

After his assistant bundled up the body, Morris, a short man with curly gray hair and a prominent nose, spoke to me with his pronounced New Jersey accent. "Give me a little time to get you a toxicology report, Sam. I'll call as soon as I can."

I nodded. "Sure, Mo. Works for me."

"I also want to check with his doctor and pharmacist about the meds and see if he was on schedule according to the dispense dates. Sometimes they accidentally double up doses."

I nodded again. "Yeah, tough remembering the little things when you're old."

"There wasn't a mark on him, you know," he said. "But there was something funny. You saw he was dressed nicely? Sport shirt and dress slacks."

"I did."

Morris held an index finger in the air. "But he had no underwear."

"Really? Think someone dressed his nude body and forgot his skivvies?"

"Who can say?"

"Got a time of death?"

"He's into rigor, so more than ninety minutes, but they keep it so damn hot in these places, I can't be sure how much more. I'd say probably sometime late last night."

"He looked clean shaven. I thought maybe earlier this morning. Why would someone in a nursing home shave at night?"

"Who knows?"

"So, maybe he died this morning?"

"I don't think so, but I'll know more after the post."

"Thanks, Mo. Give me a jingle."

"You got it, boychek. I'll talk to ya."

I t took me more than a half hour to give the basic information about Wallace Cumberbatch to Kate and Allison, smooth over the facility administrator and assuage the ego of his attending physician. Then I found room 124 and former Detective Sergeant Al Mueller.

His room looked far from Spartan, but it wasn't posh—more like an office with a bunk than a cozy bedroom. Several framed photos hung on the walls, one of a young couple and three children. Others were police related. One picture showed Al being promoted to sergeant. Another showed him accepting a plaque from a distinguished man dressed in a dark suit. The plaque hung next to the photo. I read the inscription on the Michigan State Police Bravery and Combat Award. Another picture of a woman in her fifties stood on top of a dresser next to a mini-refrigerator. I assumed it was an old photo of Mrs. Mueller.

Al sat in his easy chair in front of a twenty-one inch TV, watching an episode of *Walker, Texas Ranger* on the Sleuth Channel.

"You watch this shit?" he asked.

"Not one of my favorites."

He used the remote to put Chuck Norris to rest and tossed it onto his bed with a look of disgust.

"So, whaddaya know?" he asked.

"That's my question. You found him. I just got here."

"You heard what I told ya. Wally was a healthy guy—all things considered."

"And now he's dead. You know anyone who didn't like him?"

"No. He was a nice enough guy. A social kinda guy, if you know what I mean."

"Did he mouth off to the staff like you?"

"Gimme a break. I pay the bills here. You gotta show 'em who's boss."

"Did Wally do that?"

He shook his head. "No. Wally was a pussycat."

A nurse's aide stuck her head in Al's doorway. "Mr. Mueller, you're goin' ta be late fer lunch."

"Yeah, yeah, okay." He answered her and turned back to me. "Listen, I gotta go. Gimme a hand getting' into this motor scooter."

I locked the rear wheel of his chair and offered him an arm.

"Okay, Al, but you're in this thing now. So, nose around and see what you can find out. But don't piss off too many people if you can help it. I'll talk to you soon."

I followed him into the hallway where he looked up at me.

"You're hot shit, ya know?"

"Yeah, I do. See ya around, Albie."

Mueller made his way to the dining room, and I left the building.

The next morning, I made a couple phone calls from home before leaving for the assisted living facility. Ten minutes after I arrived, my new partner started asking questions.

"What's your ME have to say?" Mueller asked. "He do the autopsy last night?"

"Nothing yet. They were busy yesterday."

"Busy? Here in Podunk? For chrissakes."

Al's uniform of the day: A blue plaid shirt and the same khaki pants.

"Besides Wally dying," I said, "the county handled a house fire in Friendsville. That accounted for four bodies. Troopers had a double fatal on 411, and I hear Pigeon Forge is working a homicide. Everybody uses the same UT morgue facilities, so it's standing room only—so to speak."

"So, it's twenty-four hours, and you got nuthin'?"

"No," I said. "I'm back here waiting to hear what *you* found out."

He looked at me for a long moment and then laughed.

"Hot shit! You want me to do your work for you."

"You're the one talking about being a hot-shot ex-detective. I have twelve cops working three shifts, and the city of Prospect is calling for service. You wanted to be involved. So, be involved. I need all the help I can get. What do *you* know?"

"Okay, okay, you got me. No offense."

I shrugged. "No sweat. None taken."

He rolled his wheelchair over to the mini-fridge. "You want a beer?"

"Ordinarily, I'd say yes. But it's 10 a.m. Ask me again this afternoon."

"You mind?" He held up a bottle of Yuengling lager.

"You allowed to have that?" I asked.

"Hey, I told you. I sign the checks here. Doctors just give advice. It's up to me to do what I want."

"Like participatory management."

"Yeah, right." He grinned and twisted the cap off the longneck.

"Cheers," I said.

He took a long pull from the bottle.

"Remember I told you how Wally used to make it a point to dance with the old broads here?"

"You did," I said.

"So, whaddaya think? A love triangle maybe. Love's one of the big motives. Right?"

"Could be, but I don't know yet. You're thinking poison?" How romantically involved did these women get?

"I dunno either," he said, "but take a look. They're all on the home stretch. Either they get it now, or it may be never."

"Eloquently put."

"Gimme a break. You ever been an inmate in a nursing home?"

"Resident of an assisted living facility."

"Yeah? Bullshit! It's a goddamn prison."

———

Allison Gamble had worked as the Activities Director at Prospect Pines for five years. She was a smart, pretty, thirty-something-year-old brunette who would have looked more attractive had she not worn one of those baggy, garishly-colored nurse's outfits I hate.

I walked into her office and sat in one of the guest chairs. Al Mueller followed me and brought his wheelchair to an abrupt stop inches from her desk. Allison knew why I had come. She wasn't too sure about Albert.

"Can I help you with something, Mr. Mueller?" she asked with the brightest smile in the building.

"I'm with him." Mueller growled, jerking his thumb in my direction.

She looked at me questioningly.

"I seem to have acquired a partner. He's helping out. Mind if he stays?"

Allison shrugged and opened a file folder sitting on her desk.

"Does he list any family, heirs or beneficiaries?" I asked.

"You mean someone who would benefit from his death?"

"Sounds terrible, but that's what makes the world go around."

"His listed next-of-kin as a nephew."

Al interrupted. "He never sees that guy. He's a bum."

"Why do you say that?" I asked.

"Wally told me. They didn't like each other. Guy lives up in Ohio. Owns a used car lot. You wanna be friends with a guy like that?"

I rolled my eyes and shrugged that time.

"How did he pay for his accommodations here?" I asked, turning my attention to Allison.

"He had money in an account from selling his house. He also purchased a long-term care policy. Couple that with his savings and Social Security and he seemed to be doing okay. You can check with his social worker and the accounting department for more detailed information about how long he could afford to stay here. We're pretty upscale, and sometimes people have to move to a more...modest facility if their funds get low."

"Who has a copy of his will?"

"Admin has the original. I have a copy here." She handed several sheets of paper to me.

It looked very simple. Wallace left nothing to a relative, but he specified several animal welfare organizations as co-beneficiaries.

"After the estate settles his debts, all other money goes to the animals," I said.

"Who?" Al said.

"Not who—what. Animals. Literally. ASPCA, Humane Society...a couple others."

"I'll be damned. An animal lover," Al said. "Whodda thunk it?"

Allison smiled. I think she approved.

"I've heard that perhaps Mr. Cumberbatch had been, ah...romantically involved with more than one of the female residents," I said.

Allison looked over at Al Mueller. I guess she considered him the source of my information. He met her stare with the hard eyes of a former tough cop and made her blink first.

"Wallace was a very socially conscious person," she said. "He attended all the events we organized. But I don't know anything about his romantic life. I leave at five o'clock. I assume that would take place later on."

"Can you give me names of the people he socialized with most? I need people who knew him and may be able to give me information about his last few days."

She provided six names. Mueller and I went back to his room.

"Okay, Albert, here's the list. What do you think? Do we have a complete roster? Want to add anyone?"

He pulled a pair of reading glasses from his shirt pocket, looked at Allison's hand-written list and began nodding.

"This looks pretty good. These two guys—forget them." He tapped the paper in two spots. "They played cards with him. So did I. They're just two old guys."

"There ever a problem with the card games? Was Wally a big loser? He good about paying up? Money is another big motive in homicides."

"We played for plastic chips—no cash involved. I told you. Forget them. Waste of time."

He slapped the joystick and rolled his chair up to the fridge and yanked open the door. He showed me another bottle of Yuengling. "Beer?"

"Yes, it is."

He scowled. "Wise guy."

"No, thanks," I said.

"Yeah, okay." He took a long drink.

"I'm giving you your head here, Al, because I think you know what you're doing. I hope you're right about this. But don't abuse my trust."

He held the beer in one hand and thrust the other to his side. "Trust me. I know what I'm doin'."

"Jeez. You sound like me."

"Ha! Ya see."

I shook my head.

He looked back at the list. "Okay, check out the women. Felsie Huffman. Local girl. Pushing ninety. She got a chair like me. Forget her. She's almost a vegetable. Wally was nice to her, is all. He used to wheel her to bingo."

"A vegetable?"

"Yeah. Ya understand what I'm sayin'?"

"Explain so I do."

"Felsie just puts in her time. There was no involvement with Wally other than him being a nice guy. She's not capable of anything romantic."

"And you say *I'm* hot shit."

He laughed.

"These three, they're younger broads—in their seventies." He tapped the list again. "The last one here, Lexie Fromsett. She's the youngest and pretty good-lookin'. From Bay City, Michigan, like me. I think she's hot in the ass. Wally did, too."

"Did Wally take advantage of her? She pissed at him for some reason?"

"Not that I know. She's nice. He treated her okay."

"You're no help."

"Kiss my ass."

"Who's next?"

"Myrtle Rankin. She's from New Jersey. She moved here outta Florida ten years ago. Got too crowded for her and too hot. One of those we call a halfback. You know, half way back from Florida to Jersey." He laughed at the tired old joke. "Then her old man died, and she ended up in here. Myrtle's almost as tall as you. She can get nasty at times."

"Nasty sounds promising. A woman scorned? The jealous type? You know where I'm going?"

"Yeah, I do, but I got nothing to add."

"Okay, on to number three."

"Luretta Parsley. She's from somewhere in Kentucky. Real southern belle. A real cutesy. Watch out for her. You know what I'm sayin'?"

"No, I don't, but I'll talk to these ladies, and let you know."

"Hey, you said I was your partner. Now I can't come to the interrogation. What's with you?"

"Albert, so far it's just an interview. If they were involved in something kinky but innocent, they might admit it to me. I leave here, and they may never see me again. You're here every day. Why embarrass them? Get my meaning?"

"Yeah, I understand. I think it's bullshit, but I understand."

———

I interviewed Felsie Huffman first. While I didn't agree with Mueller's likening her to a rutabaga, she didn't fit the mold of a nursing home femme fatal, and I pushed her onto the back burner of my investigation. The other three, Myrtle, Luretta and Lexie were different stories.

Their ages spread from seventy-three to seventy-eight. All looked pretty well-preserved and acted like they were looking for their second or third childhoods.

Lexie Fromsett, the blonde bombshell from Bay City, was, as Al Mueller said, good-looking for a woman her age. She sounded personable enough, but I doubted that Mensa had her on their waiting list.

She confirmed that Wally's abilities on the dance floor rivaled Fred Astaire and Gene Kelly, but she never spoke of any romantic involvement.

After fifteen minutes, I got the impression she tap-danced through my interview. But it wasn't my place to smack a seventy-three-year-old woman and tell her I believed she had omitted material information.

Moving on to Mildred Rankin. Al was correct. She was almost six-foot-tall, with nicely styled gray hair and a look of basic intelligence about her. But I sensed her bristly attitude immediately. I wouldn't be able to schmooze her into cooperating.

"Ms. Rankin, tell me about your relationship with Mr. Cumberbatch."

"What relationship? He lived here. So do I. What makes you think we had a relationship?" She had an annoying way of squinting and pursing her lips after speaking.

"People have told me you two were friendly."

"What people?"

"People with open eyes and good minds."

"Not true."

"If there was no friendship, was there any animosity between you two?"

"No."

"Do you dance with men you don't like?"

"We danced. Occasionally. So what? Is that a crime?"

"Thanks a bunch, Ms. Rankin. You've been very helpful."

Bitch.

I saved Ms. Parsley for last. If I was a single gentleman over seventy, confined to an adult facility and Luretta Parsley, with her honey-colored hair, wanted to be my friend, I'd jump on the opportunity. My imagination conjured up a picture of what she might have looked like as a younger woman. On the day I met her, I placed her on my list of most attractive seventy-five-year- old girls I'd ever met—physically and mentally attractive.

After a few minutes of routine questioning, I decided to try the old Jenkins' charm and see if she'd spill the beans to her new buddy Sam.

"If you're from Louisville, I'll bet your friends call you Slugger," I said.

"Nobody does yet, but you may if ya like, Sam." She fluttered her eyelashes.

"I'm having a real problem getting information about our friend Mr. Cumberbatch."

She nodded and smiled.

"More than once, I've heard you two were friendly. Perhaps very friendly."

"Wallace was a lovely man. Such a gentleman. And a fine dancer, too. Do you dance, Sam?"

I shook my head and hoped she wasn't too disappointed. "Not very well. May I infer you two were romantically involved?"

She lowered her eyes and smiled demurely. "You might say Wallace and I had something special. Is that a problem?"

I smiled. "Not for me."

"Good. Then how may I help you?"

"This is sort of an indelicate question, but did Wallace ever mention using illicit drugs?"

Her seductive expression changed completely. "Drugs? Good Lord, no. Wallace was a gentleman, not a common hooligan."

"I have reason to believe he may have taken something other than the medications his doctor prescribed. Know anything about that?"

"Goodness me."

"Is that a no, Luretta?"

She shook her head. "I cannot imagine Wallace abusing drugs. Lord have mercy."

"Why do you think he died?"

"He was seventy-eight. Heart attack, I suppose."

"Induced by?"

"Induced by? A weak heart maybe."

Lord have mercy!

———

M y cell phone rang while I sat in a visitor's lounge at Prospect Pines trying to sort out what I learned—without Al Mueller's interference.

"Sam," Bettye said, "Doctor Mo just called. I tried to write down exactly what he said, but you need to call him. He's got all kinds of technical information on the Wallace Cumberbatch death."

As I tapped in the medical examiner's phone number, I watched two colorful finches fly around an over-sized aviary in the center of the room. The lounge felt so warm, I would have fallen asleep if I stayed much longer. Maybe I should have hung out with Al Mueller. He did keep a supply of cold beer on hand.

"Morris," I said, "are you going to complicate my life or hand me a solution for this unattended death?"

"Samilah, boychek, a great big monkey wrench I've got to throw at you.

This is what I have now, but I'll know even more when the tox report comes in."

Ten minutes later, I shook my head, rubbed my eyes with the heels of my hands and asked, "Why me?"

I called Bettye and told her to meet me at Prospect Pines.

————

Five minutes after Bettye arrived, I watched ex-Detective Sergeant Albert Mueller wheel aggressively down the hall in our direction. The three dancing women waited in the lounge on our left.

"Oh, jeez," I said. "Mueller's here. Stall him while I talk to the ladies. I know he'll want to wait around, but he can't sit in on this."

"You want me to just chase him away?" Bettye asked.

"Be nice to the old guy. He's trying to be helpful."

"What can I talk to him about?"

"Ask him to list his favorite beers. That should take plenty of time."

I assembled the women we believed to be Wallace Cumberbatch's love interests. I wouldn't normally interview subjects or suspects together, but I thought I might be able to play one off the others and get someone to blurt out a material fact.

When I entered the room, I found the girls smiling.

"Hello, Chief," two of them said, Myrtle while scowling and Lexie while smiling.

"Hi there, Sam," Luretta said.

Suddenly the mood changed. "Well, aren't we getting familiar?" Myrtle Rankin, the one from New Jersey snapped, sending visual daggers toward Luretta.

So far, things were progressing nicely. Myrtle had spotted a weak link in their alliance.

"Ladies," I said to divert their attention, "I'm afraid we have to discuss a few details about your relationships with Wally that could become a little indelicate. Forgive me, but I think it's necessary."

"Wallace." Luretta said.

"I beg your pardon?"

"He liked to be called Wallace," she said.

"Yes, I called him that, too," Lexie Fromsett said.

"So did I," Myrtle Rankin chimed in with her husky voice. "Wally sounds so...low class and *buddy-buddy*."

"Heavens to Betsy," I said. "Let's not be low class."

I didn't care about the pet name they gave him, and a phone call brought our discussion to a quick halt.

Lexie and Luretta smiled when they heard the Rolling Stones sound off from my jacket pocket. Myrtle, a tough customer, scowled at the interruption.

"Excuse me, ladies. Duty calls."

I stepped to the corner of the room when I heard Dr. Rappaport speaking.

"The official and now complete results of the autopsy on your Mr. Cumberbatch are of mixed interest, Sam."

"What's that supposed to mean?"

"It means I stand by my previous statement that he died of an old-fashioned heart attack."

"With no extenuating circumstances?"

"I didn't say that."

"Are you going to make me play twenty questions?"

"Twenty Questions, ha! I remember that show."

"Morris, I'm in the middle of something important here. Please."

"Right. Your Mr. C had the better part of forty milligrams of Viagra in his system. And a little alcohol."

"Viagra? For God's sake, would that kill him?"

"Maybe. I told you about the blockages I found. He wasn't exactly a time bomb, but his heart presented potential problems."

"So what's the normal dosage?" I asked.

"From five to twenty milligrams. But the Viagra may not have been the biggest strain to his heart."

"People say he walked a couple miles a day."

"Samilah, a leisurely stroll in the woods and a wild ride in the saddle are two different things. Your average orgasm strains the heart like running a 100-yard dash in ten seconds. If he had a very active sex life, his days could have been numbered."

"Aha!"

"Yes, aha. So now you've got something to go on."

"So, he might have ODed on vitamin V?"

"Perhaps."

"The pupils dilate when a man gets sexually aroused."

"They do."

"Do you think a man his age could get a prescription for Viagra?"

"Maybe, but based on his heart condition, I doubt a legitimate one."

"Doctor, you're a prince."

"I aim to please."

Bettye had entered the room and stood close by. We spoke for a few moments before I snapped my phone shut, walked over to an armchair and sat with the three old girls. Morris' information made it easy to run a bluff on the women.

"Ladies," I said, "I'm afraid that phone call sheds much light on Wally's death. I do believe at least one of you was present when he expired or at least shortly before. I think you all know more than you're telling."

"That's offensive." Myrtle's voice had a sharp edge to it.

"Oh, my." Lexie sounded concerned.

"Can I ask you a question, Sam, darlin'?" Luretta said.

"Not right now, Luretta. I want some answers first."

Myrtle, the tough guy, said, "Suppose we refuse to answer?"

"Do I need to call a lawyer?" Lexie asked.

"You weren't thinking of roughing us up, were you, Sam?" Luretta said, offering me a strained smile.

Two excited finches leaped from branch to branch and peeped away while the three women worried. I think the birds knew we stood at a crucial point in the interrogation.

"Rough you up? Good heavens, no," I said. "Not me. I'm turning you over to her." I jerked a thumb in Bettye's direction.

———

Bettye stepped up like a drill sergeant on the first day of basic training.

"Okay, ladies," she said. "I've just spent all morning with a friend of yours, and he gave you up."

That statement surprised me. Did Al Mueller provide Bettye with new information?

"Your pal, Morgan Terp, the maintenance man," she said, "told me how he's been supplyin' y'all with black market Viagra."

That one really surprised me. And if those women's faces could have dropped any further, I would have needed a scraper to get them off the floor.

"So, ladies," she continued, "unless y'all want to spend the rest of your golden years as guests of the Tennessee prison system on a charge of manslaughter, I suggest you start talkin'—now."

I crossed my arms over my chest and sat back, hoping to enjoy the show.

"That sniveling young bastard!" Myrtle said.

"You can never trust a man," was Lexie's advice.

Then Luretta asked, "Sam, can I ask y'all that question now?"

I sat forward, wondering what she considered so important. "Go ahead, Slugger, now's a good time."

She put on her demure act. "If I gave Wallace a couple o' pills, like Viagra fer instance, ya know, so he could, uh...*puhform* a li'l better...could I get inta trouble?

———

We learned that Wallace and Luretta had arranged for a *date* on the night he died. Earlier that day, Luretta provided him with a double dose of vitamin V so he wouldn't get embarrassed like he did on their last meeting, and she would end the evening satisfied.

The problem arose, you'll pardon the expression, when forty milligrams of the erectile dysfunction drug, washed down by one of Al Mueller's beers, sent the amorous Mr. Cumberbatch into cardiac arrest.

The curious occurrence of Wally's lack of undies was explained away by all three female suspects stating he never wore skivvies on the nights of their liaisons to make himself more accessible to them. Wally liked getting down to business with minimum hassle.

"Sam, honey, what are y'all goin' ta do with us?" Luretta asked.

"Me, Slugger? Absolutely nothing. I suggest you all call your children and have them retain a good lawyer. I'm going to dump you in the lap of an assistant district attorney."

————

Bettye and I stood in the lobby of Prospect Pines.

"Where did you get that connection to Morgan Terp?" I asked.

"When your new partner, Sergeant Mueller, told me he drank three six-packs of beer a week, I thought that was kind of hard to do in a nursing home."

I did some quick math and shrugged. "That's less than three bottles a day."

"Lord have mercy, Sam."

"What?"

"I asked him how he got the beer, and he said he tipped the maintenance man, Morgan Terp. Twenty dollars a week to pick up his beer and dispose of the empties."

"And you assumed he might also be providing all the ladies here with a supercharger for their boyfriend's sex drive."

"Exactly. It was just a hunch. Viagra is pretty easy to get a hold of."

"And because these three women weren't really bad guys, they fell into your trap and gave it up?"

"They did."

"Pretty good po-leece work, Sergeant."

"Thank you, sir. I thought so myself."

"I just can't understand why they bought it from Morgan. You can go on the Internet and get it cheap without a prescription."

"And just how do you know that, Sammy?"

"Oh, uh, people tell me things. You know how it is."

"I know, darlin'. You're the chief. You know everything."

"Naturally."

"Are we ready to get outta here?" she asked.

"No reason to hang around."

"Then, Sammy, you sweet man, I'm gonna let you take me for a late lunch."

"Good. I'm starving."

———

Assistant District Attorney General Shelby Johnson accompanied me to the Blount County Jail. We walked across the parking lot from his office in the Justice Center to the poured concrete, modular building complex that looked more like a wingless starship than a local slammer.

In an institutional gray conference room, we sat on one side of a rectangular table across from Morgan Terp and his lawyer, a public defender named Leroy Gribble. Three windowless cement block walls stood at our backs and sides. A single all-glass partition allowed Shelby and me to look into the general visitation room.

Terp slouched in a battered metal chair, resting most of his weight on his lower spine. Gribble looked a few years shy of thirty and wore a cheap, wrinkled gray suit.

I began the discussion.

"Mr. Gribble, have you told your client what he can expect if this goes to court?"

"We were hopin' Mr. Johnson would be amenable to a reduced sentence for a quick plea."

"The DA will tell you I have to agree to any plea bargain before it's accepted. And I see no reason to cut Mr. Terp any slack just to save time."

Terp showed no emotion. He sat low in his chair and seemed preoccupied trying to dig the accumulated dirt from under his left thumbnail with his right index finger.

Gribble looked young and uncomfortable. He listened closely and fidgeted in his seat.

"We thought the DA might like to save the people not only time, but the expense of a trial for some basic leniency," Gribble said.

"Mighty generous of you, Counselor," I said, "but that expense can be written off as good training for us. And this case just strengthens our reputation of not losing. This one is a headshot."

"We'll never know until we give it to the jury." Gribble sounded more like he was trying to convince himself.

"Look, Mr. Gribble. Let's quit dancing. Shelby and I get paid every other Thursday no matter what we do. Personally, I'd like going to trial. We're holding all the aces. Your client is dog food if this goes to a jury. The thought of armed robbery scares the stuffing out of the average citizen. Morgan will get the max."

Gribble's shoulders dropped slightly. He looked tired of sparring and willing to concede. Terp still paid more attention to his fingernails.

"You wouldn't have asked for a meetin' if y'all weren't lookin' for somethin'," Gribble said.

Shelby looked at me before answering. I winked and took the reins. He seemed content to allow me to speak for the people of the State of Tennessee.

"Yes, sir," I said. "The magic subject. Cooperation. How does he feel about swapping some information and testimony for that leniency?"

"He's listenin', and we're more than willin' to cooperate if it's in his best interest."

"Good. We'll make you an offer you can't refuse."

———

Morgan Terp received the big deal of the day. He copped to one count of robbery in satisfaction of all three and pled guilty to distributing the ED medication. In exchange for testimony implicating his girlfriend, Opal Kinnard, a pharmacist's assistant at Blount Memorial Hospital and a formal statement about how she pilfered quantities of Viagra, Cialis and LaVitra for him to provide the amorous ladies of Prospect Pines and their gentlemen friends with enough exercise to keep them feeling young for years, Morgan's sentence for selling controlled substances would run concurrently with his time for robbery.

Virgil Terp agreed to plead guilty to armed robbery if I dropped the bogus attempted murder of a police officer charge.

The two brothers won a full scholarship to the adult behavioral modification facility commonly called Brushy Mountain State Prison for five fun-filled years. But because of overcrowding, if they behaved themselves, they'd probably only do one-third of that.

Our three aging heroines posed a different problem. Technically, they were guilty of selling a controlled substance. In the eyes of the law, even giving equals selling. But no one wanted to place them in the same category as your everyday, run-of-the-mill drug dealer. So, with some creative courtroom antics, the lawyers arranged for them to plead guilty to a lesser charge of dispensing pharmaceuticals without a license. Because of their advanced ages and first offender status, a benevolent judge agreed to hold his verdict in abeyance for eleven months and twenty-nine days. As long as the girls didn't get into any trouble during that time, the arrest would go away as if it never happened.

Two DA investigators built a case against Opal Kinnard and put her out of business and into the court system.

Kate was able to mend my damaged jacket and donated it to the annual Coats for the Needy program. I took money from my uniform allowance fund and made Mr. L.L. Bean happy by ordering a replacement.

Meanwhile back at Prospect Pines, the administrator recognized a problem in dealing with the active libidos of some of his clients. Staff doctors agreed to provide confidential physical examinations for those determined to engage in intra-residential sex. Once certified as fit for romantic activity, the gentlemen would be provided with their ED medication of choice at list prices or directed to a volunteer resident with a personal computer who showed his comrades how to purchase their drugs from a cut-rate Internet pharmacy in Bangladesh.

A few days after wrapping up the Cumberbatch case, I stopped in to see Al Mueller and have a beer.

"Yeah, you're welcome," he said. "Happy to do all that free police work for you. But what about me? You locked up the only guy willing to go out and pick up my beer."

I had hoped for a little more camaraderie and less bitching. "I brought you a six-pack."

"I appreciate it. But how long's that gonna last?"

"You ever think about going on the wagon?"

He stuck his nose up at that suggestion. "What are you, my doctor, now?"

Before I called him an ingrate, I looked at the plaque hanging on the wall. Bravery and Combat Awards don't grow on trees.

"Albert, you're a giant pain in the ass, but I'll tell you what I'm gonna do."

Mueller smiled and sucked half his bottle dry.

Every week now, a Prospect cop smuggles three six-packs of beer into Prospect Pines for Detective Sergeant Albert Mueller, Michigan State Police, retired. He pays, but saves the twenty-dollar tip he had been giving to Morgan Terp.

I'm getting too easy in my old age.

THE END

FATE OF A FLOOZY

On a cloudy Thursday morning in late May, I stood in Helene Redpath's bedroom looking down at her naked body lying next to a man more than twenty years her junior. They were dead, of course. Killed by two blasts from a horribly expensive double-barreled shotgun.

A pair of tall double-hung windows in the second floor bedroom overlooked an Italianate garden at the back of the house. An alabaster statue of Mercury stood at the intersection of six narrow brick walks. Short and neatly trimmed boxwoods bordered pie-shaped beds of topsoil that held hundreds of colorful annuals planted no more than two weeks ago. Beyond the floral garden, stone steps led to an expansive lawn sloping to the south, terminating at the banks of the Little River.

I knew the homeowner. Not intimately, but I'd seen her around for years.

Helene Redpath had spent more than four decades portraying a floozy. She appeared in major motion pictures, TV movies, cable features and even on British television where they've never been squeamish about primetime sex or showing lots of skin. As a young actress, everyone remembered her face, but I'd be surprised if many people knew her name. Helene worked steadily for years, but spent most of that time on the "B" list. Whenever a studio needed a beautiful girl with a figure to make Miss Universe jealous, they cast Helene as a cheating housewife, an oversexed career woman, a hooker with a heart of gold or a scrumptious drunk.

Then, as she aged and the world watched her career declining, Ms. Redpath landed a part in the film *Cover-up*, playing the alcoholic mother of a soldier killed by friendly fire in Afghanistan. Suddenly the critics realized Helene could act, and she won an Oscar for best supporting role.

Jackie Shuman and David Sparks, crime scene investigators from the county Sheriff's office, worked the bedroom with the efficiency of well-trained automatons. The deputy medical examiner, Dr. Morris Rappaport, and his assistant, Earl W. Ogle, conducted field tests on the bodies and prepared them for their trip to the University of Tennessee's forensics lab.

"Got a time of death, Mo?" I asked the pathologist.

"For once, Sam, I can give you a definite answer. This young man likes to make love wearing a watch. A shotgun pellet stopped his Tag Huerer at exactly 10:28 last night."

I raised my eyebrows. "Hard to controvert that."

"By this afternoon, I'll be able to tell you if there are any factors beyond the obvious."

"Thank you, Morris. You're my favorite M.E."

He shrugged. "Such an honor."

I next spoke to the evidence technicians.

"Talk to me, Jackie. What do you know so far?"

"Well, as y'all kin see fer yer own self, there weren't no break. Either the door was open, or the shooter had him a key. The shotgun, it's layin' over yonder." He pointed just beyond the foot of the bed. "It's one sweet weapon. Musta cost more'n I make in a month. I believe it came from the cabinet downstairs in the den. Check it out. You'll find the door open an' only seven of the eight slots filled."

"Dust it yet?"

"David did. Wiped clean. Cabinet, too."

"Okay. When you finish and write all this up, stop at the PD."

"You got it, Chief."

The bedroom looked like a featured display from a museum of Early American furniture. Not the kind of things you'd buy in an antique mall, but rather what you'd acquire from a dealer who wore a double-breasted blazer and silk bow tie and paid fifty bucks for a short haircut every three weeks. A lot of thought went into decorating the room, but Helene would never enjoy it again.

Prospect, Tennessee had always been one of the vacation spots favored by some of the nine million people who visited the Great Smoky Mountains National Park annually. Those who desired a more tranquil atmosphere, a place without music halls, outlet malls or bumper car rides, visited my town. The travel brochures called us "the Peaceful side of the Smokies." It *is* peaceful...if we're not investigating double homicides.

When a small resort named Blackberry Farm, a place not far from where I lived, was named the number one holiday destination in North America by a famous travel magazine, the rich and famous began invading the hotel in force, totally oblivious to the nightly rates that topped off at $3,500.00. As Blackberry Farm gained popularity with people whose faces appeared regularly on shows like *Entertainment Tonight* and *Access Hollywood*, these celebrities decided they'd like a chunk of the Smokies for themselves and started purchasing their own private getaways.

Soon, the demand outweighed the supply, and farmers owning land with spectacular mountain views put the family homesteads on the market. Realtors began making commissions that allowed them to replace their four-door Chevys with top-of-the-line Range Rovers. Upper-crust subdivisions called Yorkshire Dales, Worthington Cove and The Cedars at Whispering Mountain overshadowed little communities within the Prospect postal district with traditional names like Gamble's Woods, Cutter's Gap or Keeble's Chapel.

Helene Redpath, herself a country girl originally from North Carolina, was one of the glamorous west coast celebrities who had discovered our corner of east Tennessee. In the years following her Oscar Award, she landed several more parts that made her a multi-millionaire. Two years ago, she and her husband paid a premium for the property I found myself now visiting, a 200-year-old farmhouse surrounded by 100 acres of choice land. Once she saw the house in which she eventually died, Helene became determined to buy it out from under a horde of hungry developers bent on carving up the land and creating another up-scale neighborhood in beautiful Prospect.

———

I found Helene Redpath's husband, Trevor Ridley, owner of a California movie production company, sitting on a love seat in the living room only a fraction of an inch away from draining a glass once full of expensive scotch. PO Bobby Crockett sat across from him on the matching sofa keeping Trevor from wandering around to places where the evidence technicians hadn't already been. Bobby had gotten the call at 9:53 that morning and investigated. After taking all the information Ridley could offer, the two men sat in silence, Bobby killing time and the victim's husband sucking down the single-malt. I took a seat next to Crockett.

"Mr. Ridley," I said. "I'm Sam Jenkins, chief at Prospect PD. I'll be investigating your wife's murder."

He nodded and looked at me with hooded, pale blue eyes. I made him for about mid-fifties. His dirty-blond hair was stylishly cut in fashionable spikes and shined up with mousse or a mono-unsaturated cooking oil. His clothing appeared beyond expensive and, from the style, probably purchased in the U.K. He was a good-looking man who had gone soft around the edges.

"Who did this?" he asked, in what I took for a working-class London accent.

"I'll have to get back to you on that, Mr. Ridley. I just got here. But I will find out who killed your wife...I always do."

I said that to either reassure him or shake him up. Husbands often kill wives—especially when they find them in bed with another man.

"I know how this must look," he said.

I shook my head. "Tell me how it looks."

He spoke as if he was reading a tabloid headline. "Husband finds wife with other man. Husband kills both. Yeah?"

"Gee," I said. "I could make a TV movie out of that."

"Yeah, right, mate. Only that ain't the way it happened."

He reached for an eighty-dollar bottle of Lagavulin and poured at least ten bucks worth into his glass.

"Want one?" he asked.

"It's a little early, "I said, "even for me."

He shrugged that off and took a long sip.

"Husbands have been known to kill unfaithful wives," I said with no sound of a threat or rancor.

"Only she wasn't unfaithful, yeah?"

"What do you think two naked people were doing up there between your sheets?"

"Christ, mate, you don't understand, do ya?"

I turned two palms up. "Help me out."

"She wasn't being unfaithful. Helly loves me. She was just getting laid. No big deal, right?"

"You're losing me, Trevor. Your wife having sex with another man is no big deal?"

"That's the way we live, mate. She loves me. I love her. Helly's a very sexual woman. She's not making love. She's just getting fucked, yeah?"

"Hollywood rules?"

"Our rules. No rules." He killed half the remaining single-malt. "Sure you don't want one?"

"Yeah. What the hell."

"How 'bout you, mate?" he asked Bobby.

Young Crockett shook his head.

Trevor pointed to an antique sideboard. "Glasses are on the buffet."

I fetched a matching glass and set it on the cocktail table. "Just a splash," I said. "I have to stay awake until at least five o'clock."

He poured two fingers.

"Good stuff, mate."

"Yeah, I know."

Trevor took another healthy pull. "Cheers."

I sipped the peat-flavored Western Isles whisky.

"Where were you last night?" I asked.

"On a red-eye from the coast. Landed this morning around 8:45 and drove right home...after I waited a year and a bloody day for my bloody luggage."

"What do you think about the lack of forced entry and your Merkel being used to shoot them?"

"Helly was a beautiful woman and a great actress, but she was something of a twit. She never remembered to lock doors."

Trevor swallowed the remainder of his drink and let out a long, "Ahh."

"Everything you're telling me holds a lot of coincidence. I'm still wondering who walked through an unlocked door, grabbed your shotgun and presumably ammunition you had handy, found two people in bed and killed them. Sounds like extraordinary timing and knowledge of the house. And for what reason?"

He popped the cork on the Lagavulin and began to pour. The neck of the bottle chattered against the rim of the glass. When the booze reached the halfway mark, he stopped.

"You gonna be okay?" I asked.

"Christ, mate, I don't know. Bit of a shock, ain't it?"

"I hope you don't mind, but let's get back to your sex life."

He shrugged and sipped.

"Did you sleep around, too?" I asked.

"Didn't have to, did I? I told ya—Helly was very sexual. What years ago blokes like you would call a nymphomaniac. I got all I could handle."

"And her extra-marital sex never bothered you?"

"Look, mate, you may not understand, but I don't mind explaining. Listen careful now. It wasn't just okay with me...I enjoyed it. It's my thing, yeah?"

"You're right. I don't understand."

After Trevor's last comment, Bobby got up quietly and stepped behind the sofa while the grieving husband sampled more of his drink.

Crocket lowered his head and whispered in my ear. "Sounds more like sumthin' you should hear than me. TMI. I'm goin' outside ta eat the Moon Pie I picked up this mornin'."

I nodded as Trevor continued his story.

"Christ, mate, Helly shagging other guys turned me on, see?"

"Uh-huh. I'm listening," I said, not really grasping the concept of his fetish. "No prurient interest on my part. Just convince me you didn't kill the guy upstairs out of jealousy."

"Okay. Where do I begin?" he said. "Right. I met her in 1979, yeah?"

He sloshed another quarter cup of whisky down the hatch.

"We've been married twenty years," he said. "But we've known each other much longer—out on the coast. Back then, we dated a few times, off and on. Had sex off and on. You know how it is."

I nodded, just to let him know he still had my attention.

"Then one day I see this bloke looking at the *Playboy* Helly posed for—June 1980 issue. She had just turned thirty. Bloody beautiful, she was."

After a little more scotch, Trevor began a running dissertation. "'You seen this?' the bloke says, showing me a page of Helly's pictures. 'I have,' says I. 'You're doing her, right?' says he. 'My business, mate,' I says."

Trevor paused long enough to take another healthy pull on his scotch. I wondered if he had a hollow leg.

"But you know what?" His question was for me. "Him looking at Helly's nude pictures turned me on. I mean, really, yeah?"

"Did you and Helly discuss the fetish after your marriage?" I asked.

"Sure we did. And we talked about her sexploits. She liked talking about it. I liked listening. Understand?"

"I hear you, Trevor. Let's change the subject for a minute, okay?"

"You're the copper, mate."

"Who's the guy upstairs?"

"A.J. Gunther. Everyone calls him Chip."

"A.J.? As in Andrew Jackson Gunther? The lawyer's son?"

"Right, mate. Big-time lawyer."

Trevor downed the remainder of his scotch like gravel sliding off a dump truck.

He was already reaching for the bottle as I asked, "Don't you think you should go a little easy with that, partner?"

"When's the last time you came home and found your wife shotgunned to death?"

———

As I headed back to the second floor, I met Earl Ogle who told me he and the doctor were ready to transport the two bodies for their final medical exam. I rounded up two uniformed cops to assist as Sergeant Stanley Rose walked in the front door.

"You're in early," I said. "What's up?" I didn't give him a chance to answer. "You look like an oversized Tiger Woods."

I looked up at Stan. He's six-foot-four with shoulders wide enough to support a steel I-beam. As I spoke, he took off a black Nike ball cap and ran a hand over his short natural. He wore a red polo shirt, black pleated trousers and black and white wing-tips.

"But I haven't been caught cheatin' and thrown out of my happy home," he said.

"Way to go."

"I stopped into the office to pick up my check, and Bettye told me what you had. Need any help?"

"Yeah, I think this one may be right up your alley."

"Good."

"Does Hollywood have its own PD?" I asked.

"No. Hollywood Division of LAPD handles it. Why?"

Stanley worked for LAPD before bringing his homesick bride back to her native East Tennessee and taking a police job in Prospect.

"We've got film industry connections here. You know anyone out there who would do a little snooping for us?"

"The guy who was my sergeant in the Metro Squad is a lieutenant now at Hollywood detectives. I think he'd help out."

"Great. Here's what I need."

I told Stan about Trevor and Helene's sex life and asked him to enlist Joe Friday or some other California cop to check around and find people who could verify Trevor's story and make sure no one else in the entertainment business thought Trevor kept a hit list.

———

I planned my next stop in the Old Town section of Knoxville where I'd break the bad news to Chip's father, Andrew Jackson Gunther III.

A uniformed valet parked my Crown Victoria in the underground garage of the Riverview Tower. I took the elevator to the penthouse.

The doors opened to the reception area of Gunther, Baxter, Josephs and Starnberg. The receptionist was a sleek number of around thirty who might have been recruited from the ranks of former beauty pageant contestants. Blonde, shapely, perky and proper, she called Gunther's secretary to announce my presence.

With a dazzling smile, the beauty queen pointed me in the general direction, but I traveled under my own steam and found Andrew the Third's executive assistant sitting behind a big walnut desk. Her nameplate read Elizabeth A. Hammontree, and she immediately jumped onto my list of top picks for the most attractive women in East Tennessee. She stood as I approached her desk and extended a hand, which I promptly shook. I placed her at pushing fifty, but who would care? An expert who knew how to fit a style to a face had cut her dark, moderately short hair. And what a face—beauty, intelligence, and loads of character. Put that on top of a figure any cheerleader would be proud of and clothe it in timeless fashion. If I thought the receptionist was good-looking, this woman was a walking aphrodisiac.

I took her smile as my cue to release her hand.

"Melissa didn't tell me the reason for your visit, sir."

"I only told her it was urgent, but didn't elaborate. I'm afraid I have bad news for Mr. Gunther."

Her smile faded. "May I ask what it is?"

"Normally I'd say no, but I think he'll need a little support after I leave. But first, tell me if there's a Mrs. Gunther."

"There was. She passed away a few years ago."

She shifted uncomfortably, looking like she didn't know what to do with her hands.

"Have you worked for him long?"

"Almost twenty years."

"Then sit down, and I'll tell you first."

She dropped into a pleated leather chair. I took one of the guest seats and pulled it close.

"I'm sorry, but there's no easy way. There was a shooting, and Mr. Gunther's son..."

"Chip? What happened?"

"He was killed. I'm sorry."

She looked shocked. Her shoulders dropped two inches, and she closed her eyes for a moment.

"Lord have mercy." Her voice held only a hint of East Tennessee accent—just enough to enhance her appearance.

"May I see him now?"

"Of course."

Andrew Gunther's office looked beyond posh, but I didn't like it. Too modern. Too many hard angles. Too much chrome. Black, white and gray. Unlike the traditional lobby and hallways I passed through. Gunther was a bit beyond posh himself, and at first glance, I didn't like him either.

I'm six-foot and one-eighty. He had me by two inches and twenty pounds. I knew him to be sixty-seven-years old, but he looked younger, even with snow white hair and a tan you can only get near the equator. His $4,000.00 gray suit shined like the scales on a black mamba.

Ms. Hammontree stood next to me as Gunther asked, "What can I do for you, Chief?"

I told him and watched his face change from a country club smile to an appropriate sadness. He took a step back and sat in a leather swivel chair, which if sold could have fed the homeless for three weeks.

"Where? How?" he asked.

I filled him in.

Elizabeth asked, "Andrew, may I get you something?"

Gunther nodded and wiggled a manicured finger in the direction of a row of crystal decanters sitting on the combination built-in cabinet and bookcase off to his right. She fetched him half a glass of honey-colored liquid, straight up.

"May I get you something, Mr. Jenkins?" she asked.

"No, thanks."

"Liz," he said. "Leave us, please."

"Are you all right, Andrew?"

"I'm fine."

His answer to someone trying to be kind sounded a bit too curt for my taste. Ms. Hammontree seemed to take no offense and left.

"I want him caught and charged." Gunther spoke with authority of one who's used to bossing around the hired hands.

"Him?"

"The man who did this."

"Might be a woman."

"Don't be ridiculous."

I generally give grieving relatives a bit of slack when they're rude.

"Is there something you know that I don't?"

"Her husband, of course."

"That's your best guess?"

"It's obvious, isn't it?"

"Not yet."

He tossed down a third of the liquor in his glass. I took him for a bourbon drinker.

Gunther tilted his head back and shook it. I looked out the windows of his corner office at a sky the color of faded denim.

"Who will be investigating the murder? The county? The TBI?" he asked.

"I will."

"And how many people are in Prospect P.D.?"

"A dozen and me. Why?"

"Why aren't you giving this to a larger agency?"

I took offense to that. "They're not as good as I am."

———

G unther the elder had been as much help as a BB gun against a rhino. So, the next day, while I waited to hear what LAPD had learned, I looked for Helene's gardener, one of the few regulars who could be found wandering around those hundred acres several times a week. Ernest Roy Dubbins was a local specimen who held down several part-time jobs. I found him working at the Crystal Creek Beef Jerky factory in north central Prospect.

A supervisor led me onto the work floor where Ernest Roy stood packing twenty-four envelopes of teriyaki-flavored meat strips into each cardboard box someone else had assembled.

Dubbins was fifty-three-years-old and looked anywhere between that and a hundred-and-six. He wore blue denim overalls, a plaid shirt with the sleeves cut off at the shoulders and a faded UT ball cap. At first, I thought I could hear *Dueling Banjos* playing somewhere in the background and doubted he was really an alumnus.

"Ernest Roy," the supervisor said. "This man's the po-leece. Wants ta talk with ya."

Dubbins finished counting his two-dozen packets of jerky, closed the box flaps and pushed the carton toward others waiting to be sealed by a woman with a tape dispenser.

He turned and gave me a suspicious look. The supervisor left us alone.

"You do the garden work at Helene Redpath's home?" I asked.

"Uh-huh." He squinted at me, obviously still suspicious.

"Damn good work," I said. "Everything complements the old house.

Looks like something from a historical restoration. You're a talented gardener."

The frown turned into a smile. I noticed his right canine and the molar behind it were missing.

"Have you heard that she was killed yesterday?"

"Yes, sir. Seen it on the news."

"I need to speak with you about what you may have seen or heard while you worked on the property."

His frown returned.

"Don't know nuthin' about this. No, sir."

"If you weren't there yesterday, there's no way you could. But let's sit down over there and see if I can jog your memory about what may be important from other times. Okay?"

Ernest Roy didn't look confident in my ability to draw out his memory, but he joined me at the lunch table on the far side of the small factory.

I left him almost an hour later with a few descriptions of people and vehicles. He had worked on the property often enough to witness the innocent routine and the notable exceptions. Speaking with Ernest Roy certainly wasn't a waste of time, but he didn't lead me to a smoking gun hidden in a potted palm either.

————

Back at the PD, Sergeant Bettye Lambert clicked away on her computer, doing the routine but necessary background investigation on our two victims and Trevor Ridley. Given enough time, my lovely blonde desk sergeant would learn everything from prior local and nationwide police involvement, credit bureau and bank information, and even a list of overdue library books.

Stan Rose interrupted his morning off to help Bettye with any telephone work generated by her data searches. So far, a personal photo with the word *killer* branded across someone's forehead hadn't flashed onto the computer screen.

A few minutes before five o'clock, when we'd normally close up shop,

Stan received a call from his LAPD friend, a third generation cop named Lieutenant Bernard Ohls. Ohls said a pair of Hollywood detectives interviewed numerous acquaintances of the Redpath/Ridley couple and learned that their marriage was not all liberal sex and domestic bliss. Apparently, Trevor was not always cool with Helene's relationships, and they were no strangers to the patrol cops assigned to handle their domestic disputes.

Our closing time stretched to almost six o'clock when Stan and Bettye left, and I called Trevor Ridley.

––––––

The sun had long ago disappeared, and dark clouds spotted the dirty gray sky like bruises on a small boy's legs. As I drove over the long entryway to Ridley's estate, raindrops spattered my windshield.

I parked next to a black Maserati Gran Turismo Cabrio and jogged up the brick walk to the porch where I found Trevor sitting in a rocking chair to the right of the front door.

He didn't get up, but raised his glass. "Cheers, mate."

"I've got to say, Trevor, you're the most likable homicide suspect I've ever met. Cheers yourself."

"You still looking at me for killing Helly?"

"I received some helpful information today from LAPD. They tell me your marriage wasn't all boxwood and roses. When you're living in your home out there, the Brentwood cops get plenty of training in handling domestic disputes."

"Bullocks! You ever fight wiff your wife? Course you 'ave. It don't mean nuffin'."

He slurred his words slightly, and I noticed a redness and glaze to his eyes. That made me think the half-empty bottle of Lagavulin sitting on the table between him and the unoccupied rocker next to it had been full when it arrived on the porch. That or he'd been crying—or both. He didn't look very happy.

"Let's talk about what I know."

"Yeah, right. But don't just stand there, mate. Sit down, and pull up a glass."

He pointed to the table and a tray holding the bottle, a second glass and a small pitcher of water.

"I guess it's about that time, isn't it?" I said.

He picked up the bottle and twisted off the cork. I held out a glass, and he poured. Then I slumped into the second rocking chair.

"Sun's over the yardarm, yeah? Time for our grog ration and all that Royal Navy rot," he said. Trevor offered a weak smile while a soft tattoo of rain pattered on the porch roof.

An hour and two glasses of whisky later, I asked, "If, as you say, you're totally innocent here, who else would want to kill your wife?"

"Beats the hell outta me, mate. That idea's been hauntin' me since it happened. I mean, who could stay mad at a girl who, if you snapped your fingers and told her she was beautiful, would jump into bed wiff ya? And there were times when she didn't need the bed, weren't there?"

"How about a *wife* who didn't want to share her hubby with Helene?"

"Good point. But Helly liked younger, unattached blokes. Sorry, mate, but an old married guy like you wouldn't stand a chance."

What do you say to an observation like that?

I sipped my scotch before asking another question. "Tell me about Andrew Jackson the fourth. Could he have been the target?"

"Petulant young bastard, that. Thirty-five years old going on nineteen. Spoiled rich kid and a useless little sod."

"You liked him?"

"Give over. He was a nasty little shit. Never could see what Helly saw in him. But he wasn't one of her regulars—not someone she really gave a toss for."

I obtained a list of several "regulars" from Helene's stable that Bettye and Stan could run backgrounds on and spent the rest of the evening with Trevor matching the descriptions of people and cars Ernest Roy provided with names he knew. With that complete, he dashed my hopes by saying there were others he never met. And before I adjourned for the night, one vehicle remained unaccounted for. A dark red Cadillac, probably a CTS.

Not as expensive as Trevor's Maserati, but on par with Chip Gunther's 2010 Corvette. I definitely wasn't playing in a pickup truck world.

———

I had two bodies, killed with an $8,000.00 shotgun, owned by a Hollywood producer who drove a $150,000.00 Italian sports car, whose wife had been in bed with a man almost thirty years younger than her, and he said he didn't do it. Fool that I am, I believed him. So, who killed the amorous pair? Damned if I knew.

I spent the next day tracking down and grilling the young men on Helene Redpath's Tennessee A-list of hot lovers. No one looked like the jealous type, and no one wanted to rat out someone else that Helly may have spoken of whilst between the sheets. And everyone seemed to have a good alibi for the night she and Chip Gunther took two magnum loads of 12 gauge goose-shot in the sensitive parts of their bodies.

My undeveloped leads fizzled into dead ends. Even Trevor Ridley, my prime suspect, was forensically cleared when the test for gunshot residue came back negative. That provided me with mixed emotions. Trevor had it all. Seemingly motive, definitely means and coincidentally, opportunity. A real headshot for the harried homicide investigator. The problem: I liked the guy and really didn't think he killed his sexy wife and the young man he called a useless little sod.

So, where did that leave me? I still had a red Cadillac to find, and I wanted to learn more about the useless little sod.

———

The next morning, I called Elizabeth Hammontree and made an appointment to see Andrew Gunther at 3 p.m.

That gave me most of the day to look for loose ends and missing threads. I read over the crime scene reports and learned nothing. The ME's report only restated the obvious. Then, in my own notes, I found an inconsistency. Ernest Roy Dubbins told me he saw a gray Corvette parked at the

Redpath/Ridley home several times. Originally, I wrote that off as Chip Gunther's car, the one we found parked under an old oak tree the day he died. But was it? The dealer I spoke to called Gunther's Vette blade silver. A small point, perhaps, but from my perspective, worth exploring. I wondered if there could be another car.

I took a photo of Chip's convertible back to the beef jerky factory and found Ernest Roy.

The same supervisor walked me through the building to where Mr. Dubbins stood at a small workstation, weighing up twelve-ounce portions of jerky, stuffing them into plastic bags and sealing them with a machine that let out a sigh each time he pressed a handle. Ernest Roy had swapped his orange ball cap for a hygienic doo-rag and wore a pair of surgical gloves. We stepped away from the dried meat to speak.

I showed him the photo.

"Is this the gray Corvette you saw at the Redpath home?"

"Nope, it weren't no ragtop. Darker gray, too, and a different shape. Kindly like a fastback—y'all know what I mean?"

"You sure it was a Corvette?"

He scratched a two-day stubble with his latex-gloved hand and put some thought into my question. At that point, I decided never to buy Crystal Creek jerky.

"Well," he said, "looked like it could be. I guessed it was a Corvette, but I ain't never been much inta sports cars."

One step forward and two back. It's always a possibility in police work. Now I needed owners for a red Caddy and a gray...sporty something.

———

The same valet parked my Ford at Riverview Tower, and I rode the same elevator to the penthouse. The former Miss Tennessee smiled for me after calling Elizabeth Hammontree.

"Mr. Gunther is waiting," she said.

At the end of the hallway, Ms. Hammontree led me into Big Andy's office.

Gunther's suit of the day was an olive green affair that covered a yellow shirt with a white collar and cuffs. Throwing in the cost of his silk paisley tie and Italian loafers, I calculated the cost of his outfit could have paid for open-heart surgery.

He brusquely waved me toward a guest chair.

"Let's make this quick," he said. "I have a deposition at four, and I can't be late."

"I'm looking at the possibility that your son may have been the target and Ms. Redpath only collateral damage."

"My son was only a boy. No one would want to kill him."

"Mr. Gunther, your son was thirty-five and having sex with a married woman. No offense, but we're not talking about a Cub Scout."

"That was offensive. And so far, you haven't shown me much ability in solving this."

Oh, he was certainly doing his best to get on my good side.

"And you're not offering much help. A detective does not find a killer by using a crystal ball or Ouija board. I need information from you, and so far, you've been uncooperative."

"That's ridiculous."

"No, it's not. I understand how a father needs to grieve for a lost son, but in my experience, most parents offer too much information. You're the exception."

He rolled his eyes and turned a palm up. "Ask."

"Tell me about his personal life. Besides Helene Redpath, who did he see? Where did he work? What did he do for kicks?"

"For God's sake, that could take us all day."

"We've got to start somewhere."

He spoke for more than thirty minutes. I learned that after Chip received his M.B.A. ten years earlier, Dad found him a job with one of the major commercial contractors in the southeast. But that didn't last, and Chip had been between gigs—for approximately four years. He had also been engaged to the daughter of one of the partners at Roma Construction, that major contracting company, but the wedding was on hold until Chip found gainful employment.

At 3:40, Gunther's phone rang.

"Excuse me," he said. "I have to take this."

After a few seconds of listening, Gunther hung up.

"My four o'clock and his client are here early. I'm afraid this will have to do."

I neither answered nor rose immediately, but rather looked at him with mild disbelief. He stood and picked up a short stack of file folders.

"Liz will show you out," he said.

He walked out, and I took my time standing. Outside his office door, I looked at Ms. Hammontree. She stood when I reached her desk. A midnight blue wraparound dress accentuated her figure. I sighed. "Gee, that went well."

She must have sensed my frustration.

"He can be brusque at times."

"Brusque I can live with. I'd call him an obstructionist."

"What do you need?" She sounded concerned and understanding.

"I'm just trying to catch his son's killer. I need information, and he's more interested in tossing my jelly beans in the toilet."

She smiled and stepped from behind her desk. We met on an oriental carpet thick enough to lose a small animal in the nap.

"Perhaps I can help," she offered.

"I hope someone can."

"Let's use Andrew's office. He'll be in the conference room for some time."

"Sure." I followed her.

She closed the door, and I sat in the chair I had already warmed up.

"How about a drink?" she asked. "Or are you not allowed while on duty?"

"I'm the boss. You'd be surprised what I can get away with while on duty."

She laughed. "Bourbon, scotch, vodka?"

"Scotch would be lovely, with just a splash of water."

She fixed two drinks, handed me one and turned a guest chair around to face me. I noticed a blue sapphire cocktail ring on her left hand—no wedding band.

"So, what can I tell you?" she asked.

I ignored the question for a moment. "Thanks for the drink. Your boss could turn a temperance worker into an alcoholic."

She chuckled again and looked at me with dark brown eyes; tiny smile lines showed at the corners.

"That's a beautiful ring you have, Miss Hammontree."

"Thank you. It was my mother's. No one else has ever given me a ring."

I took that as a hint.

"Please call me Beth."

"Gunther calls you Liz."

"He's the only one who does. My father has called me Beth since I was a little girl. He said if I used Liz, people would think my name was Lizard."

"Makes sense." I smiled and sipped what came from a bottle of thirty-three-year old Glendronach she had taken from behind closed doors.

She showed me a big smile and shook her head. "No, it doesn't."

I found it hard to believe she'd never been married.

"You're right...Beth. I often lapse into periods of foolishness."

Another moment passed, and neither of us spoke.

"You wanted information on Chip?" she asked.

"Please."

For forty minutes, I heard things that led me to believe Chip was just one of the new generation of good ol' boys—a nice guy but not worth a hoot —a useless little sod.

The interesting story came last. Beth told me about Chip's engagement to Anita DeVersa, daughter of Victor and Angela, Victor being half-owner of Roma Construction and Chip's former boss. Beth's version of the break-up differed from Andrew's. Rather than a mutual agreement to wait until Chip found a job, I learned that after a big row, Chip got the engagement ring sent back to his father's office via a bonded courier.

"That's strange. What caused the big production?" I asked.

"I really can't comment. I don't know. It looked so formal. I mean, why not just hand the ring back?"

She tightened another loose end by connecting the players. They all belonged to the Cherokee Country Club, a high-class setting on the Tennessee River, situated along the fashionable Lyon's View Pike in Knoxville.

At 4:45, I prepared to leave.

"I really appreciate your help." I handed her my card. "If you think of anything I might be interested in, please give me a call."

We stood, and Beth offered her hand. "You're quite welcome...Sam. I enjoyed talking with you. And I promise to think of *something* interesting and give you a call."

She closed Gunther's office and walked with me toward the lobby.

"Oh, I forgot to ask," I lied. "Does Andrew drive that red Caddy down in the garage? Sharp-looking car."

"Cadillac? No. Andrew is into sports cars. He just bought a new Jaguar two-seater. A gray one. But it *is* downstairs."

"Oh, okay. Well, thanks again."

The valet pulled my car up to the garage booth and hopped out. With the door open, we heard the police radio sound off.

"Here you go, officer," he said, probably figuring a cop would never give him a tip.

I handed him two bucks and said, "Thanks. Oh, hey, I hear Mr. Gunther just got a new Jag. Mind if I take a look? I'm kind of into sports cars myself."

"Sure. It's over in spot twelve, left of the elevator. But I can't unlock it without permission."

"No problem. I just want to take a peek at something I can't afford."

"Help yourself. And thanks." He held up the two singles.

A medium gray Jaguar XK-R coupe sat in spot number twelve. Gorgeous car—long, low, sleek and a fastback. I took two shots with my cell phone camera to show Ernest Roy and see if he recognized it.

I took the long way home and stopped at the Jag dealer on Kingston Pike. From a young salesman, I learned that Andrew Gunther had purchased his car there and ordered the color lunar grey metallic which cost an extra thousand dollars. According to their records, it was the only one delivered locally in that color.

"You get one hell of a car for around a hundred grand," he said. "The R Type comes standard with 510 horsepower."

"Wow," I said. "I'll bet he can get from home to work in 5.6 seconds."

———

The next morning, I got lucky and found Ernest Roy Dubbins working on the grounds at Trevor Ridley's home.

"Look at a photo for me, would you, Mr. Dubbins?"

He let the long handle of a cultivator rest against his shoulder as he pulled off the leather gloves that protected his hands from blisters and rose thorns.

"I believe that's the Corvette I seen here a few times. Yes, sir, color's right, and the lines look right, too."

"You're sure? This is Jaguar, not a Corvette."

"Don't matter what ya call it, mister. That's the car I seen, parked right over yonder."

He pointed to the graveled spot beneath the old red oak adjacent to the main driveway.

I arrived prior to 10 a.m., catching Trevor before he had started drinking and obtained a few coherent responses from him.

"'Course I've met Andrew Gunther," he said. "We used someone from his office to close on this property when we bought it."

"Did you socialize with him afterwards?"

Trevor and I sat on the front porch again, drinking strong coffee from Royal Doulton cups, poured from a French press.

"Sure, but not much. Once in a while," he said. "Used to see him at the country club, though, didn't we?"

I interrupted. "You belong to the Cherokee Country Club?" Beth Hammontree didn't mention that.

"Yeah, right."

"You didn't tell me this before." I must have sounded exasperated.

"You didn't ask, did ya, mate? Helly liked the place. Quite posh."

To emphasize his statement, Trevor exaggerated a smile and raised his pinky as he sipped delicately from the fine china cup.

"And the Tudor-style buildings reminded me of Old Blighty, don't ya know," he said.

"Were you ever at Gunther's home, or has he come here?"

"Both, mate. Andrew was a decent bloke...a good man. Not like his gobshite son. He gave a party wiff that bit o' class. Know what I'm sayin'?"

Trevor wore a black silk robe tied at the waist and a pair of bright red pajama pants. His eyes were terribly bloodshot, and he had yet to shave or comb his hair.

"You think Helly ever had an affair with old Andrew?" I asked.

"Not that I know. Not really her type. But, hey, I used to fly out to the coast a lot."

"Jesus Christ!"

"Come on, now, mate. Don't go getting judgmental on me."

I shook my head, thinking about all the time I might have saved.

"What do you know about Chip's fiancée, Anita DaVersa?

"Oh, that's a looker, that one. Dark hair. Dark eyes. Pair o' knockers I'd like to get hold of. Exotic is what I'd call her."

I heard an engine start somewhere behind the house. A few moments later, I saw Ernest Roy navigate a big Kubota tractor with a hydraulic mower deck attached to the rear along the eastern boundary of the grassed area. After a few passes, the fragrance of newly mown lawn drifted to the porch.

"How about her parents? Know much about them?"

"Vic the Godfather and Angie Baby? Yeah, I know them. Met them at Andrew's house a couple of times. Been here, too. Hot stuff, they are."

"How so?"

"Well, he'd like you to believe he's part of the Mafia. Might be, for all I know, but I doubt it. Kind of a stereotype, really. You know, open shirt, gold chains, curly hair, swarthy good looks. Kinda bloke who thinks he's got to put the make on every woman he meets."

"He go after Helly?"

"Everybody went after Helly, mate. When a guy knows a girl takes her clothes off in the movies, he thinks she's easy. They try."

"He get anywhere?"

"Couple of times that I know of. I mean, he was sort of a novelty. Helly said he acted like a real caveman. She had lots of fun telling me about him, she did."

"What did his wife say about all the flirting?"

"The more he flirted, the less she said and the more she drank. I can only imagine what that poor bastard heard when they left. Angie looked like she could get mean if she was pissed."

"Ever hear any more about them?"

"Yeah, Vic knew I knew. He knew I was okay with his arrangement wiff Helly, too. But he was the one in danger, wasn't he? I mean if Angie ever caught him in the hay wiff someone else, I believe she'd have cut his Italian balls off."

"Either one drive a dark red Caddy?"

"Beats me, mate. More coffee?" He held up the French press.

"No, thanks. I'm good."

He poured himself a refill.

———

That morning had been the most productive in the case. I left Trevor sitting on the porch and headed back to Prospect PD, feeling that old bull-in-a-china-shop impulse surging through me. I found a hot lead and needed to exploit it—pronto.

As I hit the blacktop fronting Trevor's property, I called Stanley's cell phone.

"Where are you?" I asked.

"Home, playing catch with my son."

"Who told you to stop investigating and go back to 4-to-12 patrol?"

"Who told me not to?"

"Don't get smart. Must I think of everything?"

"Huh?"

"Drag your ass down to the office. I'm going to give you and Bettye the most important work of the case. Meet me there in five minutes."

"It takes me fifteen minutes to get to work."

"Whatever."

———

I almost sprinted to the back door of the PD and tapped in my four-digit entry code. Between the back door and Bettye's desk, I whistled the theme from *The Magnificent Seven*.

Bettye was on the phone. I put my hands on her shoulders, kissed the top of her head and said, "Hang up, woman. I have work for you. The game's afoot."

She turned around and looked at me like I was a lunatic. I love the way her hazel eyes sparkle when she thinks I've gone around the bend.

"Junior," she said into the phone, "I've gotta go. The boss just walked in, and I think he needs a cold shower."

"Stop everything," I said. "If necessary, call one of the guys in off the road to answer the phone and dispatch the cars. I need you and Stanley—he's on the way in—to run down a few things for me."

Her mouth opened—then closed. I think she knew questions were futile.

"First, print out driver's license photos for Andrew Gunther the third, Victor DaVersa, Angela DaVersa and Anita DaVersa. And you better toss in Elizabeth A. Hammontree, too."

"Spell DaVersa."

I did and then walked toward my office.

"Where are you goin'?" she asked.

"Gotta make a couple phone calls."

Ten minutes later, Stanley stood in my doorway.

"What the hell is so urgent?"

"This morning I heard the news I needed. I know who killed our two victims. Now I just have to get a confession."

"Who's going to confess to a double homicide?"

"You underestimate me, Stanley. I'll assemble the suspects, mess up their heads with some selective mumbo-jumbo, and the guilty party will crumble—just like in the movies."

Stan raised his eyebrows. "If you say so."

"I do. Now take the names I gave Bettye and do a complete background on them. Make sure you call the Cherokee Country Club and see what kind of activities they participate in. And get a recent medical history on Anita DeVersa. Don't take that 'We don't give out private information' noise from anyone. Cajole them. Threaten them. Do anything you must to get that info. Even the types of doctors she's seen will do. The insurance carrier can give you that. And I need it for nine o'clock tonight."

Stan nodded slowly. "Okay. Am I going to be part of this nine o'clock dog and pony show?"

"Of course. Bettye, too. Wear snazzy civilian clothes. We're dealing with rich people. Let's intimidate them. Inspector Cramer may not be available, so I'll take care of getting someone from the D.A.'s office to show up."

"Who's Inspector Cramer?"

"Not much of a reader, huh? Never mind."

An hour later, I took the group of driver's license photos and headed back to Trevor Ridley's place. I spent a few minutes with Ernest Roy Dubbins and several more with Trevor. After I captured his interest in my proposed extravaganza, I called Beth Hammontree.

"Hi, Sam, how are you?" She sounded happy to hear from me.

"Better than I've been in days. What are you doing tonight?"

"I, uh, have no plans. What did you have in mind?"

Her voice sounded eager. If I wasn't an old married man, as Trevor called me, I'd have felt encouraged.

"It's business, but I need your help."

"Of course."

"Can you get Andrew and the three DaVersas to come to Trevor Ridley's home tonight at nine?"

"I don't know, but I'll try."

"I'd like you there, too."

"All right, but what are we doing?"

"You're all going to help me solve the Redpath/Gunther murders."

"Really?"

"Trust me. I know what I'm doing."

It took Beth more than two hours to arrange things, but she called back and told me all the players reluctantly agreed to come.

"Why do you want me there?" she asked.

"You're an integral part of this. And I thought you'd want to know the outcome."

"You've confused me. Should I bring a lawyer?"

"Why would you ask that?"

"This sounds like something out of Agatha Christie."

"Nero Wolfe, actually."

"Who?"

"Doesn't matter. If you need a lawyer, Andrew will jump in and rescue you. Unless he needs one himself."

"That's not a comfort."

"Remember what I said."

"You've said a lot."

"Trust me."

"Who would trust a man who says 'Trust me'?"

I laughed. "This isn't exactly a formal party, but I need you to wear something especially nice. Okay?"

She sighed. "Sure. See you later."

After I knew all the necessary people would be in attendance, I called Moira Menzies, the chief assistant district attorney for Blount County. Wolfe would have invited Inspector Cramer and his assistant Sergeant Purley Stebbins, but I'd settle for Moira and figured she would ask her senior investigator, Cletus Dunn, to tag along.

"For God's sake, Sam, you're not doing one of those things again, are you?"

"No, I called you as a joke. Of course, I'm doing this. Do you want to be there or not?"

"This is so theatrical. Why can't you just...? Oh, never mind. Yes, I'll be there. Nine o'clock, you say?"

"Nine it is. Ready to copy down directions?"

———

We arrived at Trevor Ridley's place at 8:30—Bettye, Stan and I, and the second largest member of Prospect P.D., Officer Harlan Flatt, who stood a couple inches shorter than Stanley, but was just as beefy. Because of his terminally receding hairline, Harley had recently taken to shaving his head, so, with his dark mustache, he somewhat resembled Jesse Ventura with a uniform.

Bettye looked chic in a simple knee-length black dress that showed a hint of cleavage. Stan wore his dark gray suit.

Trevor had invested some time arranging the living room the way I requested. To accommodate the guests who showed up for the festivities, he augmented the regular seating with a few armchairs from the dining room. I told him where I wanted each person placed.

He also provided an impressive array of alcoholic beverages on the side-board. To handle the requests, he asked his part-time cook and house-keeper, a local woman named Verna Hoyle and her daughter Cylene to prepare and serve the drinks.

Moira Menzies arrived first and, to provide close support, she dragged along my buddy, Clete Dunn.

"The last time you pulled one of these stunts, Sam," Moira said, "you came out smelling like a rose. I sure hope you've got your ducks in a row this time. These people have formidable legal horsepower at their disposal."

She wore her favorite outfit, the one she usually saves for big case summations, an electric blue two-piece suit that showed a couple inches of knee. The color went well with her curly blonde hair.

"Oh, ye of little faith," I said. "Have a seat, and watch it work."

Moira shook her head, and Trevor led her to a seat at twelve o'clock in my circle of people.

"Good luck, bud," Clete Dunn said. "Don't wanna see all y'all git caught with yer pants down."

"Yeah, thanks."

Trevor returned and asked me about a drink order.

"You have any beer?"

"Of course I've got beer, mate. You don't like my scotch?"

"Tonight, beer's more appropriate."

He didn't seem to understand, but gave me a list of what he had available. I told him what and how I wanted it served.

At ten-to-nine, Andrew Gunther and Beth Hammontree arrived together. She looked lovely in a sleeveless purple dress. He wore a pearl gray suit over a black polo shirt.

Trevor placed her right next to me on the left with the big guy beside her. She gave me a cute little wave and smiled.

Andrew remained standing and made a comment. "This is ridiculous. A carnival, for chrissake. You're going to look like a horse's ass."

When he sat down and crossed his legs, I noticed he wore black and brown tasseled loafers without socks. *And that aging preppy thought I'd look like a horse's ass.*

Five minutes later, Trevor introduced me to the DaVersa family. Vic looked exactly as described, but a little chunkier than I would have thought—too much pasta, I supposed. Angela was an attractive but hard-looking dark-haired woman. And Trevor hit the nail on the head when he called Anita exotic—a beautiful girl, in a very Mediterranean way. They were all dressed more casually that the rest of the crowd. The threesome took seats to my right with Victor two chairs away from me, just where I wanted him.

As soon as he sat down, Bettye took the chair directly across from him and crossed her legs, showing enough knee to get a celibate monk excited. That captured Vic's attention. He smiled at her, and she returned it encouragingly. Then Old Vic, the Italian stallion, scanned the room from right to left. He checked out Moira's legs, too, and ended up looking at Beth, who sat demurely with her knees locked together.

Ernest Roy Dubbins arrived last, dressed in a chocolate brown polyester suit with his hair slicked down like a ten-year-old boy.

Stan stood behind Moira, and Harley parked himself next to the bar, looking burly in a khaki shirt and green uniform pants, thumbs hooked over the top of his gun belt.

On cue, Cylene carried a tray with two bottles of Negra Modelo and a frosty glass and placed it on the small table sitting next to my chair. I popped the cap on one, took my seat and poured half a glass.

"Good evening," I said. "Thank you all for coming tonight. As you may know, my name is Sam Jenkins. I'm the chief of police in Prospect. Mr. Ridley has been kind enough to provide us with refreshments. If you already haven't been served, one of the ladies will take your order. As you can see, I'm having beer." I even sounded like Nero Wolfe, that *other* famous New York detective.

After a few drinks were distributed, I addressed the crowd.

"I know your time is valuable, and so is mine. I'll be brief with my questions and stay on point. I request that you refrain from unnecessary comments, and I'll conclude this as quickly as possible."

I watched Vic ignore me and check out the female talent again. Angela noticed, too.

If looks could kill.

"Mr. Gunther, I think I speak for us all when I offer condolences for the loss of your son."

Andrew shifted uncomfortably in his chair. "Thank you."

"When did you take delivery of your new Jaguar?"

"What? What does that have to do with anything?"

"Indulge me, please."

He shook his head in apparent disbelief. "Middle of October last year."

"Mr. Ridley, you're a sports car fan. Have you ever seen his XK-R?"

"No."

"Mr. Gunther, what was your relationship with Helene Redpath?"

"What do you mean *relationship*?"

"A simple question, sir. If I asked about your son's relationship with her, I think it would be safe to say they were lovers. How well did *you* know her?"

"Are you implying...?"

"I imply nothing. I'm asking."

I picked up the beer glass and drank half the contents. Then slowly I poured the glass full, trying my best to eliminate a head.

"My firm represented Ms. Redpath and Mr. Ridley when they purchased this property," he said. "After that, I saw them socially several times. That's all."

"I see. So, why was your *lunar grey* Jaguar, the only 2011 XK-R that color sold in this area, seen numerous times at this home when no other guests were present?"

He stood abruptly and startled Beth.

"Damn you. This is intolerable."

"Perhaps for you, sir. But I think the others may be interested in your answer."

"Now you're suggesting—" he said.

"Yes," I interrupted his attempted tirade. "Now I am. Like your son, you were having an affair with Helene Redpath, weren't you?"

"Well, I'll be buggered," Trevor said, his bloodshot eyes now wide with surprise.

"Sit down, Mr. Gunther." I waved my hand at him. "A sexual fling between two consenting adults isn't something to get you arrested."

I drank a little more beer. Gunther took his seat and began checking the condition of his manicure.

"All right," he said. "Helene and I did have an affair. Trevor, I'm..."

Ridley interrupted. "No worries, mate. Water under the bridge and all that. Let's talk about it sometime, shall we?"

"But I didn't kill her," Gunther blurted out. "And I certainly didn't kill my son."

"I'd say that, too, if I were in your position," I said. "Now, Miss DaVersa —Anita—you were engaged to Chip Gunther. Why did you break it off?"

"What?" She sounded surprised.

"Simple question. Must I repeat it?"

"I, uh, I guess things weren't working out."

"You guess? Did you find out he was being unfaithful to you? Did you learn that Chip was having an affair with Helene Redpath?"

Victor sat forward in his chair. "Hey, wait a goddamn minute."

"Mr. DaVersa, you agreed to come here. You may leave any time you like. But please, no outbursts."

"You can't talk to my daughter like that."

"I'm being polite, and I asked a simple question. Your daughter is twenty-nine, a grown woman. She can answer for herself."

Anita decided to speak. "No, I didn't know about the affair. We just decided to call it quits."

"Federal Express has a record of your engagement ring being delivered to Mr. Gunther's law office and a signature obtained upon receipt. That wasn't just an idle gesture. Something happened between you two."

She offered no comment.

"But I believe you *didn't* know about the affair. As far as I know, those two only had a few liaisons."

Vic DaVersa lightened up. He relaxed his posture and stole another look at Bettye. She met his stare and smiled. Angela's eyes darted back and forth between the two. She was getting hotter by the minute. I decided to stall and give her a chance to simmer.

"Really, people," I said. "I asked two simple questions and witnessed evasions in both cases. This process will go faster if you respond truthfully. Ask Mr. Gunther, he knows. Would a man in my position pose a question if he didn't already know the answer?"

I looked around the room. Gunther sat forward, still checking his nails, his elbows resting on his knees. Anita hung her head. Vic was back doing his eyeball thing between Beth and Bettye and Moira. I guessed he thought Bettye was the most receptive. We planned it that way.

I finished my first bottle of beer and popped the cap on the second.

"Back to my question. Miss DaVersa, why the break up?"

She began, "I told you—"

"Stop!" I said. "You're wasting time. When was your last period?"

"What?"

"Hey!" Vic said.

Angela snapped out of her chair. "We're leaving."

"Oh, for God's sake, sit down, madam," I said. "Your daughter's pregnant. Chip was the father, and he didn't want the child. A simple story. Don't get so twisted out of shape."

Anita spoke. "That's right. He turned into a real bastard when I told him."

"As I said—very simple. He wanted you to terminate the pregnancy, didn't he? And you, being a Catholic, said no. Your body. Your choice. Not at all unreasonable. Many women would have dumped him."

Angela sat, and I turned my attention back to Andrew Gunther.

"So, Mr. Gunther, once again your son disappointed you. Then you found out about his affair with the woman with whom you, too, were having sex. That enraged you, didn't it?"

For a lawyer, Andrew disappointed me. He opened his mouth, but nothing came out. He lowered his eyes.

"You don't have to answer. Fine. I'll get back to you."

"Where are you going with this, Sam?" Moira asked.

"We'll see. I'm only half finished."

I directed my next question to Vic the Stick. "Mr. DaVersa, I'll ask you the same question as Mr. Gunther. What was your relationship with Ms. Redpath?"

He shrugged and tossed up his hands. "Since you and Trevor seem to be getting along so well, I guess you already know."

I dipped my head half an inch. "I do, but tell us."

"Yes, I had a little thing with her—couple times. Then we ended it."

"Because your wife found out." I made it a statement, not a question.

"Yeah."

"And you promised to end it."

"Yes, again."

"But you didn't."

He hesitated. "Not exactly."

"Would you care to comment, Mrs. DaVersa?"

"I would not."

"Then I'll answer for you. And please, let me know how I'm doing. You took steps to end the affair your husband couldn't by visiting Helene Redpath to speak woman-to-woman. And the day you did, you found the house open—unlocked. Helene admitted two things to you. She was having an affair with your husband and that she was terrible about locking doors."

Angela locked eyes with me and refused to blink. Tough cookie.

"Really, people, you amaze me. You all seem to disregard the obvious, the fly on the wall, so to speak. I didn't invite Mr. Dubbins tonight because I thought he killed Helene Redpath, but because he could comment on what he saw while working here as the gardener. He watched you, but you never noticed him."

"So what's your point?" Angela asked, bristling with attitude.

"My point, Mrs. DaVersa, is after your first meeting with Helene, the affair *still* didn't end. Your husband couldn't help himself, and you were enraged. Not only with your husband, but with Helene. And because of what he did to your daughter—with Chip Gunther. Your mind was in turmoil."

"You're crazy," she said.

"My sanity has nothing to do with your actions."

I watched Harley Flatt move around the room and take up a spot behind Angela DaVersa.

"Now, it's my turn again," I said. "I'll explain exactly what happened. Each time you and your husband attended a social gathering here, you arrived in his black Escalade. That's the vehicle people associated with you. But based on my information, a red Cadillac CTS-V—your car, Mrs. DaVersa—was seen here, too, but at different times. Twice, your husband used it when he had his get-togethers with Helene and twice when you came here alone. The first time, you demanded she terminate the relationship with Victor. The second time, after the affair continued, you came back, that time to kill Helene. But you ended getting two birds with one stone. Or should I say two with both barrels?"

Everyone looked at Angela who defiantly stared at me.

"When Sergeant Rose spoke to people at the Cherokee Country Club,"

I said. "He learned that you and your husband take advantage of their reciprocal agreement with the Oak Ridge Shooting Sports Center. You shoot trap and skeet. You're no stranger to shotguns."

Clete Dunn leaned over and whispered in Moira's ear. She nodded.

"I don't know if killing Helene was your intention from the start that day," I said, "but it was the result. And you used the extra shell on Chip. How convenient."

Her eyes looked like a pair of burning coals. Harley stepped closer to her. I shook my head.

"I heard about your short temper, Mrs. DaVersa, and I understand how a person can take just so much. Why not get your story on the record now? Let's hear how emotionally distraught you were. That could make a big difference in court."

"You're damn right I was pissed," she said. "First that good-for-nothing Chip does this to Anita."

She pointed to her daughter's stomach.

"Then, this one can't keep it in his pants."

She jerked a thumb toward her husband.

"You saw how he couldn't keep his eyes off that blonde."

She pointed at Bettye, who uncrossed her legs and sat up.

"No, I didn't intend to kill the slut. I may have wanted to knock her block off, but when I found Chip's car there, I snapped. The house was wide open, and I heard them upstairs. Helene was very vocal up there in the sack. It was obvious what they were doing. And the Englishman, the one so proud of his expensive guns, left the cabinet open. You know the rest."

"Yes, I do. You're under arrest, Mrs. DaVersa. Officer Flatt and Investigator Dunn will process your paperwork. Perhaps Mr. Gunther can recommend a good criminal attorney."

I looked at Andrew who scowled.

He stood and looked at Beth. "I'll be outside."

She stood. Vic and Anita began to follow Angela and the two cops, but Moira Menzies stopped them.

Beth turned to me "You make me sorry I didn't get a job in a prosecutor's office," she said. "It feels good watching a criminal confess."

"Thanks for your help," I said. "I doubt they would have shown up if I asked."

"You're welcome. I'm glad you invited me. This was certainly more exciting than watching *American Idol*."

I gave her an appreciative smile. "I hope so."

She stood there for a long moment. Then Trevor walked over.

"I guess I'd better go," she said. "Andrew's waiting."

"Sure."

After she left, Trevor said, "Good-looking woman, that."

"You betcha."

"You looking to get a bit of that?"

"I'll send her flowers as thanks for the help, but no. *My* wife wouldn't understand."

He laughed. "Then I just might need to give Andrew more business. That would give me an excuse to be in his office, wouldn't it?"

"Sure would."

As the room cleared, Bettye and Stan joined Trevor and me.

"Sergeant Lambert," I said, "I do believe that gentleman was making eyes at you."

She wrinkled her nose as she often does when I mention something distasteful. "That was no gentleman."

"You did a great job leading him on."

"Strictly for God and country, Sammy. And maybe for you."

"And now the fun begins," Stan said.

"What do you mean, mate?" Trevor asked.

"Now we have to get the forensics men back to find things that corroborate her confession," Bettye said.

"Not so easy, is it?" Trevor said.

I shook my head and gave Stanley a friendly slap on the shoulder. "Thanks, guys. I couldn't have done this without you."

"Do we get a raise?" Stan asked.

I laughed. "Are you on drugs?"

"Listen," Trevor said, "I appreciate all the work you've done. And I think Helly would, too. I'd like to do somefing for you in return."

"That's not necessary," Bettye said.

"Look, I know the Chief here likes his scotch. How about I send a case to the police station, and you all have a drink on me?"

"No, we can't take a gift," I said, "but you can do me a favor."

"Name it, mate."

"Let me take the Maserati for a spin."

"Anytime you want."

"Hey, what about us?" Bettye said.

"I'll take *you* for a ride, but I doubt Stanley could fit in the jump seat."

THE END

THE GREAT SMOKY MOUNTAIN
BANK JOB

Things happened in 1968. Assassins killed Bobby Kennedy and Martin Luther King. I was a young soldier waiting for my twelve-month vacation to the Republic of South Vietnam. And Prospect, Tennessee, a small town in the foothills of the Smokies, gained prominence. Thanks to the national media, an armed robbery that took place in Prospect became known as The Great Smoky Mountain Bank Job.

Forty-three years later, Sergeant Bettye Lambert buzzed my intercom.

"Chief, there's a Miss Lucy Frobisher here to see you."

"About what?" I asked.

"Something you'll want to hear."

I get suspicious when a good-looking woman walks into my office carrying a briefcase. I expect her to hand me a document and say the magic words, "You've been served."

That didn't happen.

Instead, she offered me a hand. "Hi, I'm Lucy Frobisher. I've got a problem, and Special Agent Ralph Oliveri thinks you can help me."

I grimaced at the mention of Oliveri. "Obviously you already know I'm Sam Jenkins."

She nodded. "I do."

I shook her hand.

"Sit down," I said, pointing to one of the tan leather-covered guest chairs in front of my desk. "Tell me about your problem."

Lucy took a seat and looked at me with expressive light brown eyes. Her two-piece navy blue suit appeared expensive; the skirt landed only an inch above her knees, which she held together very properly.

"My father was murdered," she said. "I'd like you to help me find the killers."

That's not the kind of request you hear every day in a small Tennessee police department. I'd ask how Ralph Oliveri, my pal from the FBI's Knoxville field office, got involved, but I started with a few more basic questions.

"Did this happen in Prospect?"

"It did."

"When?" I sounded surprised. No one had mentioned it to me.

"April 15th, 1968."

After that, I *was* surprised. I did some quick math and came up with a figure. I would have placed Lucy Frobisher in her late thirties, but with her father getting killed forty-three years ago, she had to be at least forty-two.

"I assume your father's death was reported back then?"

"Of course. My father was the guard at the Prospect Citizen's Bank and Trust when it was robbed. Are you familiar with what the papers called The Great Smoky Mountain Bank Job?"

"No. I'm sorry. In 1968, I was stationed at Fort Bragg, North Carolina and not reading too many newspapers."

"The robbers were anarchists—anti-war types. They killed my father when he tried to stop the robbery."

"And you spoke to Oliveri because the FBI assumed responsibility for the case?"

"Yes."

I noticed her looking around the room—at the flintlock Tennessee rifle hanging on the wall behind my desk, at the shadow box with the medals and badges from my time in the Army and at the counter where the mini-refrigerator, coffee maker and a vase of artificial flowers sat.

"And no one was arrested for the robbery or your father's murder?"

"No."

"Why do you think I can solve this mystery after forty-three years?"

"Because I think at least two of the robbers were from New York."

I stared at her. She pushed a few strands of shoulder-length dark brown hair behind her right ear and smiled. Lucy Frobisher was trim and quite pretty in a very professional way—like a tall Audrey Hepburn.

"And Oliveri told you I was a cop in New York for a long time."

She nodded. "He did."

"And you think I can resurrect an old case and track down former SDS or Black Panther members or other anti-war, anti-government thugs when the entire FBI couldn't?"

"They were part of the Revolutionary Youth Movement, and I have new information."

I heard the radio crackle out in the lobby. Bettye dispatched PO Jamey Hawkins to a first aid case at a trailer park off Doc Beasley Road.

"Why won't the Feds act on this information?" I asked.

"They say it's not sufficient to reopen an old case."

That sounded like rubbish to me.

"Ms. Frobisher, I'm sorry your father was killed, but I'm only one guy with a small police department to run. Even though it happened in Prospect, I doubt I can..." I let my sentence trail off.

"May I tell you the whole story?" she asked.

She sat back and crossed her legs. I think she anticipated my answer. That or she knew a big smile and a few extra inches of lovely knee would influence my decision.

"Sure." Then thinking she may take more than a few minutes, I said, "Would you like coffee? I have a fresh pot."

"Thank you. Dark—no sugar—please."

I fixed two cups and watched her take a stack of newspaper clippings and official reports from her briefcase.

I sat behind my desk, took a sip of an extremely hot Indonesian blend and listened to Lucy tell me her father, Douglas "Buck" Frobisher, not only worked as a bank guard, but also served as a Blount County deputy sheriff —the security job being a part-time gig.

According to Ms. Frobisher, the robbery went off like something from a 1970s heist movie. Three males and one female entered the bank just before closing time carrying shotguns and pistols. All wore rubber Halloween masks. After an attention-getting shot went off and Buck Frobisher stepped out of the men's room, he drew his revolver and foolishly told the four armed felons to drop their guns. One of the males fired his shotgun, and Frobisher bought the farm. The anarchists made off with $46,000 before a bank employee could trip a silent alarm connected to the police station.

Two days later, in a message sent to the *Knoxville News-Sentinel*, members of the RYM claimed responsibility for the robbery.

The former Prospect police chief, one Eli 'Peanut' Crowder, called in FBI assistance. Lucy said the investigation lasted for months, but as with many crimes perpetrated by a crop of home-grown anarchists from the late '60s, it remained unsolved.

"You don't seem to have a problem talking about your father's death," I said.

"No, I've lived with the fact all my life. And I never knew him. My mother was pregnant when he died."

"You're certainly tenacious."

"Unfinished business." Lucy slowly nodded with a look of resolution crossing her pretty face. "I think these people should pay for what they did to my mother."

She looked at me over the top of her coffee mug.

"No argument there. But the same question keeps popping up, Ms. Frobisher. Why do you think I can solve this?"

"Please," she said, batting her eyelashes, "call me Lucy."

"Okay, Lucy, back to my question."

A little more eyelash action, then, "May I call you Sam?"

"Sure, everyone else does."

"Well, Sam, I believe you know one of the killers."

That gave me a pause that did not refresh.

I began to think I was being conned—by a real pro.

"Lucy, darling," I said, "the average housewife doesn't waltz into a police station and lay something like this on the chief. Who are you, besides Buck Frobisher's daughter? And why did that Italian rat fink, Oliveri, send you here? Who do you work for?"

She smiled again—something worth at least seven figures. She was getting prettier every minute.

"That's a lot of questions, Sam. Let's see if I can remember. One: I'm no housewife, thanks. Two: Oliveri owes me a favor. *A big one.* And he says you owe him several. *Also biggies.* If you help me, two favors will be cancelled out among three people. And lastly: I'm an agent with IRS Intelligence. Hence, I know something about you and that you and your wife went to high school with one Wanda Potemkin—the female everyone believes participated in the Smoky Mountain Bank Job.

"You used your position with the IRS to get information on me?" I tried to sound outraged.

She made a dismissive face and waved her hand. "And you've never used your police resources to check into someone's background? Perhaps for less-than-professional reasons?"

A snort was the best response I could offer.

A brief moment later, I asked, "You think Wanda Potemkin was involved?"

"The FBI does," she said.

"I'm not surprised. She had a lot to say back in the earlier '60s. A real young political reformer."

Lucy nodded. "The agents who investigated this named her and two of the three others as probables. Since then, they've all dropped off the grid."

I looked toward my office door. Bettye walked past carrying a couple file folders, glanced in and frowned. I guess she wanted to see if I was behaving myself with the good-looking visitor.

"When I was in the Academy," I said, "two FBI agents gave a lecture about what the Feds could do for local cops. They brought in the 1972 Ten Most Wanted board. I noticed Wanda figured prominently on the FBI's hit parade. She was associated with the Weather Underground then."

"She was on the list for a long time."

Lucy held her cup in two hands and took another sip of coffee. Everything she did looked very feminine.

"And she's still in the wind?"

"Apparently."

"And you think I can find her?"

"Oliveri does."

"Oh, jeez! I really don't want to get involved."

"I know, Sam. But I'd really appreciate it if you did." Flutter, flutter.

"I'll bet you would."

———

I spent another half hour with Lucy Frobisher and learned that the Feds not only thought Wanda, the Long Island girl, had participated in the Prospect bank job, but liked her for other robberies in Alabama, Texas, California and Idaho in the early to mid '70s. All that brought up the question: Where is she now? And how the hell could I find her?

I envisioned Wanda more prone to be hiding out somewhere in the Haight-Ashbury district of San Francisco or totally dropping out of society into the mountains of Idaho than being anywhere near beautiful downtown Prospect, Tennessee.

After Lucy left my office, I called Ralph Oliveri.

"You creep," I said.

"What's wrong with you? Don't like the cute IRS cop I sent your way?"

"Oh, she's more than cute. Damn near beautiful, in fact. I just don't like the job she wants me to do."

"You're not shy about saying you can do the impossible. And besides, it will knock a favor off my list."

"Hey, goombah, clearing a forty-three-year-old robbery-homicide should wipe my slate clean."

"Yeah, okay. You clear up this one and I'll say we're even. I only do that because I know you'll need another favor soon enough."

I dropped my feet from the edge of my desk and sat upright in my swivel chair.

"You're a mercenary bastard, Ralph."

"That hurt."

"Yeah? Screw you. What's this new information Lucy spoke of?"

"The evidence technicians recovered an unidentified fingerprint at the bank back in '68. One of the robbers fired his shotgun into the ceiling to get everyone's attention. He was stupid enough to eject the shell. His print was on the brass base. And for all these years no one could match it to a name. But last week a suspect in a DUI manslaughter—an older guy—matched the print. I think we've got our fourth, previously unknown bank robber."

"The print connects him to the shot shell, not the bank."

"A minor point. One a world-class interrogator like you could overcome easily, no?"

"Pfui. Your flummery is lost on me."

"Flummery?"

"He's in custody?"

"Yep."

"So, why don't you deal with it?"

"The robbery is officially a cold case. Has been for a long time. And everyone from the director on down would rather not reopen it."

"I know I'll regret asking. Why?"

I sat through a long moment of silence.

"It's from those Hoover days when agents did some embarrassing things. J. Edgar got upset with the anti-war groups. He ordered Bureau people to do some dodgy stuff. Some may have even been illegal."

I interrupted with a snide remark. "Goodness, that's hard to believe."

"Yeah, right. Anyway, the bosses would rather leave things under the rug, so to speak."

"Might get a little embarrassing if a defense attorney snuck in annoying but little-known facts about things like the Chicago convention, the Columbia sit-in, the big demonstration on the mall in DC, and please don't mention that black day in July, huh?"

"Hey, not so loud. Those events were all way before my time, so I've got nothing to worry about—but if these people were that heavily involved, they just may know stuff we need to keep quiet."

"But you'd like me to drag out the dust and see what I can find? If a local cop clears a once local case, the defense has no reason to mention irrelevant things about you evil Feds."

"Sure. You have no ties to J. Edgar. You're just a small town cop who gets lucky more often than not. Besides, it's from your era. Nostalgic, right?"

"Up yours, Ralphie.

————

J ust east of Nashville, the Wilson County sheriff held Ira Allen Wolfe without bail for the deaths of two teenagers that he caused in a motor vehicle accident while driving at three times the legal limit of intoxication.

It took me three hours to drive from Prospect, over the Cumberland Plateau, and into middle Tennessee.

"You've got yourself one hell of a jackpot here, Ira," I said.

"Tell me about it." He spoke with a New Jersey accent. "By the way, I use my middle name. Call me Allen."

I grinned like I cared. "Want some help?"

"What's your big interest? Where'd you say you're from?"

"Prospect. Ring a bell?"

He hung his head and didn't answer.

Sixty-three-year-old Ira Wolfe didn't look a day under seventy. He wore long gray hair pulled back in a ponytail. His face had more lines than a map of the metro New York road system. And I'd bet the drugs and alcohol he used in those sixty-three years had partially fried and pickled his brain.

I planted a few thoughts in his mind. "You have a lousy driving record in this state. Top that off with the reckless manslaughter of two clean-cut local kids and you're looking at some major jail time, partner."

"And you drove from east Tennessee to tell me that?"

We sat in scarred-up metal chairs at a three-by-four foot utility table in a small and shabby interview room with gray cement block walls. Through a glass panel in the door, I saw a jail guard waiting in the hallway, chewing gum.

"You've lived in Lebanon, Tennessee for ten years, but any jury will know you're not a local. They'll see you as just another northern carpetbagger, but one who habitually drinks too much and killed a boy and girl from Mount Juliet. If you don't have a friend, Allen, you're dog food."

He dropped his eyes again and nodded.

"You have money for a sharp lawyer, or are you relying on a public defender?" I asked.

"Do I look like I can afford F. Lee Bailey?"

"No offense, sport, but you don't look like you could afford his pool boy. Want to talk a deal for cooperation, or do you like the idea of being a guest of the Tennessee corrections system for seven years?"

"Whatchya think I can do for you?"

I explained how his fingerprint was linked to the Smoky Mountain Bank Job.

"Goddamn," he said. "That's more than forty years ago."

"Forty-three years and one month, but who's counting? And there's no statute of limitations on a felony murder. John and Jane Doe warrants were applied for way back then, so you're still on the hook for the stick-up, too."

"You want me to plead guilty to a bank robbery where a guard was killed and you'll help me out with a vehicular homicide? Are you nuts?"

The overhead fluorescent lighting gave Wolfe's pale skin a gray-green tinge.

"You wouldn't be the first to ask that. Hey, I'm only a local cop, but I can bring in FBI horsepower if you help me clear the bank robbery. You're gonna do time. Where you do it and how long is up to you."

"You want me to rat out my brothers?"

"Don't forget your sister, Wanda."

He looked at me with wide, bloodshot eyes.

"You know a lot."

"You betcha."

"People in prison don't like informants," he said. "I could be gettin' a death sentence."

"The people you're giving up are as old as you and me. They don't have any friends in the GP nowadays. You'll be protected. Trust me."

"Yeah, right." He still looked skeptical.

"Look, the Feds want this cleared and are ready to give you a sweetheart deal. They'll clean you up and send you to one of those federal country clubs with a new identity. You do your time and get out to live like a new man under Federal protection."

"You sure?"

"Would I lie to you?"

After another thirty minutes of persuasion, Ira Allen Wolfe provided me with the names of his three accomplices from the Prospect bank robbery, identified the shooter and told me where he last saw two of them.

After years of revolutionary campaigning, Wanda Ruth Potemkin tied up romantically and philosophically with another Long Island boy, Joel David Lipinsky. Wolfe met up with them, not long ago, in the great state of Tennessee. The fourth member of the ring was Francis Xavier "Frank" Cleary who, like Wolfe, was also from New Jersey.

In the late 1960s, the CIA recruited students from various colleges around the country to carry out matters of national security. So did assorted domestic dissident groups who opposed the Vietnam War and the government in general.

The foursome who carried out The Great Smoky Mountain Bank Job was initially card-carrying members of the Students for a Democratic Society, then the Revolutionary Youth Movement and later still, the Weather Underground Organization.

"Where can I find Wanda and Lipinsky?" I asked.

"We don't exactly meet at the Olive Garden once a month for lunch, ya know."

"Have a nice time in the slammer, Ira." I rose to leave.

"Wait, wait, wait. Hang on a minute," he said. "The last time I heard about them, they were living in Sparta."

"Sparta, Tennessee?"

"Uh-huh."

"Be more specific."

"Hell, I don't know. Like I told you, I don't socialize with them anymore."

"How did you find out they were in Sparta?"

"I met them at a craft show. It's how I make a living. I do leather work. Wanda makes jewelry. I was walking around, and I recognized her. Joel was there, too. They're a couple, still."

"Thank you. That wasn't hard, was it?"

He shrugged.

"Now," I said, "what names are they using?"

"It's like the Army, man—don't ask, don't tell."

"If you want a deal, you better tell."

"Hey look, I'm tryin', man. I didn't ask them for a bio for the years since I saw them last."

"Okay, how about Cleary?"

"Last I heard, he's out West. Oregon or Idaho or some shit. A place easy to deal pot."

"Jesus, Allen. Talk about a time warp. After seeing how Jerry Rubin went mainstream, do you feel left behind?"

"Gimme a break, man."

"Okay, don't go anywhere, pal. If we find the Lipinskys in Sparta, I'll let you know."

———

The day after I called Ralph Oliveri with Wolfe's information, a platoon of deputies from the White County Sheriff's Office combed Sparta, Tennessee for seventy-two hours looking for Wanda and Joel. The best they could do was find a double-wide occupied by a young married couple who had been there for nine months after the Lipinskys boogied. Neighbors and the absentee landlord of the mobile home said Wanda and Joel bailed out one night, leaving no forwarding address.

I went back to the Wilson County lock-up.

"Strike one, Ira. No luck. When did you see the Lipinskys at this craft show you mentioned?" I asked.

"It's Allen, please. Ira was my father. We weren't close."

I shrugged. "Yeah, okay."

"At the annual Labor Day thing in McMinnville."

"That was about nine months ago?"

He did a little thinking.

"Yeah, I guess."

"How do you sign up for the craft show?"

"I've done it for three years now. I get an application in the mail. New people apply to the Chamber of Commerce. It's a juried event. Quality stuff only. They keep out the riff-raff."

I wanted to look aghast and roll my eyes, but I kept a straight face.

"Tell me about Wanda's jewelry."

"Classy stuff. Mostly gemstones set in sterling with a lot of silver wire. High-end glass beads, too. She was good. No, even better—a real pro. She told me they do the Foothills Craft Guild show in Knoxville each year. You gotta be tops to get in there. I tried, but never got accepted."

"Okay. McMinnville Chamber of Commerce may have info on them. And maybe the Foothills Craft Guild. You're doing good, Allen. Maybe I'll get you out of jail before you turn eighty."

"Come on, man. You said if I helped, you'd get me a deal."

"So far you haven't helped much."

———

A short, stodgy-looking woman at the McMinnville C of C looked over the applications from their last craft fair. She found a Joni Mitchell and Leonard Cohen on their roster with a Sparta post office box who applied to sell jewelry and paid for their spot with a postal money order. Those names also showed up during the White County cops' investigation. Joni and Leonard settled up with the Tennessee Department of Revenue after the craft show by paying the required sales tax they collected over the weekend. So, being vendors in good standing, McMinnville planned on inviting them back again in September. No one picked up on the similarity of their names to a famous musical pair.

When I checked with a representative of the Foothills Craft Guild, I heard a similar story. However, they recently received a change of address for Joni. Now she was using a post office box in Gatlinburg.

I jumped in my gray unmarked Ford and drove the riverside road through the Smoky Mountains National Park to the touristy town of Gatlinburg in adjoining Sevier County. The post office, a small chalet-styled building on a side street, wasn't hard to find.

On the way, I tuned in the '60s station on satellite radio—just to get me in the proper mood. As I pulled into the post office parking lot, Barry McGuire was singing 'The Eve of Destruction'.

"Sure," the postmaster said. "Joni Mitchell and Leonard Cohen have Box 349."

"Think anything sounded funny about the names?" I asked.

"Well, I guess Cohen sounds Jewish. But I've met a few Jewish folks around here before."

"Uh-huh. What form of ID did she or he use when they applied for the box?"

"I remember them," he said. "Jest moved here from middle Tennessee. My card says a Tennessee driver's license with a Sparta address. Said they was livin' in a camper, lookin' fer a place ta rent."

"You only saw one form of ID?"

"That's all I need."

A young man of no more than thirty-five, the postmaster looked slightly overweight and sounded very local. He seemed content with how he did his job.

"Do they get much mail?' I asked.

"Not that I've noticed. One or two first class ever' once in a while. No second class to speak of. No magazines or advertisements yet."

"How about credit card statements, utility bills, telephone bills—all the stuff everyone else on the planet gets?"

He scratched his dirty-blond crew cut. "Cain't remember."

"They come back to give you a new local address?"

"Nope."

I was back to square one. I'd ask the Feds to watch the PO Box if they could spare an agent, and maybe they'd get lucky. But maybe they couldn't spare a body. They seemed happy to let me do all the work.

Then, on the off-chance someone there would know something, I stopped at the Gatlinburg Chamber of Commerce and spoke to a cute blonde named Tonya Carpenter.

"I'm trying to track down a couple who use a Gatlinburg PO Box, but didn't leave a local address with the postmaster."

"How in the world can I he'p ya?" She sounded like I asked her to name the Lindbergh kidnapper.

"The woman makes jewelry. She uses the name Mitchell. She lives with a guy named Cohen. Do you have a list of artists who work in town?"

"I have a list of businesses—if they joined the chamber, but no one is obligated to do that."

"Rats," I said.

She frowned. "Have you checked for a county business license?"

"Someone from my office called, but the clerk had nothing under those names."

"Are they in trouble?" she asked.

I nodded. "Sort of."

"Somethin' bad?"

"She passed a couple of bad checks in Prospect," I lied. "I'd like to find her. The people she stiffed can't afford to lose the money."

"That's terrible, stiffin' somebody with a bad check. I really wish I could he'p ya."

"Well, thanks anyway." I turned to leave.

"Hang on a minute," she said. "Maybe I can find something for ya. I've got a list of people who have shops out on Artisan's Loop. The Loop Association sends us somethin', and from their list, we make up the annual brochure."

"Great. I'll take a look."

Halfway through the list of seventy-odd names, something jumped out at me. "Aha! It's gotta be."

"Found them?"

"Yeah, they changed names again. Ms. Carpenter, I love you!"

"Do what?"

"I found what I need. Thanks a million. If my hunch pans out, I'll recommend you for the Medal of Freedom."

"Really?"

———

"Wanda was in my senior seminar group," my wife said.

Kate sat in an upholstered garden chair on the porch of our house, sipping her first gin and tonic of the season. She wore a filmy blouse of several earth tones and a pair of washed-off jeans.

"Don't broadcast that," I said. "The Feds may take a close look at you."

"She was a very intelligent person."

"Too bad she didn't join the Peace Corps instead of focusing on violently overthrowing the government."

I took a long drink of my own G&T and put my feet up on a low table.

"Amazing, isn't it?" Kate said. "We went to school with a famous anarchist."

"Make sure you call her an acquaintance and not a friend."

"Sammy, I'm about as much an anarchist as you are."

"I'm a genuine war hero and all-American boy."

"And dreadfully modest," Kate observed.

"Of course I am. Just remember, the rest of the world considers your former classmate a bad apple. The Ten Most Wanted list is populated by some real characters."

"I'm not surprised."

"I wonder if she remembers me," I asked.

"Trust me, she'll remember you."

"She'll remember *you*," I said. "I didn't hang out with your intellectual crowd. And you've looked the same for years. Maybe a little extra gray, but still the slinky brown-eyed beauty I married when we were just kids."

"Aren't you sweet?"

"What do you think she'll say if I show up with the team that arrests her?"

"She'll call you a fascist pig."

My feeling of nostalgia kicked along in high gear. I had turned on XM radio again, of course, listening to the '60s station. Scott McKenzie sang 'San Francisco'.

"Oh well, nobody's perfect, sweetie," I said.

"You're not perfect, my little piggy, but you can cook."

"Yes, I can."

"And you're pretty good in bed."

I winked. "Just pretty good?"

"Well..."

Scott crooned in the background "...be sure to wear some flowers in your hair. You're gonna meet some gentle people there."

"You knew Wanda as well as anyone," I said. "Think you could ID her if we got up close and personal?"

"Maybe. What do I get if I help you?"

"A night of shoddy pleasure with that all-American boy you think is good in bed."

"I'd get that anyway."

"Two nights."

"Oh, boy. Deal!"

———

I sat in the FBI conference room at 710 Locust Street in Knoxville. Ralph Oliveri, Lucy Frobisher and Special Agent in Charge Carl Harmon occupied three other chairs in the room. Harmon and Oliveri wore standard-issue FBI uniform—medium gray suits, white shirts and dull ties. Lucy looked lovely in a dark green wraparound dress. She used a matching green ribbon to hold her hair in a ponytail. Wearing moderate heels, she stood all of five-ten.

"What do we have to give Wolfe for this info, Sam?" Harmon asked.

I sat back in my seat and took a breath before making my thoughts known. "He thinks he'll get a full seven years for the DUI manslaughter Wilson County has hanging over his head. Depends on how badly you want the other two or three people. It's been forty-three years. We'd have squat without his tip."

Carl nodded. His steel gray hair fell in a comma over his forehead. I thought he looked more like a dentist than a cop.

"Give him a slide on the bank job as long as he wasn't the shooter," I said. "Tennessee won't care if you pick up his motel bill for those seven years at a minimum security facility in satisfaction for the manslaughter. Sign him in under an assumed name and when he gets out, put him in Wit Sec for the rest of his pinko life. He'll be seventy when he gets out of jail. If he dries out inside, he'll be no danger to anyone else when he drives."

"We've given away worse," Harmon said. "You okay with that, Lucy?"

She looked from Carl to me and nodded. "Better than nothing."

"Ralph," he said, "you have any thoughts?"

"Sounds okay to me," he said. "How often do you clear up a few slots on the Most Wanted list in one day? What happens to the other three?"

"Who cares?" I said. "They're fugitives. You had reasonable suspicion they were involved forty-three years ago. Based on what Wolfe told me, I may find Potemkin and Lipinsky. Cleary is still an unknown. They go to trial and take their chances with a jury. Maybe Wanda and Joel will deal and give up Cleary if they know anything at this late date."

I shifted in the overstuffed swivel chair. The FBI conference room looked more like something you'd find in a Fortune Five-Hundred company or the offices of a five-hundred-dollar-an-hour attorney. Our tax dollars at work.

"It sounds like good information," Lucy said. "We'll probably get two of them. And if they have no location for the last guy, at least you can put out a BOLO on Cleary."

"Lucy, I love it when you use that modern cop talk," I said.

"Sam, darlin', if we collar this trio, I'll buy you the finest dinner you've ever seen." She added a little extra 'country' to her accent.

"I'll hold you to that, Special Agent Frobisher."

"Uh, do you two mind if we interrupt?" Ralph said.

"By all means, Ralphie," I said. "And I'll take you to lunch, too, but on a different day."

Carl Harmon decided to interrupt our clever conversation. "Okay, Sam, according to your information and what you suspect, Potemkin and Lipinsky are living somewhere in Gatlinburg and operating a jewelry shop on the Artisan's Loop off US 321?"

"Correct," I said. "I believe they call themselves Wendy and Bobby Zimmerman. It makes sense to me."

"Zimmerman?" Lucy said. "Unbelievable."

"What?" Ralph said.

"Ralphie, you're from a different generation, but don't you remember the song, 'The Subterranean Homesick Blues?'"

"A song about a sewer?"

Ralph is forty-five and fancies himself an Italian stallion, but obviously, he wasn't into oldies but goodies.

"Don't be obtuse. Remember the lyrics, "You don't need a weatherman to know which way the wind blows. Don't follow leaders, watch the parkin' meters?"

"Yeah, so?"

"So who wrote it and sang it?"

"Bob Dylan, right?"

"And what was Bob Dylan's real name?"

"Who knows?"

"Apparently Lucy and I do. Bobby Zimmerman, the young folk singer from Minnesota. When I saw the name, I knew it was them."

"No kiddin'?"

"No kiddin'."

"What do you suggest, Sam?" Carl asked.

"My wife knew Wanda Potemkin as well as anyone," I said. "Kate and I can go into the jewelry shop, buy a pair of earrings and then leave and give the arrest team the signal. Voila! You nab Wanda and Joel. Then see if your AUSA wants to strike a deal to locate Frank Cleary."

My Federal comrades liked the idea.

When Bob Dylan sang, "You don't need a weatherman to know which way the wind blows," he referred to the revolutionary group. But the Weathermen gained too many female operatives to keep the sexist organizational name. So, somewhere around 1970, they officially changed it to the Weather Underground Organization. Knowing Wanda Potemkin, I assumed she had considerable input with the name conversion. Wanda always had a big mouth.

———

On a sunny Thursday morning in late May, Kate and I drove through the National Park in my restored '67 Austin-Healey 3000. Wildflowers bloomed along the verge and into the tree line. The Little Pigeon River gurgled noisily over rocks and boulders worn smooth over the centuries, and all looked right in the world. I would have put the top down, but the pine pollen would have attacked me, and I hate to arrest Federal fugitives with runny eyes.

The eight-track tape player hanging beneath the glove box of the Healey played Johnny Rivers—at the moment singing 'Going Back To Big Sur'.

We met our back-up team at the Gatlinburg PD. Two of their uniformed officers would accompany us, as would two uniforms from the Sevier County Sheriff's Office. Two of their detectives would actually make the arrest. Ralph Oliveri and his partner Bonny Rowatt stopped by to provide instant FBI liaison after the fugitives were in custody—assuming the Zimmermans were in fact the fugitives.

Our little convoy of law enforcement professionals turned off US 321 onto the country lane called Artisan's Loop. Among the tall pines and assorted deciduous trees, an occasional log cabin or rustic-looking frame building sat on the roadside next to small parking lots. We saw pottery and painter's studios, chain saw artists, soup and sandwich shops, fudge and ice cream stores and a small cabin with a dark green shingle roof, sage green-stained Texture 111 plywood siding and a yellow homemade sign naming the business The Mellow Submarine, Eclectic Jewelry and Crafts. The lettering had been done freehand using several colors. Brightly painted flowers randomly covered the empty spaces. It reminded me of something from the flower power days of the late '60s.

Kate and I pulled in and parked next to an old Winnebago with a heavy-duty electric cord running from the motor home into a back window. Ralph led the four unmarked police cars down the road a'piece to wait for our signal.

I wore a wire, allowing Ralph to hear our conversation, and an earplug that would pick up anything Ralph had to tell me.

The interior of the shop looked as I expected. Several glass-fronted display cases full of necklaces, brooches and other jewelry, a few racks of earrings on the counters, a few framed photos with price tags on the off-white sheetrock walls and a half dozen woodcarvings scattered around the room. I assumed the woodwork to be Joel's contributions to the business. Everything looked tidy.

A woman in her sixties stood behind the counter writing something on an order pad. Her long, gray hair was parted in the middle and pulled tightly into a ponytail. She wore no makeup and looked vaguely like the Wanda Potemkin I remembered, but I'd hate to send her to jail for life based on my ability to see only a passing resemblance. I looked at Kate and shrugged. She gave me a surreptitious shake of her head indicating that she was unsure, too.

The woman looked up. "Hi. If you want to see anything or need help, just let me know."

Her accent was northeast, but I couldn't remember what Wanda sounded like.

"Thanks," Kate said, and began looking at earrings on a rack not ten feet from the woman.

I looked around the shop. A door marked private led to somewhere: a storeroom, office, restroom? Neither Joel nor Bobby nor Leonard was in attendance.

"How much are these?" Kate asked, holding up a pair of dangly earrings mounted on a card.

The woman finished writing, placed her pen on the pad and started walking over.

My stroll down memory lane just wouldn't quit. A CD played music through two small speakers on opposite corners of the shop. The Animals were singing 'The House of the Rising Sun'.

"Everything on that rack is twelve," she said.

"They're beautiful," Kate said.

"Thanks. That's all sterling, and the beads are mille fiori from Italy. I make all the jewelry."

"You're very talented," Kate said.

The woman smiled.

I stood there grinning like the village idiot or Kate's chauffeur and hired muscle. I noticed the woman's bell-bottomed jeans and linen peasant's blouse—straight out of the '6os.

"Where are you folks from?" she asked.

"We live over in Blount County," I said and poked a thumb in the general direction of West.

"We just opened the shop. We're new to the area ourselves," she said. "You don't sound like locals."

"No," I said. "I retired a few years back, and we moved here from New York."

"Big difference?" she asked.

"You bet."

"Have you been in before? You look familiar."

"No, first time," I said.

"What did you do in New York?"

"I worked in civil service."

"So did my father. He's still up there, but retired," she said. "What did you do?"

Liar. Wanda Potemkin's father was a furrier.

"I was in pest control."

"Oh."

As Kate hung the card of earrings back on the rack, the front door opened. A short woman carrying an armful of framed photographs walked in.

She nodded at us. "How y'all doin' today? Hi, Wendy."

"Okay, Lulu. What have you got for me?"

Lulu looked like an odd duck, dumpy with spiky hair the color of an over-ripe carrot and dressed in nature photographer's garb—khaki pants with large cargo pockets, an olive green shirt, and a khaki vest with half-a-million pockets.

"Brought a few more pitchers if you have the room."

"Sure. You make out a consignment sheet for me?"

"I did."

"Excuse me, folks," the shop owner said, once again looking in our direction, "you need me, give a yell."

Kate and I stared at each other again. Before I could suggest leaving, the door to the back rooms opened and a thin man, also in his sixties, walked in. He wore a black baseball cap with a red Rolling Stones tongue logo on the crown. The gray hair sticking out underneath needed a cutting. His Levis hadn't seen soap for a while, and his faded Grateful Dead T-shirt looked decades old.

"Morning," he said to us. "Hey, Lulu, how're you today?"

Lulu answered, and Kate and I both said hello.

"That your Healey in the lot?" he asked.

"Sure is," I said. "Like British cars?"

"Like everything from the '60s."

I decided to engage him in conversation.

"Wendy said she makes the jewelry. Looks like Lulu is the photographer. Are you the woodcarver?"

"I am."

"Nice work." I took a few steps and picked up an eighteen-inch-tall bear stained black. "This is a good time of year to see these critters in the park."

"Yep."

Joel was a man of few words.

A cell phone attached to his belt sounded off. He answered.

"Yeah." He listened for a few moments. "Oh, yeah? You sure?" More listening. "Okay. Hang on a second. Yeah, I gotta go to the back room."

Joel disappeared.

———

K ate looked at Wanda or Joni or Wendy or whomever.

"May I see these yellow earrings in the case, please?"

"Sure," Wanda said. "Be right there."

Kate pointed out what she wanted to see. "The yellow twisted beads. Yes, next to the agate necklace."

"These are called Nueva Cadiz beads. They're old and pretty rare. I got them in New Mexico."

"Beautiful," Kate said. "How much are they?"

"They're thirty."

"I think I need these. What do you think, sweetie?"

I'd been looking where Bobby or Leonard or Joel had gone.

"Huh?" I said.

"These are pretty. May I get them?"

"Uh, sure." I wondered if the FBI would pay.

Kate placed the earrings on the counter. Wanda picked them up.

"I'll put them over by the register."

"Okay. I'm still looking," Kate said.

Dollar signs rolled around in my head like the symbols on a slot machine.

Joel interrupted my thought process. He burst out of the back room wearing a tan windbreaker not unlike the one I wore. I used mine to hide the small Smith & Wesson Chief's Special I tucked into my waistband. I wondered what he was hiding.

"Uh-oh." I whispered into my microphone.

"Excuse me, Lulu," Joel said. "I just got an important call. Sorry, but we're gonna have to close."

"What's going on, Sam?" I heard Ralph loud and clear in my ear piece.

"Do we have time to pay for the earrings?" I asked.

"Of course," Wanda said.

"I'll just come back tomorrow," Lulu said, reaching into her multi-pocketed vest for a set of truck keys.

As she approached the door, I saw Ralph's silver Crown Victoria pull up close to the entrance. Bonny Rowatt, a good-looking young redhead was out of the passenger's side in a flash, Ralph only a few steps behind her. Joel beat Lulu to the door and opened it.

As Lulu exited, he spoke to Ralph and Bonny.

"Sorry, folks," he said. "We have to close early. Family emergency. Sorry."

He closed and locked the door immediately. I had the feeling we might be hostages.

As I watched Ralph and Bonny drive off, I heard Ralph in my left ear. "Talk to me, Sam."

"Do you take charge cards?" I asked.

Ralph said, "Jesus, Sam."

"Sure we do," Wanda said.

Joel stepped close to me. "Let's knock off the bullshit, shall we, Mr. Jenkins?"

He pulled a well-used GI .45 automatic from the small of his back, probably something he stole from a state armory forty-five years ago.

"I wonder who called your cell phone?" I said.

"Jenkins?" Wanda asked and looked at me closely. A brief moment passed, and she turned her attention on Kate. "Sam Jenkins? Kate? Kate Wisniewski?"

"Small world, huh, Wanda?" I said.

"What the hell's going on, Joel?" Wanda asked.

"Jenkins here is a cop," he said. "From Prospect."

"Prospect?" she said. "Oh, shit."

Joel raised the .45 to about my chest level. Kate was sharp enough to take a step away from me to the right.

"As they used to say in the old cowboy movies, Joel, you seem to have the drop on me. Mind lowering your gun? That's an awfully big hole I'm looking at."

"Not a chance, pal. What are you doing here? You think you can arrest us?"

In my ear, I heard, "Hang in there, buddy. We're right here."

"The thought had crossed my mind," I said. "You're both Federal fugitives, you know."

"You're both cops?" Wanda asked.

"No, Wanda," I said. "We're married. I'm the only cop. I figured if we could ID you two, I'd go back to my little police station, call my buddy from the FBI, and I'd be a hero."

"I always thought you were a fascist bastard," she said. "I'll bet you stay home on weekends and watch John Wayne movies."

Kate looked at me. "What did I tell you?"

"Not now, Kats." I turned to Wanda. "You'd be surprised. I haven't rented *The Green Berets* in years, and I don't have anti-Jane Fonda bumper stickers on any of our cars."

"We should just kill you and leave," Wanda said, adding a little venom to her voice.

"You'd do that to your old Long Island school chums?" I asked.

"I never liked you, Sam," Wanda said.

My eyes darted around the room looking out the windows for our reinforcements. I knew Ralph was hearing me, but so far, the cavalry hadn't ridden up.

"Pigs!" Wanda spat out.

Somehow, I didn't see Ms. Potemkin as a sympathetic ear. I'd try negotiating with her partner.

"Look, Joel," I said. "I'm the pig—no argument. Although I'd prefer you call me the fuzz. How about you let Kate leave and you and Wanda and me talk about this?"

"Talk about what?" he said. "I'm holding this cannon, and you're standing there shittin' in your pants."

Actually, I hadn't soiled my knickers, and I forced myself to concentrate on Joel and his pistol because in the background, the McCoys were doing 'Hang on Sloopy', and I wanted to sing along. But quickly I noticed that the hammer of Joel's 1911 Colt wasn't cocked. He held the heavy gun unsteadily at arm's length and didn't have a very tight-looking grip on the old thing. If I made a move for my revolver and he was any good with a gun, it would take him at least two or three seconds, plus reaction time, to cock and fire the pistol—assuming he had a round in the chamber. If he didn't, by the time he racked a round into battery, I could take a short nap and still put a bullet in his head. I decided the former revolutionary was just an old man and sufficiently unsure of himself for me to try a trick that always worked before.

"Joel, I get your point," I said, "but I've gotta ask, hasn't anyone ever told you, a... wet...bird...never...flies...at...night?"

I noticed the confused look on his face. As soon as I spoke the word "night," I pulled the Chief's Special, took a half step to my left, assumed a combat stance and fired a bullet into his thigh.

"Oh, Jesus Christ!" he cried. "Fucking Christ! That hurts!"

One hundred and fifty-eight grains of hollow point .38 would do that. The .45 fell to the floor. So did Joel.

When my gun went off, Kate screamed and grabbed her ears. She stood far enough away to be safe.

Wanda sprinted between the counters toward her partner. I stood ten feet away and moved closer.

Just as she arrived next to Joel, Wanda reached for the fallen automatic. By then I was only a step away. The sound of me cocking the hammer on my revolver echoed in the room.

"Don't touch it," I said.

She hesitated. I held my ground, the barrel of my gun less than a foot from Wanda's head.

"He's just wounded," I said. "You'll die. Still wanna try?"

Neither she nor I moved. The few seconds she spent thinking seemed like an eternity. I looked at her eyes as she stared intently at the gun. No doubt, she wanted to punch my ticket. Wanda Potemkin was a cool customer.

Joel moaned, trying to hold two hands tightly on his thigh. Blood oozed from the wound to the floor.

"He's bleeding to death while you're screwing around," I said.

"Oh, fuck you," she said and backed off.

Glass in the front door broke. An arm reached in and unlocked the bolt. Four uniformed cops burst in with guns drawn. Two of them pulled Joel Lipinsky away and administered first aid. A third used his portable radio to call for an ambulance. The fourth put handcuffs on Wanda.

I picked up the .45 and checked the chamber. Whoops. I found a round seated and ready to go.

Ralph Oliveri and Bonny Rowatt followed the two Sevier County dicks into the store. Kate stepped over and put her arms around me.

———

I sat at the same three-by-four table in the same battered metal chair in the Wilson County jail gazing through the glass into the hallway. The door opened, and a jail guard wearing a gray uniform escorted Ira Allen Wolfe into the room, his hands cuffed in front with the shackles attached to a chain around his waist that puckered the cloth of his orange prison jumpsuit. Wolfe shuffled as he walked, jingling the chains and manacles around his ankles. His bird-like face looked drawn and ashen. The guard pulled the chair away from the table and pointed for him to sit. He hesitated.

"Have a seat, Allen," I said without enthusiasm.

He smiled weakly. "Did you find Wanda and Joel?"

I didn't return the smile; nor did I answer.

"What's up? They get away?" He tried to look serious now.

"Aren't you wondering why you're chained up today like the *Prisoner of Zenda*?"

"Uh, yeah. Last time it was just handcuffs. What's up?"

"What's up, Allen, is that you're on my shit list."

"You didn't find them? Hey, man, I tried my best. That was all right-eous info I gave you. You can't find them, it ain't my fault."

"They gave out the Academy Awards in February, so cut the crap."

"Huh?"

"Don't huh me, you skinny little bastard. You dropped a dime on Lipinsky and told him I was coming. Did a good job of describing me, too."

"No, man, you're crazy. It wasn't me. I'm in jail, for chrissakes. How am I gonna do that?"

"Don't insult me, Allen. You could call the White House from any jail in the country."

I took a cell phone from my pocket and dropped it on the table. The guard, who remained in the room and stood with his back against the wall, cracked a smile. Wolfe's head dropped.

"This is a prepaid cell phone, smart guy," I said. "We couldn't trace calls going out from it, but it stores incoming calls in memory. Guess what phone called this cell last?"

"Hey, man, I..."

"Shut up, moron. This is Lipinsky's cell. And one of the public phones in this correctional facility was used to call him. Surprise, surprise."

"Man, you gotta understand..."

"I told you to shut up. I don't want to put this officer in a position where he sees you ricochet off these concrete walls, so stop talking, and I won't hit you."

He nodded.

"As luck would have it, I did find Joel and Wanda. And you, you duplicitous bastard, called him while I was standing there. But you know that. And you probably know Joel intended to shoot me. And my wife, you prick." My volume went up drastically. A jail trustee sweeping the floor in the hall stopped and looked toward the interview room. I slammed my hand down hard on the table. Wolfe jumped. The guard's grin widened.

"Man, you gotta understand," he repeated. "We were soldiers fighting for this country, too. We went through a lot together. I couldn't leave my brother and sister hangin' out there."

"Most things in life, Allen, come down to choice. I understand that. You made a choice. I offered a sweet deal to get you off a major hook. You betrayed my trust. So, I say to you exactly what Wanda said to me, 'Fuck you'."

"But you said..."

"Tough shit, partner. Your deal is off the table. But you know what the good news is?"

"Good news? What?" He sounded a little encouraged.

"You won't have to concern yourself with the manslaughter charge Wilson County has on you."

"What?"

"Not for a long while, anyway. And the Feds are waiving prosecution on the bank job."

"Feds?"

"The Blount County District Attorney will have deputies pick you up and drive east where you and Joel and Wanda will stand trial in state court for the armed robbery you admitted to and complicity in the murder of Douglas Frobisher."

"But I didn't kill anybody!"

"Remember these words, Allen. Tough shit. You robbed the bank. You say Frank Cleary killed the guard. Why should I believe that? You all wore masks. The witnesses wouldn't know Frank Cleary from H. Rap Brown. And so what? In the eyes of the law, you're as guilty as Cleary. So are Joel and Wanda."

"Come on, man."

"I offered you a seven-year vacation in a Federal country club if you did the right thing. Now you're looking at a trial for two serious crimes in a very conservative, pro-America county. How do you think a jury will view three people who wanted to violently overthrow the government?"

His mouth opened, and I held up a hand to silence him.

"Remember one more thing while you're trying to sleep for the next few nights. Frobisher wasn't only a bank guard. He was an off-duty deputy where you're going to spend your pre-trial confinement. And Tennessee still has the death penalty for cases like this. Still think your choice was a good one?"

He hung his head.

"By the way, you don't need a weatherman to know which way the wind blows...just ask me."

I waved my hand for the guard to take him away.

"Have a good life, Ira."

———

We all sat in Carl Harmon's office in comfortable chairs, looking at walnut tongue-and-groove paneling that must have cost the taxpayers a small fortune—Ralph, Bonny, Lucy Frobisher, me and Moira Menzies, the chief assistant district attorney general for Blount County.

"Thank you, Sam," Carl said. "Very well done. I expect you'll get a letter from the Director shortly."

I shrugged and tried to look humble. "Aw, shucks, folks, it was nuthin'."

Ralph rolled his eyes. "Oh, jeez."

Bonny and Lucy smiled. Girls usually like my self-effacing behavior.

"I'm surprised you didn't kill Lipinsky. That's more your style," Moira said.

"Don't be such a wet blanket. I was thinking of the public relations value. Old man spared by humane cop."

She shook her head. "Please."

Maybe not all girls.

"Sure you didn't jerk the trigger and miss his chest?" Ralph asked with an obnoxious grin.

"Don't even think it," I said.

Carl interrupted. "Are you looking for the death penalty, Moira?"

"We'd like the defendants to think so. As far as we know, Cleary was the shooter. Wolfe seems like the weakest link. He's scared. Maybe he'll help us find Cleary. If we get any leads out of state, can we count on Bureau assistance?"

"I'm sure we can arrange that," Carl said.

"Good. I'll keep you informed."

There was a long moment of silence.

"I think we're done here," Carl said.

We all shook hands and left. In the agent's squad room, Lucy and I stopped at Ralph's desk.

"Thank you, Sam," she said. "I know my father would be pleased with the work you did for me." She kissed my cheek.

"He does good work for an old man," Ralph said. "Little of it, but what's there is good."

"Thanks, I think," I said.

"Don't forget that dinner I promised you," Lucy said.

"Let's make it a lunch. At my age, I hate to drive at night."

She smiled.

After having seen three of her outfits, I wondered where she kept her issue Glock.

I looked at Oliveri. "And may I assume my slate is now clean?"

"Sure. But you'll be back soon enough."

"Thanks."

"Hey," he said. "I've got something for Kate."

He handed me the earrings with the twisted yellow beads.

"Did you pay for these?" I asked.

"Of course I did. I left thirty bucks in the register."

"My wife and I thank you, Ralphie. But what about the sales tax?"

THE END

HURRICANE BLOW-UP

Hurricane Irene slammed the South Carolina coast the night before. Forecasters said it wasn't the most powerful storm, but it was the largest, with about as much square footage as Europe.

I strolled from the parking lot to the back door, tapped in my four-digit code, and entered Prospect PD.

When I reached our lobby, Bettye Lambert asked, "How is it out there?"

"Beautiful. About seventy-five and dry. A twenty-mile-an-hour breeze is blowing, but no one would know a hurricane is hammering the coast."

We were working on a Saturday, and Bettye had abandoned her Monday-to-Friday police uniform for a blue knitted blouse and tan slacks. A sergeant's badge hung on her belt along with a .40 caliber Glock automatic. She looked like my idea of a sexy TV detective.

"We could use some rain," she said.

"Don't hold your breath. Not a cloud overhead, but the sky looks like a war zone. The Air Force is sending oodles of C-130s from bases on the coast to McGhee-Tyson, and the Army has squadrons of choppers heading to the aviation support facility. They want to keep their aircraft safe. Makes me want to raise a band of mercenaries and attack Kentucky."

"Of course you do, Sammy."

"Before I plan a military operation, I should run all these tourists out of town. Every motel, B&B and RV park from here to Pigeon Forge is packed with evacuees, NASCAR fans going to Bristol and all the usual late summer merrymakers.

"The guys handled six fender-benders before I got here at eight this morning," she said. "These visitors just don't know where they're going."

"And I hate every one of them for making us work overtime."

"You're not exactly a good candidate for ambassador of tourism, are you?"

"Ah, nuts. Screw'em all."

Bettye laughed, and the radio crackled.

On the other end, PO Junior Huskey yelled into his microphone, "Lord have mercy! This is 501. I'm drivin' by the Foothills View Mo-tel, an' a car jest blew up."

As he held the transmit button down, we heard his tires squeal when he turned the cruiser toward the motel.

"Je-sus, look at that smoke and fire!" Junior said. "Stand by, I'll check it out."

I've never seen Bettye get rattled. "10-4, five-zero-one," she said, as calm as an ER nurse facing a spurting artery. "I'll send the fire department. Advise if you need medics."

"10-4," Junior said. "I'm 10-36 now. I'll advise."

Sergeant Stan Rose spoke calmly from his car. "535, headquarters, I'll respond and assist. Other units, remain on patrol until I know if we need additional cars."

"10-4, five-three-five," Bettye said. "Prospect-One is here and knows the situation."

"535, 10-4," Stanley said.

"507, copy." And "511, me, too," came from POs Bobby Crockett and Jamey Hawkins, respectively.

Then Junior's voice came over the radio. "501, headquarters, send medics. I got an adult male with glass cuts."

Bettye typed a quick line into her computer and transmitted the information to Rural Metro Ambulance Service.

"10-4, five-zero-one," she said. "Paramedics on the way."

"Damn," I said. "Aren't you and our troops just so disciplined and efficient?"

"'Cause we have a great leader, darlin'," Bettye said.

"Thank you, my dear. Since I'm Prospect-One, I'll just mosey over to the motel and see what's up. By the time I get there, the firemen should have the situation under control."

"Call me when you know," she said.

———

The Best Western Foothills View Motel looked like something transplanted from Innsbruck, Austria to Prospect, Tennessee. Chalet-styled with dark wood siding and rustic white shutters and colorful flower boxes hung under the windows. The glass panes were so clean they sparkled in the sunlight. Charming. Simply charming.

When I pulled into the parking lot, I noticed a smoldering white Cadillac DeVille with South Carolina plates had scarred the tranquility of the alpine setting.

The Blount County Fire Department had dispatched two trucks and an assistant chief's car from the nearby Walland substation. Hoses from the pumper covered the blacktop surface, and two firefighters in turnout gear stood near the still-smoking car. Streams of water trickled down the sloping pavement.

The Rural Metro ambulance was parked halfway between the office and the scene of the explosion. A man in his early thirties sat on the tailgate of the ambulance. A man and a woman in paramedic uniforms tended to the wound on the back of his head, and a tall young woman dressed in shorts and a T-shirt stood close by, looking concerned. I showed the four my badge.

"That your Caddy?" I asked the injured man.

"No. Jesus, I just backed into that car, and it went up. Honest, I didn't know I was that close."

The stress showed on his face and in his voice.

"I was backing out of the spot across from him. I guess I wasn't paying attention, and then—wham! The damn thing blew, and there was glass everywhere. I'm sorry, but..."

"Take it easy," I said. "Which car is yours?"

The female medic used long tweezers to pick glass fragments out of the man's hair.

"The red Dodge," he said. "I pulled away from the Cadillac best I could, but my back window blew out. I..."

"Okay. You're lucky you weren't looking to the rear, or that glass would be in your face."

He nodded. "I know."

"Y'all need ta hold still," the medic with the tweezers said.

"Let these people finish fixing you up, and we'll talk again. What's your name and room number?"

"Jeremy Bullen. We're in 212."

"Okay, Jeremy, hang in there."

Junior Huskey and Stan Rose stood thirty feet from the burned-out hulk of the once-white Cadillac, next to a middle-aged man wrapped in a terrycloth robe. The man's dark hair was streaked with gray, wet and slicked straight back. I assumed he had been in the pool when the car went up. It only took me a few more steps to get a close look at the man.

I thought he could have been George Hamilton's stunt double. Add pearly white teeth and a well-cultivated tan to the hair, and anyone would assume he'd have a closet full of Brooks Brothers double-breasted blazers.

The windows of two first-floor rooms had been blown out. The drapes moved slightly in the breeze, showing scorch marks on the white backing. The other guests had vacated the pool area, but plenty of them stood around watching the action.

A half-dozen firemen waited patiently as a man wearing a blue jumpsuit rolled from under the Caddy on a mechanic's creeper. I recognized him as Delbert Ousley, the assistant fire chief.

He reached the two uniformed cops and Mr. Hamilton just as I did.

"Gennlemen," the assistant chief said, "I'm afraid I got bad news fer ya. It appears there was an explosive device planted under the driver's seat. No doubt in my mind. Y'all need ta have a bomb expert look at this."

———

An hour later—after I learned the George Hamilton look-alike's real name was Lloyd Corwen—he sat in my office wearing an expensive Hawaiian shirt and a pair of natural linen trousers. The woman sharing his motel room, a basket case named Stella Pawlowski, waited in the lobby where Bettye tried her best to offer comfort.

Right after telling me his name, Corwen identified himself as a retired New York detective. He didn't look too upset for a guy who almost went up in smoke.

"Jeez, nice office you got here," he said.

"Thanks. The job is nice, too."

"Like it better than up in New York?"

I shrugged. "Whole different world."

"I guess you don't remember, but I met you once. I used to work organized crime in Manhattan and then Brooklyn South."

"Where did we meet?"

"Syracuse, at a school on gambling and loan sharks. We never actually spoke, but I recognized you as the guy who took off Sonny Masucci."

"Wow, a name from the past."

"Yeah, a real shitball," he said.

I didn't want to start talking old times, so I only smiled.

"Does this car bomb have something to do with the job?" I asked.

"Who the hell knows?" he said. "I've been retired a couple years, and nobody's tried to kill me before."

"This was no accident. As soon as Ned the Fed gets back to me about the bomb, I may know something."

"Ned the Fed?"

"Ned Greznik, an ATF agent from Knoxville. Best bomb guy I've ever met. He can piece together little fragments and tell you all about the bomb and the guy who made it."

"Sounds good."

"You've got no idea who wants you dead?"

"Nope."

Maybe it was his oily good looks or his twenty-thousand-dollar smile, but Lloyd Corwen just didn't ring true.

"How about your girlfriend?"

"She doesn't know anything."

"Not what I meant. Would anyone want to kill her?"

"I've known her four years. We've lived together since I retired. No. She don't piss anyone off."

I nodded.

"And we don't know anyone over here," he said. "We just came from Myrtle Beach."

"What do you do in Myrtle Beach?"

"Play golf. I've had a condo there for six years. Moved in full-time when I retired."

"Got run outta Dodge by Irene?"

"Mandatory evacuation. I figured, what the hell, who wants to get his jock knocked off by a hurricane? So, we came over here. Spent yesterday looking at your town and then went over to the casino in Cherokee. Had dinner there and drove back."

"What's next?"

"Can't go back home just yet. I suppose we'll play one or two of the local courses, maybe gamble some. You get the idea."

"Even if you cheat at golf or cards, that's no reason to blow you up."

He shrugged.

"You think it's wise wandering around the county if someone wants to punch your ticket?"

"I think this was just a case of mistaken identity."

"You'd be better off relocating somewhere else. Look at all the angles. They may try again, and you don't want to sit in the same spot. You can find a place other than Prospect. Get a hotel in Knoxville or fly to...anywhere."

"You guys seem to be doing a good job. I'd hate for us to get caught on an Interstate or in an airport without backup. If you don't mind, we'll hang out here."

"We'll keep an eye on you as best we can, but if someone wants you dead, they can do it."

"I know. We'll be careful." His big Hollywood grin came back. "And I figure I'm safe with you," he said. "Kind of an ego thing. You'd hate to see me killed in your town."

"Quit smiling, or I'll kill you myself."

"Ha! I knew I could count on you."

I shook my head in disbelief and wondered: *How do I get into these situations?*

"Can I give you a ride to a car rental place?" I asked. "You'll need some wheels."

"Yeah, thanks."

"I'll call in one of the road cops."

I picked up the phone, but Corwen spoke before I buzzed the intercom.

"That blonde in the lobby one of your detectives?"

"She's the regular desk sergeant. We're on OT today because of the unusual crowd. That's why she's in plainclothes."

"Pretty woman," he said. "She's no kid, but got an ass like a twenty-year-old. And some set of—"

I interrupted. "Yeah, she's a good cop. Good partner when I need one. She'd do well in any PD."

His lecherous smile flashed like a neon billboard. "If you say so."

I dropped the phone back onto the cradle. "Let's go outside and get you a ride."

We approached the reception desk, and I said, "Betts, call in one of the guys to take these folks to the car rental desk at the airport, please."

Bettye nodded and keyed the microphone.

I asked, "You doing all right, Ms. Pawlowski?"

"I don't mind tellin' ya, sir," she said, "this scared the stuffin's outta me.

Who would do this? I mean, my God." Stella spoke with a classic *Nu Yawk* accent.

"I don't know yet," I said, "but we're not the third-world PD we look like. It's a good bet we'll find the bomber sooner than later."

"I pray ta God ya do. This was awful."

Stella Pawlowski was in her early fifties, in good shape, but had some hard edges on her. She wore clothes more appropriate for a girl in her twenties. Too much unnecessary makeup caked her pretty face, and she should have paid more attention to her dark roots.

"Lloyd and I couldn't come up with a reasonable theory," I said. "You have any thoughts about our bomber?"

"Me?" Stella sounded shocked that I'd ask. "You guys are the cops. I'm just, well, ya know... How should I know?"

I shifted my eyes to Bettye who offered a barely perceptible shrug.

"Thanks anyway," I said.

"Ya know," she said, "ya sound like yah from Nu Yawk. Where'd ya live before heah?"

"I'm from Long Guyland, dahling. Do I really sound like it?"

Stella smiled. "Yeah, I guess."

I offered a little more information. "Lloyd will tell you all about me. I see your ride is here."

PO Bobby John Crockett entered the lobby and stood with his thumbs hooked over his gun belt.

"What a good-looking boy," Stella said, and looked at me. "He looks like a youngah version o' you. Ya son?"

Bettye snickered. Crockett smiled.

"Not that I remember," I said.

Corwen and his girlfriend had been as helpful as antlers on a frog. Neither one offered an idea about who might want to kill them. I found that difficult to believe.

Once they cleared the lobby, Bettye said, "Clay sent over a list of all the guests at the Foothills View."

"Good. We'll need a bio on everyone, and look for a connection with Lloyd or Stella.

"Lucky me."

"If you think the phones and radio will get too busy, call in someone who'd like more OT."

"Okay, darlin'."

"I'll get a list from the manager of the Comfort Inn, too. It's only a hundred yards away from the blast."

"The coast gets a hurricane, and we get a firestorm."

"That was almost poetic, Sergeant."

———

After I dropped a second formidable list of motel guests on Bettye's desk, I called an old friend from NYPD. Jim Doheney had been a sergeant in the Intelligence Unit since Julius Caesar was a PFC.

"Christ Almighty. Sam Jenkins. I thought you were dead."

"Only the good die young, Jimmy."

"I hear somebody actually hired you as a police chief. Jesus Christ, what a mistake."

"Don't get snotty, you old fart."

"You're callin' me old?" He took a moment to laugh. "So, what can I do for ya?"

I told him my bomb story and asked for help covering the New York angles on the background investigation of my targeted victims.

"I remember Corwen from when he worked in Manhattan," Doheney said. "No ball of fire, but he did his job. I heard he got his gold shield through a rabbi his old man had in City Hall."

"What else is new?"

"Yeah, right. But I understand he actually made a name for himself when he went to Brooklyn. Supposedly, he really screwed with those Ruskies in Brighton Beach."

"Good for him. You think the Russian mob would blow him up now?" I asked.

"Who knows? I'll ask."

"Corwen had a woman with him. The name Pawlowski ring any bells?"

"I know that name from somewhere. Can't place it, though. She on the job?"

"When I met her, she couldn't walk and chew gum at the same time. She was no cop. Did say she used to live in Whitestone. So did Corwen. First name's Stella."

I gave Jimmy all the personal information I had on my unlucky pair.

"I'll search every nook and cranny for you, kid. Call ya back."

———

Ned Greznik sat in my office stretched out in one of the guest chairs, a coffee mug in his left hand. He was a short, dark man who looked more like a clockmaker than a Federal agent and bomb expert.

"We have a pretty simple device here," he said, speaking with an Upper Peninsula/Michigan accent. "Fabricated mercury switch ignites explosive and—boom."

"How difficult is it to get the parts?"

"Everybody from Radio Shack to Wal-Mart sells things you can use to make a detonator."

"What about the explosive? Even black powder is regulated."

"This is Tennessee, man. Just drive to any of the surrounding counties, and you can buy enough fireworks to light up half the world."

Greznik gulped down some hot coffee. *Asbestos mouth.*

"My guess is the bomber bought a few six-packs of M-8os to cannibalize," he said. "Those little bastards are each a quarter stick of dynamite."

"You're not making it easy for me."

"Sorry."

"Can you lend a hand trying to find the origin of the bomb?"

He smiled. "Sure. Your Federal tax dollars at work."

"Think we're dealing with a pro or some hacker following directions in *The Anarchist's Cookbook?*"

"Guy's a pro. This is not his first bomb."

———

"How you making out with the computer work?" I asked Bettye.

"We're lucky. Things are moving fast today."

"Thanks for small favors."

"I've still got hours more to go," she said.

"Don't burn yourself out. There's always tomorrow. And get a helper in here to do the phones and radio."

"I will. I just wanted to save the overtime budget a little."

"We're civil servants. We spend money, not save it."

"Sometimes I wonder how you get away with things."

"I'm cute. Nobody gets mad at me."

She laughed then asked, "Did you learn *anything* from Corwen?"

"He thinks you have a great figure."

"Oh, Lord have mercy! He told you that?"

"Sort of. I cut him off. Defending your honor, so to speak."

"My hero."

"That's me, baby."

"Thanks."

"He probably fell in love with your new haircut."

Bettye had recently gone from a long ponytail to something very sophisticated that ended an inch above her shoulders.

"I thought all you men liked long hair."

"Maybe those steak-and-potatoes guys who like women barefoot and pregnant do. I think hair should be cut to suit the face."

"Does this suit my face?"

"You betcha." I raised my eyebrows twice to emphasize my opinion.

"Am I going to be safe here when we're alone?"

I shook my head. "Not a chance."

"Bless your heart, Sammy." She smiled and adjusted her eyeglasses. "You goin' to lunch?"

"Why don't you go first?" I said. "You need a break."

"I won't say no."

"Bring something back for me?"

"What would you like?"

"Surprise me."

"Okey dokey, sugar. See ya later."

———

Stanley Rose dropped all six-foot-four inches of himself into one of my guest chairs. His biceps filled out the short sleeves of the khaki uniform shirt that contrasted sharply with his dark brown skin.

"What do we know about the bomber?" he asked.

"Greznik says a pro. Simple but effective mercury switch affair."

"So when that poor guy backed into the Caddy, the mercury moved and completed the circuit and...boom."

"That's about it."

"You call some old friend to learn about ex-Detective Corwen?"

"In the works. The friend says Corwen worked Russian mob cases in Brooklyn."

"Don't want them here."

"Hardly."

"Lemme know whatcha need."

"Make up a roster of guys to keep watch on Corwen's room. I do not want anyone getting whacked under our noses."

"You got it."

Two hours later, Jim Doheney called back.

"Okay, kid, here's the scoop on Lloyd Corwen. Very simple, he impressed the bosses at Brooklyn South by taking down a bunch of low-level Russian hoods."

"You think the bomb was retribution?"

"I didn't see anyone big enough to warrant killing an ex-cop."

"I thought those guys had no rules."

"Compared to the goombahs we know and love, the Russians are barbarians. But I don't think so. All the soldiers he arrested were expendable cannon fodder. Just a boss's overhead. Know what I mean?"

"And you promised me a smoking gun."

"I promised nothing but the straight skinny. I don't like the Ruskies for this, but hang onto your hat. I got more."

I swung my feet from the desktop and sat upright in my chair.

"This sounds promising."

"Ya anywhere near ya back door?" he asked.

"Not even close."

"Got a window in ya office?"

"Stop the foreplay."

"I want ya to look in your own backyard."

"Keep talking."

"Remember I said Pawlowski rang a bell?"

"I do."

"A guy named Pawlowski from the job here, won a Medal of Honor seven, eight years back."

"I didn't hear about it."

"Ya wouldn't down there in hillbilly land. Ta make a long story short, Pawlowski was a sergeant in Emergency Services. Some kid was screwing around at a construction site and got stuck in an excavated hole or some shit. When they found the kid and tried to get him out, the sand walls started caving in. So this guy, Tony Pawlowski, almost got buried 'cause he wouldn't leave the kid until he got him free and hooked to a rope. A true hero...and the ex-husband of Corwen's girlfriend, Stella."

"And?"

"And as you know, many ES people are bomb techs—Pawlowski included."

"Is this all conjecture or are we heading somewhere interesting?"

"Circumstantial maybe, but very interesting. Pawlowski's old lieutenant told me that Corwen and Mrs. Pawlowski were caught having an affair."

"Yikes!"

"Well said."

"What happened next?"

"Tony considered Stella's dalliance a big problem. He walked into Brooklyn South one day in full pack and punched out Lloyd, the handsome devil."

"Tough to learn your wife is doing the horizontal mambo with another cop."

"Even tougher was when, after an attempt to reconcile, Stella picked Lloyd over Tony. She left our hero flat and moved south with the newly retired Detective Corwen."

"Aha."

"Yes, aha. Now let's move to ya backyard."

"Please do."

"As luck would have it, Sergeant Pawlowski didn't stay unmarried too long. Like so many other cops, he met a lovely waitress, fell in love or lust or something, and they hooked up. Just so happens, the now-retired Sergeant's pension checks are being sent to an address in a place called—a drum roll, please—Prospect, Tennessee."

"Jimmy, you Irish leprechaun, I believe you've found my pot o' gold."

———

P awlowski's driveway stretched almost a quarter mile through dense woods filled with Virginia pines, sweet gums and tulip poplars. As soon as I entered a clearing, I saw a large log home, honey colored by Clear Wood Finish. At the sound of my tires crunching on the gravel, a big man abandoned what he had been doing under the hood of a new Chevy pickup and looked in my direction. I parked and walked over.

"Anton Pawlowski?" I asked.

"Who wants to know?"

I just love guys like that.

Like many of the ES cops I knew, Tony Pawlowski looked like he ate small automobiles for breakfast. Besides doing bomb work, these officers made up the SWAT component of their respective departments and did all the heavy rescue work. Emergency Services is a very physical job, and many of their ranks could double as WWF members.

"My name's Jenkins. I'm the chief at Prospect PD."

"Oh, yeah." He gave me a half smile, half sneer. "I heard about you when I moved here. Retired dick lieutenant from the Island, right?"

Manhattan cops always thought they were the elite of metro New York law enforcement. I ignored his juvenile sneer—barely.

"Got a minute to talk?" I asked.

"About what?"

Pawlowski was rapidly moving toward the bottom of my hit parade.

"About where you were prior to ten o'clock this morning."

"You lookin' at me for somethin'?"

"Have you seen your ex-wife or the guy she's living with since they came to Prospect?"

The smile/sneer came back. "Didn't know they were here. Wouldn't want to see them if I did. She's past history. Good riddance."

"Somebody tried to punch their tickets earlier today. I thought you'd be interested."

"Tried? Anybody hurt?"

"Some poor schmuck who backed into their car and set off a bomb. Your wife was at the pool."

"Too bad. I assume the guy with Stella is Lloyd Corwen?"

"Good guess."

Pawlowski wiped his hands with a clean rag that came from a back pocket.

"Don't know anything about that," he said.

"Back to my question. Where were you between last night and ten this morning?"

"Shouldn't you be advising me of my rights?"

"I thought you knew them. This isn't New York, but we're still in the United States. You want a lawyer now?"

"Sure, why not?"

"Okay. I guess you'll need a few minutes with the Yellow Pages. Be in my office at 9 a.m. Monday. If you're not there, I'll send a couple of cops to get you."

I turned to leave.

"Have a nice day, Chief."

Pawlowski made *chief* sound like a four-letter word.

———

Back in the office, I sat at my desk, gritting my teeth, wishing I could find something or someone to tie Tony Pawlowski to the crime scene. Then Rachel Williamson from WNXX TV news called.

"Hey, big feller," she said, "I've been waiting for my phone call. When are you going to update me on the bomber?"

She loves to hear me do a Humphrey Bogart impression, and I aim to please.

"Sorry to disappoint you, doll face, but I just hit a brick wall in my '32 Ford roadster. I can't find a decent clue in this whole cockamamie town."

"Oh, my poor Bogey. Can I do anything for you?"

"A dangerous question, sweetheart."

She laughed.

"Sure," I said. "If you deliver, bring me a pitcher of vodka martinis, and help me drown my sorrows."

"Maybe not. You're still on duty."

"How about I tell you something on the QT? When this story breaks, a dame like you could go places...if she had an exclusive."

"Why do I subject myself to this?"

I switched back to my good old Long Island accent. "Because I'm your favorite police chief, and I trust you."

"If I didn't love you, I'd wait for the press release."

"That's no fun."

"I know," she said.

"While I'm listening to you and picturing that cute little dimple on your chin, I had an idea."

"You did?"

"Want to interview the intended victims?"

"Alleged victims." She laughed again.

"Give that a rest."

"Since you said that sweet thing about my dimple, okay."

"Great. Here's what I know, and here's what I need you to do..."

Knowing she'd never broadcast anything before I gave her the nod, I told Rachel about Pawlowski being my prime suspect.

I also suggested that she bring a cameraman so we could photograph Lloyd Corwen at the Foothills Motel. Rachel could ask questions and Corwen do the answering. Only I'd make my life easier by letting them do that in front of a room where Lloyd and Stella would not be staying. So, with luck, if Pawlowski or another assassin wanted to make a second attempt on their lives, we'd be there waiting, and my two targets would be elsewhere, protected by one of Prospect's finest.

Rachel is no stranger to some of the more innovative scams I've used to solve crimes in beautiful downtown Prospect, and she agreed to do the interview. I had no problem offering Lloyd Corwen up as a sacrificial goat. He saw merit in my plan and liked it. Stella Pawlowski seemed to have no say in the matter.

———

At 9:10 Monday morning, Tony Pawlowski walked into our lobby with a sleazy but expensive lawyer named Brack Clemmons. I think being ten minutes late was engineered to piss me off.

Clemmons flashed a phony smile. "Hello, Chief. Good ta see ya ag'in."

I'd call Brack Clemmons portly, but his high-priced suit made him appear dapper. A fifty-dollar haircut made him look like a televangelist, and a slight overbite might have fooled someone into underestimating his ability as a shyster.

"Hi there, Mr. Clemmons. Always a pleasure."

I shook his hand, but Pawlowski didn't offer one.

"Has your client told you what this is all about?" I asked.

"Yessir, yessir, he shore did. Pure coincidence. I assure ya, nothing but coincidence."

"I don't believe in coincidence, so let's talk, shall we?"

Pawlowski ran a hand over his salt-and-pepper crew cut and dropped into a guest chair without comment. Clemmons took a yellow pad from his briefcase and set the case on the floor. He unbuttoned his light gray jacket and took the other seat.

"Would you like to make an opening statement, Counselor?"

The lawyer gave me a counterfeit million-dollar smile. "Now, I know how this must look, Chief—"

I interrupted to show him who was in control. "Call me Sam. I think informality is best."

"Well, all right then. O'course, Sam. Yessir, Sam it is."

"Okay, Brack, where was Tony before the bomb detonated?"

"At home. Yessir, at home. Mindin' his own bidness."

"And someone can verify that?"

"Yessir. Yessir, indeed. His wife."

"Yeah," Pawlowski said. "The wife who's not out there screwing around."

"She'll provide a statement affirming that she and Tony were together from nightfall Friday until 10 a.m. Saturday?"

"Well, Mrs. Pawlowski can say she got home after work late Friday night and was there until Saturday mornin'," Clemmons said.

"That leaves a big window of opportunity—if her times are accurate."

"Come on, Sam," Clemmons said. "Mr. Pawlowski's a decorated po-leece officer, a gat-dag hero, fer godssakes. Why would he want to kill his ex-wife? He's got himself a new life. The past is over."

"Obvious reasons," I said. "Look, let's cut the bullshit, Tony. You know the questions I want to ask. What's the story?"

"It's not me." His obnoxious grin resurfaced. "She's a slut. He's a fuckin' backstabber. Go find someone else they cheated out o' somethin'."

Clemmons seemed content to allow his client to speak. He sat straight-faced, tapping an index finger on the legal pad.

"Look at it from a judge's point of view," I said. "You're a bomb expert. You've got motive. The proximity gives you means. And you clearly had the opportunity."

Pawlowski waved a hand dismissively.

"It's a small town," I said. "Purely by chance, you saw Stella, followed her and thought it's get-even time. How many guys on a jury would argue that? She betrayed your trust. Corwen stole your wife. Everything surged back into your mind and pissed you off again. You lost control. No big deal. Mr. Clemmons doesn't have to explain how an extreme emotional state mitigates your culpability. Let your lawyer negotiate with the DA. Maybe he can get you a charge of reckless endangerment rather than the attempted murder of Corwen and the assault on that innocent bystander. Based on your past history, he can probably swing probation."

Pawlowski sat there grinning and shaking his head.

"You walk out now, and let's-make-a-deal time is gone forever," I said.

Pawlowski chuckled. "Who the hell you think you're talkin' to? You really think I'd buy that line o' shit?"

He was too big, but I still wanted to smack him and wipe the arrogance off his face.

I stood. "Okay, gents. Thanks for your time. If I get lucky, I'll see you at sentencing."

———

While I wasted my time with Pawlowski and Clemmons, Bettye found Rita Pawlowski, Tony's second wife, working at a local home improvement store. She'd been reluctant to speak without her husband present, but Bettye smooth-talked her into admitting a few basics.

Later, in my office, Bettye said, "I think she's afraid to tell the whole truth."

"Pawlowski is a big, mean-looking bastard," I said. "Maybe she's afraid he'll tune her up."

I poured two cups of coffee and added a spoonful of Splenda and a splash of fat-free half-and-half to Bettye's.

I handed her the cup.

"Thanks, darlin'." She took a careful sip. "I'll have to dig further to see if he's been abusin' her, but I think Rita's just afraid because she *knows* Tony planted the bomb."

"A wife's testimony would confirm our suspicions, but isn't worth much in court. Clemmons is no idiot. He'll make a motion to exclude her under the spousal rule."

"Have we got anything else?" she asked.

"Since no one on our motel lists is connected to Corwen or Stella, I can send the boys out to canvas the entire area again looking for somebody who may have seen Pawlowski or his truck near the motel."

"Needle in a haystack?"

"Yeah. I'll ask the Loudon and Monroe County sheriffs to take Pawlowski's photo to their fireworks dealers. And maybe Greznik came up with something on the components."

"We've been lucky before."

I shook my head. "This guy is good. He knows what we've got. And he'll keep his mouth shut."

Bettye nodded and sipped more coffee. I realized mine was getting cold, and I hadn't touched it.

"Rita worked until closing Friday night—eleven o'clock," Bettye said. "Then she cleaned up her department and cashed out. That got her home around midnight. She said Tony was there waitin' for her."

"Plenty of time between dark and midnight for him to plant the bomb," I suggested.

"And an ex-cop would know our men will be gassin' their cars after eleven, waitin' for the midnight shift to come in. Not much patrollin' goes on close to the end of a tour."

"It only takes a minute to attach a bomb. He wouldn't hang around too long before or after," I said.

"You think he'll try again?"

"If he's angry enough to hold a grudge for a couple years...maybe. But Corwen and Stella won't be here too much longer. He'll have to do it soon."

"The storm is already north of Myrtle Beach," Bettye said. "Another couple days and they'll get cleaned up, the power will be back on, and they'll be good to go home."

"Let's call Myrtle Beach PD and the state troopers and see what kind of time we're looking at. Rachel will be here this afternoon. I hope our bomber watches the news."

She nodded. "And I guess we'd better keep an extra pair of eyes on that motel room after the interview."

"I'll call South Carolina. You call Harley. Tell him I'd like him to do the watching. And be sure he brings his rifle. My guess is Pawlowski won't try another bomb. Shooting is a nice, direct approach, and as a former SWAT member, he can do that from a distance and be gone before anyone sees him."

———

Mayor Ronnie Shields objected, for financial reasons, but finally agreed to foot the bill at the local bed and breakfast I found to house Corwen and Stella. He also rolled over and paid for one day at the Foothills View, giving me the room of my choice for Rachel's interview and our plan to lure the killer back for a second attempt.

———

At two o'clock Monday afternoon, Rachel and her cameraman, John Leckmanski, pulled into the visitor's lot behind Prospect PD. By twenty after, we all stood in front of room 124—the number conspicuous and something John assured me would show prominently in the footage destined for Rachel's five o'clock broadcast.

Rachel looked lovely in a red suit with a short skirt and a white scoop-neck T-shirt. Leckmanski wore one of his typical outfits. A Led Zeppelin T-shirt, washed-off camo fatigue pants and an Atlanta Braves ball cap.

While John got ready to tape the interview, Lloyd Corwen practiced his matinee idol smile and waited to go on stage.

Rachel began the segment with a little background. "We're at the Foothills View Motel in Prospect to speak with former New York Detective Lloyd Corwen and his friend Stella Pawlowski. On Saturday morning, Detective Corwen's car blew up not far from where we're standing. Foul play is expected in the case. The Prospect Police and agents from the Bureau of Alcohol, Tobacco, and Firearms are investigating."

Rachel turned and faced Corwen. "Detective, do you believe someone from your past has tried to kill you?"

Lloyd smiled like the star of a toothpaste commercial when Rachel stuck the microphone beneath his teeth.

"As you know," he said, "I've been retired for two years, and I seriously doubt anyone from my past wants to do me harm."

I had to hand it to Corwen. He acted like a pro for the camera. He looked at ease, said the right things and sounded believable. But I wanted to kick him in the groin because when he wasn't speaking, his eyes locked on Rachel's cleavage like a Cruise missile seeking an acquired target.

"You worked for NYPD Organized Crime Control Bureau," Rachel said. "Didn't that subject you to many dangerous characters?"

"Yes, it did, but I still doubt anyone would go to these lengths to kill me."

To emphasize the point, he looked into the camera lens and flashed his twenty-grand cap work for the audience.

He finished with, "I think it's a case of mistaken identity."

Rachel turned to Stella who stood on Corwen's left. "Ms. Pawlowski, do you have any thoughts about who may have tried to kill either Mr. Corwen or you?"

It was almost as if Rachel took Stella by surprise. It sounded like English was her second language. "Uh, I, uh, don't think...uh, Lloyd is probably right. This must be mistaken identity. The bomber was after someone else. I guess."

As Stella spoke, Lloyd's eyes went back to Rachel's bust line. A big grin crossed his face, and Stella noticed everything that happened. She finished her statement with a frown.

Rachel fired off several more questions, a few about Stella and a few more about Lloyd's former 'clients'.

Corwen stood there, his teeth twinkling, as Rachel finished. "This is Rachel Williamson in Prospect. Now back to you, Jack."

The red light on Leckmanski's camera went out, and we wrapped up the video fiasco.

PO Johnny Rutledge hurried Lloyd and Stella off to the B&B proprietors who agreed to give them shelter, and Rachel and I walked back toward my car.

"It's a damn good thing you're not like *that* New York cop," she said.

"What?"

She brushed a few strands of dark brown hair off her forehead with a free hand.

"If he tried to look any further down my blouse, he would have fallen in."

"Corwen is a snake. Don't worry about him."

"He's a pig."

"Yeah, but if you didn't wear that blouse, he couldn't have looked and—"

She quickly interrupted me. "Are you sticking up for him?"

"No, I'm just saying—"

"Are you jealous?"

"Who, me?"

"You are, aren't you?"

"Am not." That sounded juvenile.

"Ha," she said.

"Hey, you're beautiful, and he's just a guy," I said. "And guys look. I looked."

"Oh, oink."

I threw my hands in the air. "I give up."

After he packed up the camera equipment, John Leckmanski found us standing between the WNXX van and my gray unmarked Ford. He grinned, Rachel kissed my cheek, and I shook my head.

With luck, the right person would see the room number and visit 124 before too long.

———

Still marveling at my inability to understand women, I swung the Crown Victoria eastbound on McTeer's Station Pike heading toward the Municipal Building and my office. The Rolling Stones' version of *Paint it Black* coming through my phone interrupted the trip. I slowed down and answered the call.

"Hey, boss," Johnny Rutledge said. "I got these two settled inta The Mountain Mist. You want me ta play bodyguard after four o'clock, or are you sendin' a relief?"

"The mayor's agreed to spring for OT during our crisis. You good for an extra four hours?"

"Sure enough. I'll be here."

"How'd everything go? The place look easy to secure?"

"The place is fine. Nice an' easy ta watch. But I'm not sure the bomber is the only one wantin' ta kill yer buddy, Corwen."

"Not my buddy, sport. Explain."

"Him an' Stella had them one wing-ding of a fight. Never heard such language from a woman."

"Oh, shit. Do we need to talk about this face to face?"

"Well, it would save usin' up our phone minutes."

In less than fifteen minutes, I pulled up in front of The Mountain Mist Bed & Breakfast, a business owned by Milo and Goldie Huffacre. Strategically, the place couldn't have been better situated. The mammoth log structure sat atop an unnamed hill with only one road up. The grounds all around the house had been cleared of trees and offered guests unobstructed views of the Smokies and the valleys surrounding the larger mountains. Give me that handpicked group of mercenaries with whom I wanted to attack Kentucky, and I could have held that position until the food, water or ammunition ran out.

I found Johnny Rutledge, another one of my thirty-something year old cops, sitting in the lounge, reading a copy of *Knoxville Today* magazine.

"Are they willing to stay put until I say come out?" I asked.

He tossed the magazine on the coffee table and scratched his sandy hair.

"Yessir. I believe so. Miss Goldie is goin' ta make them dinner tonight and feed them long as ya say to. An' ol' De-tective Corwen, he asked me ta take him to a likker store b'fore comin' here. Got himse'f a bottle o' whiskey and seems happy enough bein' here. Now, Stella, she's another story."

"What's her bitch?"

"Lemme see if I kin give it ta ya ver-batim," Johnny said. "Now, I'm guessin' she weren't too happy with the way Lloyd behaved at Miss Rachel's interview."

I rolled my eyes, but indulged young Rutledge.

"It kinda went like this," he said. "'Lloyd, you bastard,' she said. 'You couldn't keep yer eyes off that woman's boobs. Goddamnit, Lloyd, how'd you think that made me feel?' Now, Lloyd, he says, 'Gimme a break, Stella. I was just standin' there answerin' questions.' Then Stella, she says, 'No, you bastard, you were makin' eyes at her and lookin' at her tits.' Excuse my French, boss."

"Yeah, okay," I said. "I get the picture. Was that it?"

"Uh-huh, mostly. But she did end up sayin', 'I gave up my married life for you, Lloyd. And you look at every woman who walks by. I don't trust you, damnit. You're a sneaky bastard. I'm sorry you weren't in the car when it blew up.' Then she walked off, an' I heard the door slam."

"Jesus H. Christ," I said. "I hope they have something to read in the room because I doubt they'll be doing much talking."

"Shoot, he got him enough likker ta make anything she says go in one ear an' out the other."

———

Just before dark, I met Harley Flatt in the office. He's a big man. Not as big as Stan Rose, but close. Ever since his hair began thinning out, he's shaved his head. With his neat military mustache, he looks a lot like Jesse Ventura.

When Harley walked in, I thought he planned to go turkey hunting. Dressed head to foot in Real-Tree camouflage clothing, he'd blend into the foliage that surrounded the Foothills View Motel.

"Got your rifle?" I asked.

"Yep, shotgun, too. I figger we might get us some close-in work."

"Always better to have your opponent out-gunned," I said.

He grinned, and I called Stan Rose who would take on the unenviable job of sitting inside room 124 waiting to be shot or blown apart by Tony Pawlowski or some other psycho bomb expert.

Just after dark, Harley and I parked near the motel and snuck up to the spots we determined to be tactically appropriate. Three marked Prospect cruisers were on routine patrol, and two other men waited close by in case we needed additional backup.

Harley hid in the bushes on the perimeter of the motel grounds. Dressed in dark clothing, I hung out next to the pool house—close to the room, but out of sight. We both carried night vision glasses.

Two hours passed, but it seemed like six. Surveillances are generally boring, and the time drags when you see basically nothing. A few guests moved around the parking lot, coming and going. Several people made trips to the ice or vending machines. Occasionally, I'd hear a phone ring. A muted hum from a few television sets drifted through the parking lot. If the stakeout lasted much longer, I'd struggle to stay awake.

At 10:38, Harley whispered into his portable radio.

"Y'all got someone walkin' towards the room. Somethin' looks wrong. Big guy, short hair, wearin' what looks like a raincoat. Heads up."

"10-4," I said.

Stan said, "Copy that in the room."

It was August 29th, dry and pleasant. I didn't need the long-sleeved shirt I wore. No one needed a top coat—unless they were hiding something beneath it.

The figure of a burly man showed green and luminescent in my night vision binoculars. He faced away from me, but based on size, it could have been Pawlowski.

Our intruder walked in the available shadows until he reached a spot adjacent room 124, on the corner of the motel wing. Then he disappeared between two parked cars in the row across from the first floor sidewalk and the row of vehicles outside the room doors.

I moved a few feet to my left and found him again with my glasses. From under the coat, he produced what looked like a small machine pistol and pointed it casually at the door to 124. With his free hand, he flipped open a cell phone and speed dialed a number. He made a brief statement, waited a few seconds and then spoke into the phone again.

A few moments later, Stanley's voice sounded on the radio. "An anonymous caller just said someone's trying to break into my car. Any visual on the guy with the raincoat?"

"Affirmative," I said. "He's crouching between the cars across from the room. Looks like he's armed with something full-auto. Do not open that door."

"Copy that," Stan said. "I told him I'd put my pants on and then check the car. Talks with an accent. Might be one of your Russian hoods."

"Good. Gives us a few seconds. Harley, move up, but wait for me. I can close in on him from behind."

"10-4," Harley said.

I covered the distance between the pool house and the row of parked cars in only seconds. The grass was soft, and when I reached the blacktop, my rubber soles didn't make a sound. I took a safe position behind the right rear of the car where our shooter hid.

I decided to break the ice. "Police, don't move!" I bellowed.

The man froze, wisely not turning his gun toward me.

"Put your gun on the ground!"

He didn't immediately comply. Three or four seconds passed. It seemed longer.

I cocked the hammer of my Smith & Wesson. The click sounded like the slamming of a door. "Goddamnit, drop that gun!"

"Okay, okay," he said and raised his left hand, but still held the little machine gun.

I yelled again. "Put the gun on the ground! Don't talk about it. Do it. Now!"

"Okay, don't shoot." He spoke with what sounded like an eastern European accent.

Soft footsteps tapped the ground off to my right. I hoped to hell it was Harley Flatt.

A jolt went through me when the unmistakable sound of a pump action shotgun echoed through the parking lot.

After racking a shell into the shotgun's chamber, Harley said, "I believe he told ya ta drop that gun."

Nothing grabs your attention like a round of magnum double-o buck-shot being slammed into the breach of a Remington 870. The gunman set a Heckler & Koch MP-5 on the blacktop.

Still pointing my gun at his head, I walked the car length and stood next to our prisoner. Harley used the radio to call Stanley and our two backup cars.

"Face down on the pavement, comrade," I said, assuming the man was Russian.

The big guy sprawled out, putting his hands to the side and said, "Wrong country, policeman. I am no Russian."

After I cuffed our mystery man, Stan, Harley, and I walked him back to the motel room.

I told Harley, "When our backup gets here, check the motel grounds for an accomplice. Get the three men on patrol to cruise around the area looking for a suspicious, occupied car. Everybody use extreme caution, okay? And see if there's a deputy or trooper on the road. They can help, too."

"You got it, boss."

The prisoner said, "Don't waste time. I work alone."

"Thanks for the tip," I said. "And no offense, but we'll check anyway."

"I take offense to be called a Russian. I am Albanian, thank you very much."

"Albanian it is. Do you have identification with you?"

"Yes, it is in my very nice black Mercedes in parking lot. By the way, do you know a U.S. attorney who can make me good deal? I have much to say, but not to you."

"I'll make a call. Have you got a name?"

"Of course. I am Artan Luga."

The name didn't ring a bell, and I guess I didn't seem impressed. Maybe that offended Mr. Luga, too, but he didn't show it.

Actually, he looked quite relaxed and smiled for the first time. He must have weighed about two-forty and looked like a power lifter who had a few too many beers. His dark crew cut needed a trim, and he hadn't shaved in a couple days. But Artan Luga seemed ready for a night out with the boys.

"When I call my buddy at the FBI and ask him to wake up the on-call AUSA, Artan my friend, I'll need something to pique his interest. I hope you don't want to trade your mother's recipe for Albanian-style imam bajalldi for a pass on attempted murder."

"Ha!" he said, throwing back his head. "You are funny. You know imam bajalldi? Good. I *love* eggplant. You, too?"

"My wife makes that dish so good, my ears wiggle."

"Your wife is Albanian?"

I shook my head.

"Turkish? Greek, maybe?"

"Polish-American with a cookbook and talent in the kitchen."

Stanley looked at me like I had two heads. He never likes to make friends with the bad guys.

"For a policeman," Artan said, "you are very friendly. That's good. You got me. I give up. No reason to be enemies."

"None at all. Give me a minute to call the Feds."

"Go ahead, my friendly friend. I am going nowhere." Luga threw his head back again and bellowed out a good old Balkan laugh.

Stanley shook his head.

I called Ralph Oliveri from the Knoxville FBI field office and asked him to roust a U.S. attorney for me. An hour later he showed up at Prospect PD with a young woman named Heidi Piper.

Artan, the sexist, looked at Ralph and asked, "So, you have power to offer deal?"

Oliveri, who was dressed in a polo shirt and jeans, pulled a credential case from his back pocket and identified himself. "I'm Special Agent Oliveri. This is Assistant U.S. Attorney Piper, a supervisor from the local office of the Department of Justice. She'll listen to what you have to say and decide if you have anything worth a deal."

Luga grinned and turned on some Albanian charm. "Oh, excuse me, lovely lady, I didn't know. I am Artan Luga—what our friends here would call Albanian mobster."

Heidi Piper was tall and attractive and in her late thirties. She wore her long brown hair back in a tail and had bright dark eyes.

She waited a long moment before answering. "I understand you want a deal for leniency on several serious charges. What do you know that's so important to us?"

"Maybe not important to you, pretty lady, but you call Federal people in New York or maybe other places and see what they say. I can give you information on Mr. Bujar Hasani."

No recognition registered on Heidi's face. She looked at Ralph.

"I did a little checking on Albanian organized crime," he said. "Hasani is the boss in metro New York."

"Yes, Mr. Special Agent," Luga said, "the big boss. You check more and see how big."

I jumped into the conversation. "We have Mr. Luga for possession of an automatic weapon. The overt act of making a phone call to lure his intended target outside gets us into the realm of attempted murder and based on his statement that he was hired to kill former New York Detective Lloyd Corwen, I've got a solid criminal conspiracy. And since he came here from New York, you people may want to look at him for interstate transportation of a machine gun, but as a gesture of good will, I'm going to let him slide for parking his car in a handicapped zone. I called him a Russian, and he took offense. It's the least I can do"

Heidi looked at me and frowned.

"Just a little payback for my mistake," I said.

Luga laughed again. "He is funny, no?"

"Yeah, a genuine comedian," Ralph said.

"Well, I like him," Luga said. "He is friendly. For a cop."

I looked at Heidi. "Prior to your arrival, Artan offered to provide detailed information on Albanian mob business in New York and possibly clear several homicides there and in New Jersey. Because the people he can implicate are famous for holding a grudge, he'd like witness protection and to skate on our pending charges."

"And other past crimes, please?" Artan said with another smile.

Heidi looked at me.

"I can make things happen here," I said, "but the rest is not mine to give away."

"His information has to be pretty good for that kind of favor," Ralph said.

"Is very good." Artan grinned. "Yes, very, very good."

Then he looked at me. "And, my friendly friend, because I like you, I can even make you happy with what I know."

"Tell me," I said.

"Your Mr. Ex-Detective Corwen, he's not so much a good boy. You understand?"

I turned to Ralph and Heidi. "As you walked in, we were just about to discuss why Mr. Luga had been hired to kill former Detective Corwen. So, before we get too far afield with crimes committed in New York, let's clear up what almost happened in Prospect."

Heidi turned one of my guest chairs slightly to face Luga and sat.

"Fine with me," she said.

Ralph moved a third chair between Luga and the door and sat.

"This may take a while," I said, "So, before we get going, would anyone like coffee?"

Artan answered first. "I would love cup of coffee. Black, please, and extra strong maybe."

Ralph and Stan nodded. Harley said he'd pass.

"I could use a drink," Heidi said.

"Scotch, okay?" I asked.

"I was being facetious," she said. "Coffee is fine."

Stanley spun the side chair away from my desk and sat with his forearms resting on the back. Harley had taken off his camouflage cap and field shirt and stood in the doorway wearing a Rascal Flatts T-shirt and the Real-Tree camo pants.

As I puttered around with Mr. Coffee, I spoke over my shoulder to Artan. "Corwen caused the Brighton Beach Russian mob grief. No one in New York said anything about involvement with the Albanians."

Luga shot me the biggest grin of the night. A gold tooth on the top left sparkled.

"Corwen had only one problem with Bujar Hasani, my friend, and it was big mistake." His smile disappeared, replaced by a deep frown.

"I'd love to hear this," I said.

The grin came back, and his tooth twinkled with a thousand candlepower.

"We're waiting, Artan," I said.

"I get to Hasani soon," he said. "But first you must know whole story —from start."

Mr. Coffee perked away, and I sat on the edge of my desk.

"Please—from the beginning."

"Your Detective Corwen—he arrests many Russians, yes?"

"So I hear."

"You think Corwen is smart boy? Good detective?"

"I don't know Corwen very well."

"Corwen arrests Russians, thanks to Mr. Bujar Hasani."

I didn't like the sound of that. "How so?"

"Easy. Corwen is not so smart, but Corwen is on payroll. For money, he looks other way from Albanians in Brooklyn. To make police boss happy, Bujar Hasani gives Corwen information about Russians. Good information. Corwen arrests Russians."

I swung my eyes around the room. No one looked very pleased with Luga's accusation.

"So Hasani pays for security and eliminates a little competition?" I said.

"I knew *you* were smart man," Luga said.

"I still don't see why Hasani sent you here to blow up Corwen."

"Okay, my friend, here comes good part. After Corwen is paid by Hasani and collects money for years, Corwen wants to retire as policeman. Hasani is not happy, but that's life. So, what does Corwen do? He takes all he knows about Bujar Hasani and gives it to boss policeman in Brooklyn. Soon Hasani is arrested, and Corwen is retired and gone. Hasani does two years in jail."

"And Hasani thinks Corwen set him up to go out looking good."

"And Hasani *knows* Corwen set him up. Corwen was not only cop on payroll."

My eyes took a trip around the room again.

"I can picture this," I said. "Some deputy inspector who hasn't made an arrest in ten years gets this information and exploits it, looking for his fifteen minutes of fame. Even if Hasani implicates Corwen, the DI conveniently overlooks that. He doesn't want to lessen the impact of his big arrest and doesn't want the word to get out that he had a dirty detective working in his shop." I shook my head. "Internal Affairs will have an orgasm when they hear this."

"And Bujar Hasani got out of jail one month ago," Luga said, his smile back full force. "What do you think he wants to do next?"

"It's crazy to think Hasani knew Corwen would be in Prospect."

"Bujar Hasani is not mind reader. But he gets phone call, of course. Then he calls me. I drive to Tennessee—twelve hours only. I make good time. Then I meet you. Good for Corwen. Too bad for me."

"Where have you been staying since Saturday?"

"Saturday?" Luga looked surprised. "I get phone call Sunday night. I leave Brooklyn and get here this morning. I find motel little west of the Knoxville city. I sleep a little, eat and then get second phone call from Hasani, telling me new room number. Now here I am."

"What about the car bomb?"

"Car bomb?"

"Saturday morning. Corwen's Cadillac was blown up."

"Shame to blow up nice car. I don't know bombs. I blow away people with *bullets*."

———

I spent another forty minutes trying to get Luga to confess to the bombing. He wouldn't budge. He said he was never told of an ally to contact in Prospect. Hasani never divulged who dropped the dime on Corwen, and Luga didn't want to know.

By the time two deputy U.S. marshals walked into Prospect PD, I believed him. Luga had nothing to lose. The U.S. Attorney could have written off the bombing like everything else.

The Marshal's Service would take Artan Luga back to New York so he could rat out the big boss of the local Albanian mob. After that, he might get set up for life with a single-wide and a job at Jiffy Lube in Waco, Texas. Probably better than twenty years in the slammer, but not much.

"Where does that leave you with your bomber?" Ralph Oliveri asked.

"You ever feel like someone just dumped a bucket of manure on your head?" I asked.

"Anything we can do for you?" he said.

"Sure, get someone in your New York office to look into who called Hasani's phone from beautiful downtown Prospect.

"Not so easy, paisan. You think he's only got one phone? Ever hear about throwaway cells?"

"Everyone knows where to call Bujar Hasani," Luga said. "He owns Valona House restaurant. Easy to find."

"So, start there," I said. "I don't know, Ralphie—doesn't the Bureau have some kind of spy satellite or something that can intercept communications from anywhere?"

"Sure, Sam, just for you." Ralph shook his head. "I'll ask New York to check with Telco security."

"Good. And let's try any phone Tony Pawlowski or his ex-wife, Stella, has. See if they called Hasani. Tony hates Corwen. And now Stella is pissed because Corwen got caught admiring Rachel Williamson's cleavage."

"This is more information than I need," Heidi said.

"I'll see what I can do," Ralph said. "But no promises."

Before we closed up for the night and the marshals whisked him away to a safe house, Artan Luga and I shook hands. But I didn't offer to buy him lunch some day at an Albanian fast food joint.

———

O n Tuesday afternoon, I sat in the lounge at Chesapeake's restaurant in Knoxville, knocking back a pint of Cherokee red ale. Rachel Williamson sat across the table from me in a big captain's chair, sipping a glass of chardonnay.

"I'm mad," she said. "I can't use any of this good story."

"No, you're not mad. You're only saying that. And if you told the world what actually happened, you'd probably get a very personable Albanian thug killed."

"You really owe me, Sammy."

"Of course I owe you. I've never denied that. You're the only reporter in whom I've ever confided."

She chuckled. "In whom?"

"Oh, shut up."

"Will you ever arrest Pawlowski?"

She sipped her wine, and I swallowed half the beer left in my glass.

"Probably not," I said. "We can't link him with the bombing or a call to Hasani. And I've got nothing on Stella except a little suspicion."

"And you need reasonable cause to believe, right?"

"You're a good law student. Hey, I know Pawlowski planted the bomb. And he knows I know. Someday maybe. Stranger things have happened."

"So, it was the perfect crime."

"No, only perfect if he killed Corwen and got away with it. Pawlowski came up short, too."

THE END

169

THE BUTLERS DID IT

WAYNE ZURL

Some people say, when a person completes a stretch in a Tennessee correctional facility, they've paid their debt to society. They don't know Noyd LeQuire.

After his release from Brushy Mountain State Prison and a bus ride to Knoxville, a taxi delivered him to the town square in Prospect.

As soon as he rented a single-wide on Doc Beasley Road, it became known as a bad neighborhood and property values dropped drastically.

All that happened just before Thanksgiving.

Four weeks later, I sat double-parked in my unmarked police car outside Prospect Bait & Tackle, waiting for Sergeant Bettye Lambert to purchase a Christmas gift for her son.

The city's Department of Buildings and Grounds had once again overdone the holiday decorations, with illuminated wreaths on every utility pole, millions of twinkling lights in the bare branches of trees on the town square and a Christmas tree to rival the monster at Rockefeller Center in front of the Municipal Building. If the citizens of Prospect didn't know the city's kilowatt-hour meter was spinning at warp speed, they should have.

I looked in the rearview mirror and watched a GMC Denali vacate a spot three car lengths behind me. As the big SUV drove past, I tapped the gearshift into reverse and parallel parked in the vacant spot.

Two minutes later, a twenty-year-old Chevy Caprice slid into a parking spot near the Prospect Citizen's Bank & Trust.

As I looked away from the yellow Caprice, Bettye startled me by opening the back door of the Crown Victoria and tossing in a disassembled fishing rod. Then she jumped into the passenger's seat next to me.

"Hey," I said. "That was quick."

"I sure hope you're right about what rod and reel to buy for Li'l Donnie."

"Of course I'm right. My friend Richie is a serious fisherman, and he says a Penn reel and Ugly Stik rod is the way to go."

To my left, three car doors slammed. I looked across the street just as a trio of men, wearing night-watch caps and raincoats, exited the Caprice and headed toward the bank.

"Damn it," I said. "This does not look good. Get on the radio, and tell all units we've got a 10-15 in progress at the bank."

"What?" she said.

"I'm moving up to that blue car across from the entrance. Get backup, and meet me there. And be careful."

"Gotcha, boss."

I stepped out of the car and tried to stroll to the sidewalk without drawing attention to myself. As I reached the first parked car, I ducked down and scrambled to a spot directly across from the bank. A few moments passed. Luckily, no pedestrians showed up on either side of the street. After making a radio call, Bettye hustled over and squatted down next to me on the sidewalk, her back against the Camry I hid behind.

"Come over here behind the wheel," I said. "I don't want you to get your backside shot off."

She moved, and I peeked over the hood. One man carrying a sawed-off shotgun with a cut-down stock emerged from the bank. He looked right and left through the eyes of the cap, which was now rolled down into a ski mask.

In only moments, a second man wielding a handgun emerged carrying a cloth sack.

To my right, a Prospect PD cruiser with its blue lights flashing stopped, blocking both lanes of Main Street. The robbers looked to their left as a second police car came screeching up from the opposite direction, assuming a similar posture on the roadway.

I could feel the panic emanating from the two criminals as their heads darted left and right. And then a third man hurried from the bank carrying another bag and a short-barreled riot gun.

To prevent a hostage situation, it seemed essential to keep the robbers from reentering the bank. The sporting thing to do would have been call out and give them an opportunity to surrender. But I didn't have the luxury of time to take that chance, and I couldn't talk and shoot simultaneously.

"When I tell you," I said, "as loud as you can, yell, 'Police, don't move.'"

Bettye nodded.

I braced my Smith & Wesson on the hood of the Toyota. As soon as I said, "Now," Bettye yelled. The robbers turned their guns toward us, and I squeezed off two quick shots. Each of my hollow-points struck the man with the cut-off scattergun in the chest. His weapon fell to the ground, and he crashed, face first, on the concrete.

After seeing their comrade fall, the crook with the other shotgun ran toward the Caprice, and the man with the handgun fired three quick one-handed shots at me. Two went high and shattered the plate-glass window of the store behind us. One hit the side window of the Camry. The booming reports echoed in the narrow street. I guessed a .45.

Bettye drew her Glock and began to peek over the fender just as a fourth shot hit the sheet metal of the Toyota. I grabbed her shoulder and pushed down.

Two more shots sounded from our left and right. The sharper, cracking sounds told me they came from two cops firing their .40 caliber Glocks. One hit something with a thud. The other sounded like it hit metal, but both missed the gunman.

Leather soles tapped the blacktop just before two more .45s struck the

Toyota. I dropped prone and looked under the car. The man shooting had walked toward our hiding place.

I had counted his shots. If he was using a traditional Army .45, he might have two more rounds.

I tried an old trick by firing three shots under the car at the ground in front of our assailant. If you don't have a big target to aim at, sometimes the bullets can do the finding for you. Before I could roll over and conceal myself behind the rear wheel to reload my revolver, I heard a scream.

Bettye and I peeked over the car at the masked man writhing in pain and clutching his ankles.

I stretched over the trunk lid and fired my last shot at the Caprice, but only shattered the moving car's left rear door window, as the third robber accelerated straight for PO Lenny Alcock's cruiser. The Chevy hit the rear quarter of the police car and spun it sideways. Alcock ran for cover behind a nearby Honda. After grazing another parked car, the escapee nailed the gas and took off down South Main.

I ran to the wounded man, and Bettye followed. We met Alcock there with his gun pointed at the bank robber's head. I used my foot to move the big automatic from the man's grasp.

PO Billy Puckett maneuvered his patrol car through the carnage in pursuit of the one who got away.

Bettye scurried back to the radio to alert the adjoining districts. I ejected the six spent shells from my Smith and reloaded.

"Cuff that son-of-a-bitch, Lenny. Then get something to wrap his ankles. I'll cover him."

When Alcock returned with a first aid kit, I bent down and pulled a navy blue ski mask off the prisoner's head.

He kept repeating, "Lord have mercy. Lord have mercy. Got-damn that hurts."

Bettye returned, looking a little out of breath. "I put out an alarm for that yellow Chevy—for all the good it'll do. And I called the medics for this one." She pointed to the wounded man. "I'll go back and see if Billy's called in yet."

"Okay. Lenny's got this guy. I'll check the one across the street."

She nodded.

"You okay?" I asked.

"Yes. You?"

"For a minute there, I almost soiled my knickers, but yeah, I'm fine."

She touched my arm. "I'm glad you're a good shot, darlin'."

"Just like the OK Corral."

Bettye shook her head and walked off saying, "We really don't need this."

From far off, the hi-low siren of a Rural Metro Ambulance broke the silence of the crime scene.

"I think the cavalry is coming," I said to no one in particular as I reached the second gunshot victim.

A pool of blood covered the sidewalk in front of the bank. The manager, Joe Rex Wilcox, and three of his employees stood in the doorway looking into the street.

I laid two fingers across the man's carotid artery and felt nothing. I rolled him over, looked into the lifeless blue eyes, and turned to the banker.

"Joe, stand here, and keep an eye on this shotgun and the sack of money. This guy's not going anywhere. Don't touch anything, and don't let anyone near you."

My ears were ringing from the gunfire, and I couldn't hear well. When he didn't respond, I yelled, "You hear me?"

"Yessir, yessir. I'll do it. Lord have mercy, Sam—"

"Everything's okay now. Just keep an eye on things until I can get another cop here."

Joe Rex nodded, and I walked over to Lenny and the wounded man who had calmed down a little and might have been lapsing into shock. I kneeled down next to him.

"Boss, I'm sorry," Lenny said. "I couldn't get off a second round without shootin' at Billy."

"It's okay, Lenny. Sometimes you can only do so much."

I took hold of the shooter's face and turned it.

"Hey, look at me," I said.

His glassy eyes focused on mine.

"The ambulance will be here in a minute."

He nodded.

"What's your name?"

He didn't answer.

"We'll find out soon enough."

He gave a slight shrug. "Von Butler."

"Who's the other one over there?" I gestured to the body with my head.

"You killed my brother, Wyatt." Butler spoke with as much distaste as he could muster.

I couldn't resist a little sarcasm. "Yeah, sorry for your loss."

"I'll bet."

"And the one who drove away?"

"I ain't sayin' no more."

I made a fist and rapped my knuckles against his bandaged ankle, hoping to change his mind.

"Ahhh, got-damn!"

Von Butler passed out, and I didn't get my answer.

Bettye walked over scowling. "What did you just do?"

"I was questioning him." I guess she saw me hit his leg.

"What am I gonna do with you, Sam Jenkins?" It was a rhetorical question. One she often asks.

"You have news for me, Sergeant?" I returned her scowl.

She wrinkled her nose. "Yes, I do, *Chief*. But not good news. Billy lost him."

I shook my head. "How could he lose a tub like that old Caprice?"

"On the Thirteen Curves. And there's more bad news. Billy ran off the road."

"Jeez. He get hurt?"

"No, but the car's mashed up a little."

"Mashed up?"

"The air dam got ripped off, and the grill's broken. He's not sure if the frame was bent."

"Can he drive it?"

"Stuck in the dirt."

"Super. Two cars out of commission."

"A deputy's coming up from Maryville to help out. The County's dispatching a wrecker."

"And the Caprice is?"

"Last seen headin' down Sevierville Road."

I began to open my mouth.

"Yes," she said. "I amended the alarm."

"See why you're my favorite desk sergeant?"

"I'm your only desk sergeant." She made a face again.

"You know you're beautiful when you're being sarcastic?"

"Oh, give it a rest."

I laughed. She smiled and ran a hand through her blonde hair.

———

Since the FBI claims to have a vested interest in bank robberies— Federal Deposit Insurance and all—I called Ralph Oliveri at the Knoxville field office.

"Just my luck I'm catching the squeals today." Ralph's from Queens and speaks with a very New York accent.

"For a young guy, you sound like an old squad dick. Where do you get language like that?"

"Probably from you. Sometimes I wish you had stayed in New York. My caseload would be much lighter."

"Fate brought us together, Ralphie. Hey, before you leave the office, bring additional help along with your evidence technicians. We've got one bad guy dead and one wounded."

"You guys killed one and shot another?" He sounded surprised.

"Well, actually just me. But one more got away. Sorry."

"So, you want us to investigate the shooting, too?" Now he sounded overworked.

"For chrissakes, Ralph, there's not much to investigate. I was justified. One pointed a 12-gauge at me, and the other was popping caps at Bettye and me when I took him out."

"Okay, don't get your dander up. Who's the third guy?"

"Beats me. I can't do everything for you."

———

PO Joey Gillespie was sitting at the reception desk at Prospect PD when Bettye and I walked in. I wrote down two names, Von and Wyatt Butler, and handed him the slip of paper.

"I need a full workup on these two," I said. "If we can, I'd like to find the third robber before the FBI."

Joey nodded.

"While the ambulance crew and the medical examiner worked on the Butler brothers," I said, "I noticed those assholes each had an array of jail-house tattoos. See where they did time and get me a list of cellmates. When you get the arrest records, call the PDs where they were locked up and see who's recorded as accomplices or associates."

Joey's eyes got a little wider.

"And in your spare time, see if a 1990-something yellow Caprice shows up anywhere."

"Lord have mercy." Joey looked from me to Bettye. "Y'all okay?"

"We're just peachy, son. Thanks for asking."

"Joey," Bettye said, "Don't pay any attention to the boss. He gets grumpy when he has to clean his gun."

"Do not," I said.

I noticed her hazel eyes had the twinkle they get when she's being a smartass. Even Bettye isn't beyond a little gallows humor.

Joey looked confused.

"Sergeant," I said, "would you join me in my office?"

"Right behind you, darlin'."

We entered the room, and I turned around. "Sit."

"Are you mad at me?" She sounded surprised.

"Of course not. We just had a few nasty minutes out there. Time to decompress."

"Want me to make fresh coffee?"

"Not what I had in mind."

I circled behind my desk and took two glasses and a bottle of Glenfiddich from the bottom drawer. I poured a level two fingers in each glass and handed one to Bettye.

"I never used to drink before I met you," she said.

"At least I don't have to carve that on your tombstone."

"Thank you." She sipped a little whisky.

"Comes with the job, partner."

"I wish it didn't."

I shrugged.

"How do you do it?" she asked.

"Do what?"

"Don't try to sound local. And don't say something stupid. You know what I mean, so stop."

"As The Duke would say, 'A man's gotta do what a man's gotta do.' The Army taught me all I needed to know."

After another sip of whisky and another frown, she said, "I worry about you, Sammy."

"I appreciate your concern, but I'm okay. If I need help, I'll find a mental Band-Aid."

"Promise?"

"Promise."

She smiled and pointed to the glass. "This is warming my tummy."

"You'll feel relaxed all over in a minute."

"Good."

"Be sure you call the family," I said. "You don't want them to hear about this on the news."

She nodded. "I know. And don't you forget to call Kate."

"My very next thing."

———

An hour later, Bettye walked back into my office. She had combed her hair, fixed her makeup and looked full of mischief.

"Have I got news for you, mister," she said.

"You looked pleased with yourself."

"I am. The Butler bothers are twenty-eight and twenty-six years old. Between them, they've done fifteen years hard time."

"Yikes. So young and yet so much accomplished."

Bettye took a second to smile for me. I returned the favor.

"It's mostly here in Tennessee," she said, "but Wyatt, the older one, also did ninety days up in Whitley County, Kentucky."

"Busy boys. What are they famous for?"

"Wyatt did juvie time for auto theft. Later on, he got convicted of felony assault, burglary, bein' part of a meth operation and then for haulin' a load of moonshine to Williamsburg, Kentucky. Von's another convicted burglar, and he too was involved in cookin' meth. A few more arrests, but no other convictions listed."

"Morons."

"Ya might say so. Two names keep showin' up on their paperwork. One's a local man, name of Noyd LeQuire—I remember him, a genuine bad guy. Records show he just finished six years at Brushy Mountain for manslaughter. The other's a Fentress County hard case, an older man named Quint Teffler."

"Fentress County's a long way off. You call the sheriff there?"

Bettye looked over the tops of her granny glasses. She didn't have to say, "You think you're dealin' with an amateur?" Her look said it all.

"Sorry I asked."

"Quint, or Quintillian, as it appears on his birth certificate," she said, "enjoyed a stay as guest of the Brushy Mountain Hotel at the same time Wyatt served his sentence. And, coincidentally, so did our Mr. Noyd LeQuire."

"You're amazing."

"Thank ya, darlin'. What sort of name you suppose Noyd is?"

"A strange one. But LeQuire sounds French. Either his family's been in

Tennessee since the fur trade days, or he's Cajun. I guess we'll soon find out."

"And this Teffler had his fingers into other things, including the methamphetamine business."

"Sounds like two places to start."

"Are you going to tell Oliveri about this?" she asked.

"He's got his own computer. If he can't find as much as you, shame on him."

"That's not very professional."

"Pfui. I'll check the local guy first. If we have to go to Fentress County, I may want company."

"You're bad."

"I ain't bad, but the bad don't mess with me."

"Egomaniac."

Bettye loves it when I use my James Mason accent. "Madam, the liberties you take with me are extraordinary."

"Aren't they just, m'lord."

———

M ost of Doc Beasley Road is not in the high-rent district of Prospect. Lenny Alcock and I sat in my metallic gray Ford outside the single-wide rented by Noyd LeQuire.

A parole officer had told me where to find him and described the object of our investigation as six-foot-one, covered with tattoos and a muscle-bound product of steroids and the prison gym facilities. He said LeQuire had made his required appearance after an early release, but didn't break his neck complying with the obligatory weekly visits. Noyd knew the system well enough to stretch things just shy of a parole violation. The PO categorized him as a better-than-average badass. Prison records showed he was always near the trouble, but no one ever had the courage to finger him for the odd stabbing, beating or trafficking in illicit substances within his tier. He suggested that if I had an opportunity, I should check out Noyd's collection of tattoos and count how many swastikas I could find. I just couldn't wait to meet him.

The parole officer faxed us a photo of Noyd LeQuire. He looked big and mean. I thought if I shot him six times, he'd just get pissed and bite the barrel off my gun then hand it back. But he was a good-looking man, with shoulders wide enough to make Atlas jealous who wore his dirty-blond hair in cornrows and affected the modern look of a perpetual three-day stubble.

"Boss, ya know y'all kin count on me if somethin' happens," Lenny said. "I swear, this mornin', I jest couldn't git off a safe shot when y'all needed it."

"I know. In a situation like that...I didn't see things from your angle. I'm sure you did the right thing."

In truth, I wasn't sure. At the time, I was too busy keeping Bettye safe and dodging bullets to watch my troops closely.

"Nothing's shaking here," I said. "Let's see if we can find a landlord. The four trailers are so close together, there must be one owner."

The mobile homes sat on a level stretch of property backed up by a fallow cornfield that covered more than twenty acres. At the far boundary, an ancient barn stood at the end of a gravel drive. Beyond that, a beautiful view of the Smokies spanned the horizon. The group of old and neglected trailers looked like four warts on a beautiful nose. Two of them had an assortment of brightly colored plastic toys scattered around the exterior. Landscaping was almost non-existent, and a mangy brindle dog wandered between two of the homes, sniffing the ground. After finding a suitable spot, she squatted down and watered the dallisgrass.

Lenny and I walked across the street and chose the largest trailer, one with a carport and the only vehicle present. I jotted down the plate number from an old white Impala and noted the house number, 4114. One of the cluster mailboxes with the corresponding number showed the name Spilavoy crudely painted on the hatch.

We climbed a few steps to a weathered wooden deck, and I knocked. A flea-bitten crone wearing a pink sweat suit answered the door.

I greeted her with a smile. "Mrs. Spilavoy?"

"Who wants to know?"

Why do people insist on saying that?

Alcock stood next to me, clean-cut and in full uniform, conspicuously a police officer. I showed her my badge anyway.

"Chief Jenkins, Officer Alcock, Prospect PD. We'd like a minute of your time."

"Yeah? Fer whot?"

I'd been shot at earlier in the day. I killed one person and severely wounded another. We were looking for an escaped bank robber armed with at least a shotgun. I didn't need a woman who looked like she just gnawed off the hind leg of a pit bull giving me lip.

"We're looking for your neighbor, Noyd LeQuire. He doesn't seem to be home."

The smile remained on my face, but I felt pressure building up inside my head.

"He's a tenant. And he don't check in with *me*. Try his parole officer."

She held a cigarette in her right hand with the elbow cocked at a jaunty angle. After speaking, she took a long drag and blew smoke upward from the side of her mouth. She looked so delicate—the picture of refinement.

"The PO told me we could find him here. I'm wondering if you've seen him today or know where he might be."

"Saw the lights on this mornin', but I've been ta the store fer a couple hours. I don't know where he's at."

She ran her left hand through a mop of orange hair that showed three inches of gray roots and took another hit on the cigarette.

"You see any activity at his place?" I asked.

She frowned, looking confused.

"He get any visitors?" I asked. "He behave himself?"

"He done somethin'?"

I wish people answered a question with a statement.

"I think he may know someone who just did."

"Pays his rent on time—so far. Don't know nothin' 'bout friends, 'cept Twyla and Hettie."

"Who?"

"Twyla Burgess. The one in number 4118. Don't think they was ever married, but Hettie is Noyd's kid. Twyla told him I had 4120 for rent."

"They don't live together now?"

"Nope."

"Twyla around?"

"Ain't seen her."

"Know anything derogatory about her?" Lenny asked.

Mrs. Spilavoy scratched her head. "Derogatory?"

"Yeah, anything negative?"

She scratched again and took another puff on the cigarette. "Negative?"

I broke in. "You know anything *bad* about her?"

A stream of smoke shot skyward from her mouth. "No, she's okay."

"She work?" I asked.

"Used ta. On welfare now. Or am I opposed ta say public assistance?"

For some reason, the old brindle dog took off running between two of the trailers, possibly after a squirrel.

I refocused on Mrs. Spilavoy. "Either Twyla or Noyd have a vehicle?"

"Twyla got her some piece o' Japanese junk, a li'l red one. Noyd jest got him an old black pickup. Dodge, I think. Got a goat or sumthin' as a hood ornament."

"Ever seen a yellow Caprice parked at Noyd's place?"

"What's that?"

"A big Chevy. An older car," I said.

"Nope."

"What's Noyd do for cash?"

"He ain't said. Long as he's got the rent, I don't care. None o' my bidness."

I offered her a business card. "If either Twyla or Noyd show up, will you give me a call?"

She made me wait while she expelled more smoke toward the ceiling. Then she shook her head and didn't reach for the card.

"Don't wanna git involved."

She closed the door in our faces. Had we stayed a few minutes longer, my head would have exploded.

I looked at Lenny. "What a nice lady."

W hen I turned over the information about Noyd LeQuire to the FBI, Ralph Oliveri's boss, Special Agent-in-Charge Carl Harmon, supplied two men to watch the trailer at 4120 Doc Beasley Road.

By 10 p.m. that night, Blount County deputies had recovered a burned-out yellow Caprice along the shore of Chilhowee Lake on the old moonshiner's road to North Carolina. A check of the vehicle identification number revealed that the Chevy had been reported stolen several days earlier from the parking lot of the East Town Mall in North Knoxville. The Knox County license plate on the car had been pinched from a sedan parked in a residential area less than a mile from the mall.

T hat night I dozed off easily enough, but my sleep only lasted a few hours. I awoke remembering disjointed and bizarre dreams of tattooed musclemen, walking corpses and crying soldiers lying in a field, writhing in pain. I might have slept more, but every time Kate moved or made a sound, my eyes popped open. I felt like an electric charge might shoot me out of the bed. At six o'clock, I began my day.

In the middle of eating a bowl of cereal and an English muffin, Kate brought up a topic I would rather have not broached.

"Are you doing okay with the shooting?"

"Sure. It was a clean one. I don't have to sweat the grand jury with this."

"I'm not talking about the legal ramifications, Sammy. What's going on in your head?"

Kate ate a spoonful of low-carb, low-fat and low-calorie strawberry-colada yogurt and set the container down on her placemat. She had pulled her salt and pepper hair back and up into a ponytail. Even without makeup, she looked lovely.

"I'm trying to think up a few good Christmas jokes to include with my holiday note to the troops."

"Don't act obtuse. How are you handling the shootout?"

"I was only a boy when I first fired a gun in anger. It's old hat now."

She rolled up the napkin from her lap and tossed it on the table. Her wraparound robe parted in front and showed me more than a hint of cleavage.

"Damn it. You were twenty-six years old when you got out of the Army. And how many years did it take before you got a decent night's sleep?"

"A while."

"A while? I believe it's easier to balance trauma on a pair of wide young shoulders. Aren't you the guy who tells me how his stress battery is running on fumes? You are not a kid any longer."

"I appreciate your concern, sweetie, but I'm okay. The shooting had that all-important element: necessity. I was in the right place at the right time, and I did the right thing. Everything's cool."

"The wrong place at the right time, thank you. And how many Advil did you take last night?"

"I had a tension headache. It was a long day."

"And a fist full of pain pills washed down with a glass of scotch is an acceptable remedy?"

"Seems to work."

"You're unbelievable."

"That's me. One in a million."

"Grrrrr."

———

Later that morning, at ten after nine precisely, a woman named Juretta Burgess reported her daughter, Twyla, and granddaughter, Hettie, missing. I drove to an old home in the northern section of Prospect to interview her.

"I seen her three days ago," the woman said. "But ain't heard from her since."

"Is that unusual?"

"She might call me ever' day."

"But might not?"

"No. She usually calls ever' day."

Mrs. Burgess might have been good-looking once, but a bad haircut, no makeup and the need of basic dental maintenance kept me from calling her attractive.

"Twyla say she had any Christmas plans?"

"Didn't say."

"Have you got a picture of Twyla and Hettie?"

"I'll git ya one."

A gray tabby cat jumped onto the couch next to Mrs. Burgess and rubbed his head against her forearm.

She told me Twyla was thirty-one years old. Juretta was only forty-six. Juretta's husband, a former Marine Corps reservist, had been killed in a training accident nine years earlier. Juretta looked upset when she mentioned his name.

I changed the subject. "Tell me about Noyd LeQuire."

"That godless fool. I don't even like ta speak his name."

"I hear Hettie is his child."

"She is."

"Why isn't Twyla living with him?"

"Probably sick o' bein' beat. Mighta came ta her senses after they put 'im in jail."

"Yet Twyla prompted Noyd to move in next to her when he got out."

"Sometimes I think when that girl's a'lookin' in the mirror thinkin' how perty she is, she might oughta be standin' in line collectin' the brains she done forgot ta pick up."

Bettye broadcast a missing persons alarm for Twyla and Hettie Burgess, they being our case, and Ralph put out a hold-for-questioning want on Noyd LeQuire. I took on the simple plod work of the M.P. case, while every uniformed cop in the Smoky Mountain region began looking for the six-foot-one prison weightlifter.

Just before noon, a sharp-eyed state trooper found Noyd's Dodge pickup parked in the northbound rest area and visitor's center on I-75, a mile north of the Kentucky border. Carl Harmon sent two agents and an impound wrecker to fetch the truck. An FBI evidence recovery team found nothing of use or interest after spending a couple hours looking at the vehicle.

So, assuming the worst, LeQuire abducted his daughter and ex-paramour and was making a run for it, trying to throw us off the trail by leaving one vehicle a dozen miles on the Tennessee side of North Carolina and another a mile inside Kentucky. I could hear the FBI agents sharpening their fangs over the possibility of an interstate flight.

Or, LeQuire had nothing to do with the robbery and only intended to take his daughter and her mother to visit friends in Kentucky when his old pickup crapped out on the Interstate.

Law enforcement, even in the high-tech 21st century, is not always easy.

I t wasn't difficult to track down the next player in our cast of characters. Quint Teffler waited for us in the Fentress County Jail, serving a ninety-day sentence for DUI and misdemeanor possession of the evil weed.

I met Ralph Oliveri in Knoxville and drove with him toward the Cumberland Plateau.

"If you would have given me Teffler's name, I could have had an agent locate him and saved you the time," Ralph said.

"No big deal. Bettye found him right away."

"If he was closer to Prospect would you have invited me along for the ride?"

I tried to act offended. "Ralph, what are you suggesting?"

"Don't sound shocked. I know you. You'd love to find LeQuire before we do."

"The idea never entered my mind," I said. "I am shocked. And deeply hurt. How could you think such a thing?"

"Oh, gimme a break."

Just west of the golf community of Crossville, we turned north on US 127, heading toward Jamestown. On South Smith Street, we found the sheriff's office and county jail.

After checking in with the duty officer and getting visitor's badges, Ralph and I secured our weapons in a small locker and were escorted to a private interview room. Ten minutes later, a corrections officer brought in Quint Teffler.

Teffler's rap sheet showed him as forty-six, but he looked much older. He wore long dark hair in a ponytail, slicked straight back, and hadn't shaved his narrow face in several days. We explained about needing help to locate Noyd LeQuire.

"Might be able ta he'p." He broke a slight smile and brushed a piece of lint from his orange jumpsuit. "What's in it fer me?"

"As soon as we find LeQuire," Ralph said, "You walk out of here."

"I only got fifty-nine days left."

Ralph shrugged. He's a good-looking guy in his mid-forties.

"I'll put you on my Christmas card list," I said.

Teffler laughed. "Ya got any smokes?"

Ralph shook his head.

I made him another offer. "I'll have the commissary send a carton after you give us the 4-1-1. But if you're bullshittin', I'll tell the tier boss you jerked us around. It'll be a tough fifty-nine days."

"I got no reason ta bullshit ya. Make it Marlboros, an' ya got a deal."

I smiled. "You're a fine American, Quint."

———

Teffler told us of two possible places to find Noyd—the first, his own single-wide in Pall Mall, Tennessee, just north of Jamestown. He had once told LeQuire where to find a hidden key and offered to let him hide out in an emergency or just crash if necessary. Ralph and I checked that out and came up with bupkis.

The alternative would require more time and effort, and a new name to consider—Sawyer Jack Mosby, the man who bought all the untaxed liquor Noyd and the Butler boys hauled into Kentucky.

Mosby's old haunt had been in Whitley County, just north of the Tennessee line, where he could sell all the high-quality Smoky Mountain moonshine the trio of Tennessee bootleggers could supply.

Recently, Sawyer Jack moved further east to the back of beyond in the tiny community of Chavies, deep within Kentucky coal country, where they pipe in sunshine and the Perry Country deputies preferred not to visit unless called upon to do so.

Equipped with no more than sketchy directions to the Mosby homestead, Ralph called the Perry County Sheriff's Office asking them to assist in establishing Noyd LeQuire's presence in their jurisdiction.

While Ralph waited to hear from those detectives, I pursued an angle that had been bothering me since I met the parole officer who described LeQuire.

"Betts, I know things happened quickly outside the bank," I said, "but describe the subject that got away one more time."

"Basically, sort of tall, otherwise average. Hard to get more specific with someone wearing a big black raincoat."

"How tall?"

"Compared to the others, taller than one. The same or close to the other. Might have been the tallest."

"LeQuire is six-one and a weightlifter," I said. "I didn't think the guy who drove off was exceptionally big."

"The preliminary autopsy report on Wyatt Butler shows him as 68-and-a-half inches," she said. "Von's driver's license says he's five-ten. The third one could have been six-one."

"Let's see what the bank employees can tell me," I suggested. "Maybe FBI interview techniques aren't as good as they'd like us to believe."

Any cop will tell you eyewitness descriptions can vary greatly. I've interviewed people who described Quasimodo as tall, dark, and handsome. After the heat of a robbery, it's anyone's guess what a stressed-out victim will recall.

From Joe Rex Wilcox, his platform assistant and the two tellers, I got estimates ranging from five-foot-eight to six-foot-two and weights from 150 to 200 pounds. Not exactly the help I'd hoped for.

After finishing at the bank, I returned for another chat with Juretta Burgess.

"Any new thoughts on where Twyla might be?" I asked.

"I been rackin' my brain, but cain't think of a single place."

"You call anyone?"

"Same people I tol' you about. They don't know nuthin'."

"You said Twyla never married and has no current boyfriend. Do you have the list of past boyfriends I asked for?"

"Yessir. I put the ones she lived with fer a while on top."

I tried not to lose patience or show annoyance at the late information.

"Yesterday I asked if she'd been living with anyone."

"Well, she's not livin' with no one rot now."

I let my shoulders drop an inch and sighed. "Any long-term relationships on the list?"

"Nosir. Other than Noyd, nuthin' lasted too long."

Her cat walked into the room licking its chops. He looked at me, headed straight for my navy blue slacks and rubbed against me, leaving a streak of gray hairs. I wanted to scream.

"These guys still around?" I asked.

"I 'spect so. But not Murphy Cottrell. Army Reserve done sent him to Afghanistan or some such place."

"Any brothers or sisters?"

"Murphy?"

"No, Twyla." I almost bit my lip.

"Nosir. I couldn't have any."

"Cousins?"

"Don't keep up with no one."

"Thanks. Remember to call if you hear from her."

I gave Bettye the new list of people to contact and tossed in another request.

"Run Twyla through everything you can think of to get more background. She and the kid didn't just vaporize. They're out there somewhere"

"Okey dokey, darlin". I'll treat this just like she's a wanted criminal."

"You check with the school about her kid?"

"They're on Christmas break. No absence involved."

"Twyla's not exactly the picture-perfect daughter. Maybe she just took off while school's out and didn't tell her mother."

"Maybe."

"Or she's aiding and abetting Noyd. Could be the bank money lured her back into his clutches." I raised my eyebrows twice.

"Aren't we melodramatic today?"

I snorted. "See if you can get phone numbers for a few classmates. Maybe Hettie told a friend that Twyla planned a trip for the holiday."

———

A Perry County detective phoned Ralph Oliveri with promising news. He knew about the trailer home owned by Sawyer Jack Mosby, someone on their radar as a member of a right-wing militia group calling themselves The Sons of Jefferson Davis. He found Twyla Burgess's red Nissan Sentra parked at Mosby's place when he and his partner made a quick neighborhood check. Unfortunately, they found no one at home, and his department didn't have the manpower to constantly watch the place.

So, Ralph and two other agents and I took off the next morning for beautiful downtown Chavies. The FBI's Lexington office promised to send a four-man tactical team to meet us in the county seat of Hazard—as in *Dukes of.*

From the Knoxville Federal building at 710 Locust Street, it took us only ten minutes to merge onto the Interstate and begin the drive to Kentucky. Just south of London, we left I-75 and drove east on the Hal Rogers Parkway through the Redbird section of the Daniel Boone National

Forest. Ralph drove, and I rode shotgun. Special Agents Bonnie Rowatt and Martin Saunders sat in the back.

We'd been on the road for more than ninety minutes when we entered the Federal forest land. Even driving quickly, it seemed like we could expect an additional hour on the road.

I opened a roadmap and looked over one of the poorest areas of Appalachia. Communities named Buckhorn, Quicksand, Tomahawk, Shoulderblade and Lost Creek made me think we were time-traveling back into the 18th century when men like Boone, Simon Kenton and Thomas Walker intruded upon the happy hunting grounds of the Shawnee. Signs of civilization were scarce, and the winter landscape didn't provide much to admire.

We pulled into Hazard around noon. Ralph wanted to eat in a barbeque joint he saw on Main Street called The Rabid Pig or The Sleazy Sow, I can't remember. They didn't serve beer, and I refused to drink sweet tea, so I wasn't a happy policeman. So far, my excursion into southeast Kentucky seemed less than auspicious.

After lunch, which wasn't really that bad, we met Detectives Duffy Hayes and Hershel Crabtree at the sheriff's office. At 1:30, the four agents making up our TAC team arrived. We spent a few minutes talking strategy before the detectives led the way north on Kentucky 15 toward Chavies. At Route 28, we hung a left. The road curved into wooded hills, past working and abandoned strip-mines and old, dilapidated cabins. The winding lane seemed unending; had there been foliage, the overhead canopy would have blocked all traces of sunlight.

When we arrived in Chavies, we parked in a prearranged spot behind a small community center, concealing our police cars from nosy onlookers. Single-wide mobile homes and small frame houses sat around in no discernible order. I wondered if a member of the planning commission had tossed a handful of dominoes in the air over a map and where they landed is where residents were told to set up shop. Derelict vehicles were parked here and there. Rusted bicycles and piles of weather-beaten toys littered much of the ground. Piles of coal chunks had been heaped outside each of the front doors. I saw no sense or order. Had I not been made of sterner stuff, I might have gotten another tension headache.

Duffy Hayes pointed out Mosby's trailer. An old Ford van with peeling blue paint and Kentucky plates sat next to the entrance. The red Sentra wasn't there.

As our SWAT team deployed, Ralph and the two agents spoke with Hayes and Crabtree, and my cell phone sounded off. Everyone looked at me as the Rolling Stones played *Paint it Black*. I smiled and excused myself.

"Sammy, darlin'," Bettye said, "wait 'til you hear what I learned."

———

D uffy Hayes, a burly man with brown hair falling across his forehead, tiptoed up the rickety steps to the front entrance of Mosby's home. As he knocked on the windowless door, he unzipped his leather jacket, giving him easy access to the pistol holstered on his left side.

A man called out from within the trailer. "Who is it?"

"Hey, Bubba, it's yer neighbor, Duffy. Y'all know there's two flats on yer van?"

Two agents dressed in black tactical clothing stood on either side of the steps. Two more crouched below a window a few feet away.

The door opened a crack, and a disheveled-looking man stuck his nose out.

"Who'd ya say it was?"

Hayes thrust his hand between the door and the frame, grabbed Sawyer Jack Mosby by his long hair and yanked sharply, throwing him off balance while one of the uniformed agents dragged him down the stairs.

In only seconds, two agents armed with MP-5 sub-machine guns broke into the front room. Hayes, now with gun drawn, followed, as did Ralph Oliveri and I. The remainder of our team had been watching the rear of the trailer.

The narrow interior looked like a hovel inhabited by unmarried cavemen.

The temperature inside must have been eighty degrees. Unwashed dishes were stacked around the sink. Two tied-off plastic garbage bags sat on the floor near the refrigerator. Empty beer cans lie all around the kitchen and living room.

Noyd LeQuire sat slumped on the couch with a surprised look on his face, and his young daughter, Hettie, sat next to him. A soap opera played on a flat-screen TV and a Mossberg pump shotgun lay on a scarred cocktail table. The short barrel and black plastic stock looked the same as the gun carried by the escaped bank robber.

Instead of instinctively protecting his daughter from the intruders, LeQuire lurched forward, reaching for the shotgun.

Before Noyd could grab the 12-gauge, the agent on my left growled, "Touch it, you die!"

LeQuire hesitated. His hand hovered above the wrist of the riot gun.

Only seconds passed, and the agent yelled, "Back off!"

Hettie had pushed herself against the couch and crawled close to her father. Noyd may have assumed the same thing as me. The agent speaking wouldn't have been the one shooting. The other man, the quiet one on my right, would. That put Hettie dangerously close to the potential line of fire. Maybe Noyd cared about his daughter. Or maybe he just knew there was no chance of escape and didn't like the odds of walking away from seventy rounds of hot 9 mm ammunition fired from a pair of MP-5s. Either way, Noyd LeQuire's future did not look bright.

Suddenly, the ex-convict jerked his torso back against the couch cushions. Instantly, his prison training kicked in, and he placed his hands atop his head.

"No trouble here, boss." As he spoke, a sardonic smile crossed his lips.

Hettie moved even closer to her father, probably feeling more fear than ever before.

The TAC team members hustled Noyd off the couch and cuffed him while his daughter cried and screamed, "Don't hurt my daddy!"

LeQuire didn't say a word to the girl or even look back as they led him out of the trailer.

I took a seat on the opposite end of the couch, less than three feet from the young girl. She scurried as far away from me as possible.

The kid must have looked at me as her enemy, so I showed her my badge. "We're the police. No one is going to harm you or your father."

Her expression resembled that of a frightened deer caught in the headlights of a speeding eighteen-wheeler.

"Everything's okay," I said. "Are you Hettie?"

She loosened up a little and nodded.

"Where's your mother?"

Nine-year-old Hettie was thin and tall for her age. She wore her brown hair parted in the middle and tied into pigtails on the sides.

"Is your mom okay?"

When she still didn't answer, I shifted on the couch, let out a sigh and tried again.

"I need to make sure you and your mom are okay, Hettie. Where is she?"

After a long moment she said, "She went to the store."

"Did she go alone?"

"Uh-huh."

"She drive her little red car?"

"Uh-huh."

I looked over at Bonnie Rowatt who stood near the door with Marty Saunders.

"Hettie, will you go with this lady? She'll take you to where your father is. I'll wait here for your mom."

Hettie nodded, but Bonnie wasn't sure she liked that arrangement.

"I'm not really good with kids," she said.

"I'll take her," Saunders said, stepping up and extending a hand. "Come on, sweetheart. I'll get you a soda, and we'll be waiting when your mom gets there."

White-haired Marty Saunders's kindly grandfather appearance enticed the kid. She slid off the couch and followed him out of the grungy trailer.

I turned toward Bonnie, a good-looking redhead in her early thirties. "No maternal instincts?"

"Not hardly."

I laughed. "Where's Ralph?"

"He walked out behind LeQuire."

I pulled on a pair of latex gloves, picked up the shotgun, depressed the slide release and ejected a round from the chamber into my palm. Then I pinched the retainer spring four more times and dropped the remainder of the shells into my hand.

I handed the open weapon and five shells to Bonnie. "Here ya go, Special Agent Rowatt—a crucial piece of evidence if I'm not mistaken."

She also put on a pair of gloves, giving the second one a snap against her wrist.

"Thanks ever so much, Chief Jenkins. I'll take care of this for you." That sounded a little testy, but I let it go.

I left the trailer and found Oliveri talking with Hayes and Crabtree. Noyd LeQuire sat in the back seat of an FBI sedan with a TAC team member. Sawyer Jack Mosby slouched in the rear of a marked Perry County Sheriff's car that had recently arrived.

"Ralph," I said, "got a minute?"

He excused himself and joined me twenty feet away.

"The kid says her mother went to the store. Obviously, Twyla's not a hostage. Or she's got the quickest case of Stockholm syndrome in recorded history. Since she's my missing person, I'll wait here and see what's up when she gets back."

"I suppose you want a car?"

"This isn't Brooklyn, paisan. I can't stand under a streetlight and look inconspicuous."

He handed me the keys.

"Do not, for God's sake, do anything to my car."

"You have no faith."

"That's right. That's why I'm leaving Bonnie with you."

"You're such a putz. While we're waiting, should I teach her how to be a world-class detective?"

Ralph ignored that remark.

"If Twyla is complicit in helping Noyd hide out, she's an accessory," he said. "We've got two states involved. Your M.P. case becomes an FBI matter."

"You've got a point. I'll be nice to Bonnie."

I drove Ralph's silver Crown Victoria to a spot where we could watch Mosby's trailer and still remain out of the public eye. Bonnie and I waited.

After only a couple minutes, she broke the ice. "What did you do in New York?"

I've never been sure Bonnie liked me. Nor was I sure I liked her. So, I couldn't resist responding to her question with an almost obnoxious answer.

"You mean for kicks or on the job?"

"Don't be silly. On the job. I've never asked before."

Maybe she did like me.

"After getting out of the bag, I was a general service squad dick. A sergeant in the organized crime unit, and then I had a couple of gigs as a lieutenant. I ended up running the special investigations section."

"Hmm," she said. "That last one sounds kinda vague."

"If I told you what we did, I'd have to kill you."

She rolled her green eyes. "Oh, spare me, please. How long?"

"Twenty years."

"Hmm."

"How long have you been with the Bureau?"

"Almost five years now."

I smiled. "Gettin' to be an old-timer."

She did the eye thing again. "Yeah, right."

The weather had been unusually mild for a couple weeks. Several species of birds flew around the poor neighborhood from branch to branch and bush to bush.

"Look at all these birds," I said.

"Yeah, fascinating," she said sarcastically.

After a few minutes of silence, she tilted the rearview mirror to her and looked at her chin.

"Am I getting a spot here?" she asked.

I turned to face her. "A spot?"

"You know—a spot."

"What are you talking about? Lemme see."

She turned her head, and I put on my glasses.

"My guess," I said, "tomorrow you'll have a pimple."

"Oh, gross. I hate that word."

"What? You want me to call it a spot? A spot is paint. You've got a pimple."

"Oh, shut up."

"Why do women ask questions when they don't want honest answers?"

She ignored me.

I took off my glasses and looked out the windshield again. An old red Nissan Sentra drove slowly down the street and pulled up next to Mosby's van.

"That's her," I said.

Bonnie and I stepped out of the car.

"Hurry up," I said. "Cover the back. I'll approach her."

"I get the back again? Don't you think I should—?"

"Cover the back," I snapped. "Quick. I want to be in place before she gets out of the car. And stay back there until I call you."

She sighed. "Okay."

It only took me a few seconds to trot past two trailers and approach the Nissan before Twyla switched off the ignition. Two plastic grocery bags sat on the passenger's seat. Twyla rummaged around in her handbag as I stepped next to the driver's side and jerked the door open.

"Police," I said. "Put your hands on the wheel."

In a perfect world she would have said, 'Okey dokey, sugar. Ya got me,' and things would have gone smoothly. But we weren't in a perfect world. We were in Chavies, Kentucky. Twyla Burgess brought her right hand out of the purse holding a Walther .380 semi-automatic and turned in my direction. As she twisted her body and tried to level the gun at me, I started pushing the car door closed. Her hand and the gun were too close for comfort when the window frame struck her forearm and half-slammed it against the upright strut between the front and back doors. Twyla let out a throaty scream, but held tightly to the Walther PPK. I jammed my hip against the door and pressed my weight to it as I grabbed the gun's slide with my left hand. I wrestled to disarm her, but her strong grip kept me from taking the gun. Then she pulled the trigger.

The recoil of the shot pushed the slide rearward, but my hand blocked the shell from ejecting and pushed it back into the port. The sharp edges of the automatic's slide cut into my left hand, making it hurt like hell. Luckily, the gun jammed, giving me time to slam my right hand onto the little automatic and wrench it free from her grip.

With the pistol safely tucked into my waistband, I pulled Twyla from the car, thinking the injury to her right arm had caused enough pain for her to surrender quickly.

But I was still in Chavies and nowhere near that perfect world.

Twyla swung her good left hand at my head. I checked the punch with my right, twisted my forearm over hers, and trapped her left arm under my right. Still she struggled, so for good measure, I drove a left hand into her solar plexus. I often think of those guys who balk at hitting a woman and how they might suffer the consequences for being squeamish.

Bonnie finally reached the Nissan just as my punch landed, and Twyla let out a healthy, "Oof."

Blood from my left palm stained Twyla's jacket as I spun her around to face the car and pushed her against the rear door. Bonnie stood three feet away, grinning and holding a pair of handcuffs.

"You can get pretty rough on a girl," she said.

"I thought I told you to stay in the rear." I felt a little out of breath.

"I can go back if you'd like."

"Smartass."

Bonnie cuffed the prisoner and dragged her a few feet from the car. Standing upright, Twyla Burgess looked almost as tall as me. She had reported being five-feet-eight-inches on her driver's license application, but in reality stood at least five-ten. And her mother had been correct, she looked quite pretty—for someone who just tried to shoot me.

———

After dropping Twyla off at the Perry County Sheriff's Office with a quick explanation of what happened and a little about what I had learned from Bettye, Bonnie drove me to the Appalachian Regional Medical Center to get my hand attended to.

An hour later, back at the county detective's squad room, we found our team completing the necessary paperwork. Ralph Oliveri had called the special agent-in-charge of the Lexington FBI office and arranged for a pair of deputy U.S. marshals to meet us in Hazard with a big government SUV and transport the prisoners back to Knoxville. The TAC team would remain with us as security for our little convoy.

A couple hours later, the two marshals arrived—a young guy with a white cowboy hat and scruffy Vandyke and a short black woman. They both spoke with Kentucky accents. After the marshals loaded our three prisoners into the SUV, we hit the road.

Ralph hadn't said much for the first fifteen minutes, but as we pulled onto the Hal Rogers Parkway, heading into the setting sun, he asked a reasonable question.

"How did you know Twyla Burgess was the third subject at the bank robbery, and why didn't you tell me?"

"I didn't know until we were in Chavies."

"How so?" Marty Saunders asked.

"Bettye called me. I had asked her to learn everything she could about Twyla. When she went into the state birth records, she found a glitch—no one named Twyla Burgess with a conventional birth certificate. However, she did find adoption records. Juretta and Thurman Burgess adopted a little girl with the same DOB. More checking revealed the girl had been born to a fifteen-year-old named Emma Lee Butler. Like Twyla, Emma Lee never married, but she lived with a few different men. And a few years after giving away her daughter, she gave birth to a couple of sons who she didn't put up for adoption—Wyatt and Vonnie—our two bank robbers. Twyla, who is tall enough to look like a man, joined her two half-brothers in their scheme to make extra holiday cash. Noyd LeQuire, although a real badass, is only guilty as an accessory after the crime. But it's enough to put him back into the slammer."

"And you were going to tell us this when?" Ralph asked.

"I wanted to verify my information. You wouldn't want me to sound like an alarmist. I told you when I handed over the prisoner."

"I knew you wanted to close this before us."

"Nonsense."

"I should charge you for withholding information."

"That's ridiculous. And you'd never do that."

"Oh, yeah?"

"Yes, because my first phone call from the Federal holding cells would be to my friend at WNXX TV News. She'd make a broadcast telling the world how I found the third bank robber before you. Prospect robbery—Prospect PD closeout. It would make a great local interest story."

Marty Saunders chuckled.

Then Bonnie stuck in her two cents. "Twyla didn't seem too pleased when you punched her in the stomach. How'd you get her to roll over and admit being part of the robbery?"

Ralph came back to life after Bonnie let the cat out of the bag. "You punched a woman in the stomach?"

"Oh, bug off, Oliveri. She didn't try to shoot you."

He must have thought that was humorous and snorted out a forced laugh.

With Ralph out of the way, I answered Bonnie. "Getting cooperation wasn't hard. I offered to arrange for her mother to take custody of Hettie instead of calling in Child Protective Services to put the kid in foster care. Unlike some people I know, Twyla has maternal instincts."

"You think you're so smart," Bonnie said.

"I do," I said. "And I'm generous. My Christmas present to you, Ralphie—take full credit. Forget I was ever here. You drove—it's your collar."

"You're all heart," Ralph said.

"Right again. I call it friendship. I phone you for a favor, and you piss and moan, but you always come through. This is the least I can do as repayment."

Ralph remained silent for a long moment.

"Well...thanks."

"You're welcome. Now I won't feel bad when I call for the next favor."

"Oh, jeez!"

"Stop complaining. 'Tis the season to be jolly."

"Yeah, right." He affected another laugh. "Okay, Mr. Smart guy, where's the sack of money Twyla got away with?"

"How should I know? Ask her. Do I have to do everything for you?"

THE END

THANK YOU FOR READING

Did you enjoy this book?

We invite you to leave a review at the site from which this book was purchased.

DID YOU KNOW THAT LEAVING A REVIEW...

- Helps other readers find books they may enjoy.
- Gives you a chance to let your voice be heard.
- Gives authors recognition for their hard work.
- Doesn't have to be long. A sentence or two about why you liked the book will do.

If you enjoyed *The Great Smoky Mountain Bank Job and Other Sam Jenkins Mysteries* and would like a free copy of the award winning *A New Prospect*, simply go to
http://waynezurl.authorreach.com

Don't miss out on your next favorite book!

Join the Melange Books mailing list at
www.melange-books.com/mail.html

Perks include:

- First peeks at upcoming releases.
- Exclusive giveaways.
- News of book sales and freebies right in your inbox.
- And more!

ABOUT THE AUTHOR

Wayne Zurl grew up on Long Island and retired after twenty years with the Suffolk County Police Department, one of the largest municipal law enforcement agencies in New York and the nation. For thirteen of those years he served as a section commander, supervising investigators. He is a graduate of SUNY,  Empire State College and served on active duty in the US Army during the Vietnam War and later in the reserves. Zurl left New York to live in the foothills of the Great Smoky Mountains of Tennessee with his wife, Barbara.

Zurl has won Eric Hoffer and Indie Book Awards, and was named a finalist for a Montaigne Medal and First Horizon Book Award. He has written seven novels and more than twenty novelettes in the Sam Jenkins mystery series.

www.waynezurlbooks.net
www.facebook.com/waynezurl
www.twitter.com/waynezurl

ALSO BY WAYNE ZURL

A New Prospect

A Leprechaun's Lament

Heroes and Lovers

Pigeon River Blues

A Touch of Morning Calm

A Can of Worms

Honor Among Thieves

From New York to the Smokies: A Collection of Sam Jenkins Mysteries

Murder in Knoxville and Other Sam Jenkins Mysteries

The Great Smoky Mountain Bank Job and Other Sam Jenkins Mysteries

Coming Soon...

Graceland on Wheels and More Sam Jenkins Mysteries

www.ingramcontent.com/pod-product-compliance
Lightning Source LLC
Chambersburg PA
CBHW030450250626
47154CB00003BA/1207